GAMMA QUEST

BOOK 2

SEARCH AND RESCUE

MARVEL®

SPIDER-MAN: THE VENOM FACTOR
by Diane Duane

THE ULTIMATE SPIDER-MAN,
Stan Lee, Editor

IRON MAN: THE ARMOR TRAP
by Greg Cox

SPIDER-MAN: CARNAGE IN NEW YORK
by David Michelinie & Dean Wesley Smith

THE INCREDIBLE HULK:
WHAT SAVAGE BEAST by Peter David

SPIDER-MAN: THE LIZARD SANCTION
by Diane Duane

THE ULTIMATE SILVER SURFER,
Stan Lee, Editor

FANTASTIC FOUR: TO FREE ATLANTIS
by Nancy A. Collins

DAREDEVIL: PREDATOR'S SMILE
by Christopher Golden

X-MEN: MUTANT EMPIRE
Book 1: SIEGE by Christopher Golden

THE ULTIMATE SUPER-VILLAINS,
Stan Lee, Editor

SPIDER-MAN & THE INCREDIBLE HULK:
RAMPAGE by Danny Fingeroth & Eric Fein
(Doom's Day Book 1)

SPIDER-MAN: GOBLIN'S REVENGE
by Dean Wesley Smith

THE ULTIMATE X-MEN, Stan Lee, Editor

SPIDER-MAN: THE OCTOPUS AGENDA
by Diane Duane

X-MEN: MUTANT EMPIRE
Book 2: SANCTUARY by Christopher Golden

IRON MAN: OPERATION A.I.M.
by Greg Cox

SPIDER-MAN & IRON MAN: SABOTAGE
by Pierce Askegren & Danny Fingeroth
(Doom's Day Book 2)

X-MEN: MUTANT EMPIRE
Book 3: SALVATION by Christopher Golden

GENERATION X
by Scott Lobdell & Elliot S! Maggin

FANTASTIC FOUR: REDEMPTION OF THE
SILVER SURFER by Michael Jan Friedman

THE INCREDIBLE HULK:
ABOMINATIONS by Jason Henderson

X-MEN: SMOKE AND MIRRORS
by eluki bes shahar

UNTOLD TALES OF SPIDER-MAN,
Stan Lee & Kurt Busiek, Editors

X-MEN: EMPIRE'S END by Diane Duane

SPIDER-MAN & FANTASTIC FOUR:
WRECKAGE by Eric Fein & Pierce Askegren
(Doom's Day Book 3)
X-MEN: THE JEWELS OF CYTTORAK
by Dean Wesley Smith

SPIDER-MAN: VALLEY OF THE LIZARD
by John Vornholt

X-MEN: LAW OF THE JUNGLE
by Dave Smeds

SPIDER-MAN: WANTED: DEAD OR ALIVE
by Craig Shaw Gardner

X-MEN: PRISONER X by Ann Nocenti

FANTASTIC FOUR: COUNTDOWN TO
CHAOS by Pierce Askegren

X-MEN & SPIDER-MAN: TIME'S
ARROW Book 1: THE PAST
by Tom DeFalco & Jason Henderson

X-MEN & SPIDER-MAN: TIME'S
ARROW Book 2: THE PRESENT
by Tom DeFalco & Adam-Troy Castro

X-MEN & SPIDER-MAN: TIME'S
ARROW Book 3: THE FUTURE
by Tom DeFalco & eluki bes shahar

SPIDER-MAN: VENOM'S WRATH
by Keith R.A. DeCandido & José R. Nieto

THE ULTIMATE HULK
Stan Lee & Peter David, Editors

X-MEN: CODENAME WOLVERINE
by Christopher Golden

GENERATION X: CROSSROADS
by J. Steven York

CAPTAIN AMERICA: LIBERTY'S TORCH
by Tony Isabella & Bob Ingersoll

THE AVENGERS & THE THUNDER-
BOLTS by Pierce Askegren

X-MEN: SOUL KILLER by Richard Lee Byers

SPIDER-MAN: THE GATHERING OF
THE SINISTER SIX by Adam-Troy Castro

DAREDEVIL: THE CUTTING EDGE
by Madeleine E. Robins

X-MEN & THE AVENGERS:
GAMMA QUEST: Book 1: LOST AND
FOUND by Greg Cox

SPIDER-MAN: GOBLIN MOON
by Kurt Busiek & Nathan Archer

X-MEN & THE AVENGERS: GAMMA
QUEST: Book 2: SEARCH AND RESCUE
by Greg Cox

X-MEN & THE AVENGERS: GAMMA
QUEST: Book 3: FRIEND OR FOE?
by Greg Cox

X-MEN LEGENDS,
Stan Lee, Editor

COMING SOON:

NICK FURY, AGENT OF S.H.I.E.L.D.:
EMPYRE by Will Murray

GENERATION X: GENOGOTHS
by J. Steven York

SPIDER-MAN: EMERALD MYSTERY
by Dean Wesley Smith

GAMMA QUEST

BOOK 2
SEARCH AND RESCUE

Greg Cox

Illustrations by George Pérez

MARVEL®

BP BOOKS, INC.
NEW YORK

BERKLEY BOULEVARD BOOKS, NEW YORK

If you purchased this book without a cover you should be aware that this book is stolen property. It was reported as "unsold and destroyed" to the publisher and neither the author nor the publisher has received any payment for this "stripped book."

Special thanks to Ginjer Buchanan, John Morgan, Ursula Ward, Mike Thomas, and Steve Behling.

X-MEN & THE AVENGERS: GAMMA QUEST:
Book 2: SEARCH AND RESCUE

A Berkley Boulevard Book
A BP Books, Inc. Book

This is a work of fiction. Names, characters, places, and incidents are either the product of the author's imagination or are used fictitiously, and any resemblance to actual persons, living or dead, business establishments, events, or locales is entirely coincidental.

PRINTING HISTORY
Berkley Boulevard paperback edition / August 1999

All rights reserved.
Copyright © 1999 Marvel Characters, Inc.
Edited by Dwight Jon Zimmerman.
Cover art by Julie Bell.
Cover design by Claude Goodwin.
Book design by Michael Mendelsohn.
This book may not be reproduced in whole or in part, by mimeograph or any other means, without permission.
For information address: BP Books, Inc.,
24 West 25th Street, New York, New York 10010.

The Penguin Putnam Inc. World Wide Web site address is
http://www.penguinputnam.com

Check out the Ace Science Fiction/Fantasy newsletter,
and much more, at Club PPI!

ISBN: 0-425-16989-8

BERKLEY BOULEVARD
Berkley Boulevard Books are published by The Berkley Publishing Group,
a division of Penguin Putnam Inc., 375 Hudson Street, New York, New York 10014.
BERKLEY BOULEVARD and its logo
are trademarks belonging to Penguin Putnam Inc.

PRINTED IN THE UNITED STATES OF AMERICA

10 9 8 7 6 5 4 3

"But search the land of living men,
"Where wilt thou find their like again?"
—Sir Walter Scott (1808)

"If there are people in need—mutate, mutant, human or otherwise—the Avengers are there!"
—Steve Rogers (1993)

ACKNOWLEDGMENTS

Thanks to Keith R.A. DeCandido for jump-starting this project, and to Steve Roman and Ginjer Buchanan for seeing it through.

GAMMA QUEST

BOOK 2

SEARCH AND RESCUE

Prologue

"They also serve who only stand and wait." Milton's immortal words came readily to Edwin Jarvis's thoughts as he worriedly watched an emergency news bulletin on television. He often turned to that particular quotation in times of trouble; indeed, over the course of his long tenure as butler to the mighty Avengers, it had practically become his credo.

Alas, that seldom made the waiting any easier....

His hands kept busy polishing a silver tea service while his gaze stayed glued to a small television monitor mounted above the kitchen counter. The middle-aged Englishman wore an apron over his starched proper attire. At the moment, he had the spotless kitchen to himself, along with the rest of Avengers Mansion. On the screen overhead, live footage from Niagara Falls revealed that a trio of his superheroic employers were once more pitted against formidable antagonists in a battle of epic proportions; to be more specific, the combined strength and extraordinary abilities of the champion of liberty, Captain America, the high-tech knight, Iron Man, and the synthetic human, the Vision, were now matched against both the notorious outlaw mutants known as the uncanny X-Men and the fearsome green man-monster called the incredible Hulk. *A daunting combination,* the butler assessed, although he clung steadfastly to his faith that the Avengers would emerge triumphant in the end, as they so often had before. *They have consistently prevailed over even greater odds,* he recalled, *and against far more merciless foes.*

Both the X-Men and the Hulk, in fact, had sometimes fought beside the Avengers as allies, for all that such partnerships tended to be strained and somewhat fractious. Whatever cruel combination of circumstances had led to this present conflict, Jarvis held onto the hope that neither the Hulk nor the X-Men truly desired the Avengers' total destruction, as might, say, the Grim Reaper or Ultron, although where the undeniably volatile Hulk was concerned, anything was possible. Nor could such reassurances rule out the possibility of a tragic accident, particularly in so hazardous a setting.

The awesome heights of Niagara Falls, over which torrents of frothing white water cascaded impressively, provided a scenic backdrop to the spectacular struggle, but also obvious opportunities for the various combatants to come to harm. Even now, as Jarvis methodically buffed the exterior of a tarnished tea kettle, the Hulk had fearlessly taken up a position along the very crest of the famed Horseshoe Falls, tempting fate, not to mention the raging current, to topple him from his precarious perch. Jarvis gulped involuntarily as the Vision alighted in the rapids above the Falls, only a few feet away from the bestial green goliath known as the Hulk. *I certainly hope Master Vision knows what he is doing,* Jarvis fretted. Never mind the Falls, for a moment; on his own, the Hulk could be as savage as he was inhumanly powerful.

TV newspeople speculated shamelessly about what might have brought all these costumed champions to this titanic clash, the reporters's urgent voiceovers accompanying vivid action footage from cameras on the shore. Jarvis turned down the volume. He already knew far more than the commentators about the origins of this latest adventure.

It had all started yesterday, when Mistress Wanda, professionally known as the Scarlet Witch, failed to return from a morning's outing to a local museum. Subsequent investigation revealed that the mutant heroine had been attacked and abducted by, of all things, one of the displays of a coterie of wooden marionettes. As though this were not puzzling enough, Iron Man's sophisticated electronic sensors had detected lingering traces of radiation at the site of the Scarlet Witch's disappearance. *Gamma* radiation, to be precise, of the sort associated with both the rampaging Hulk and his more rational alter ego, Dr. Robert Bruce Banner.

Led by Captain America, the Avengers had already resolved to seek out the Hulk and/or Banner to question him (them?) about the incident at the museum when word came that the S.H.I.E.L.D. Helicarrier, airborne headquarters of the world's premiere intelligence and anti-terrorism organization, had been invaded by several super-powered mutants linked to the X-Men. According to Nicholas Fury, the irascible director of S.H.I.E.L.D., the mutant renegades had stolen the top-secret prototypes of the Gamma Sentinels, a new generation of robot enforcers powered by the same form of gamma radiation that had created the Hulk. Given that the Gamma Sentinels were expressly designed to seek out and contain dangerous mutants, a preemptive strike by the X-Men seemed a plausible explanation for the assault on the Helicarrier, even if Captain America continued to entertain doubts about the X-Men's guilt, judging them innocent until proven otherwise—according to the best tradition of British and American justice.

How very like the Captain to give the X-Men the benefit of the doubt, Jarvis reflected. *But whatever could the stolen*

SEARCH AND RESCUE

Sentinels, and the X-Men, have to do with Mistress Wanda's abduction, especially since the mutant-hunting robots were purloined several hours after the Scarlet Witch's bizarre encounter with the animated puppets? Her Avenging teammates had been equally baffled by the peculiar chain of events.

Then the evening news had reported that Bruce Banner, a wanted fugitive, had been spotted in Niagara Falls, just south of the Canadian border. The three Avengers on hand, including Mistress Wanda's estranged husband, the Vision, had immediately winged toward Niagara, only to land squarely in the middle of a tense confrontation involving the Hulk, the X-Men, and the armed forces of both the United States and Canada. Precisely whose side the X-Men were on remained unclear to both the on-the-air commentators and Jarvis himself; at various points in the ongoing crisis, they had appeared to be both allied and opposed to the Hulk, who seemed typically ill-deposed to all concerned. Jarvis did not know the X-Men well, having in the past had but fleeting contact with those of their number, but past encounters with the Hulk led him to suspect that the brutish Hulk was on the side of nothing save yet more chaos and strife. Jarvis had cleaned up after the Hulk enough to know that where that uncouth ogre went, violence and wanton destruction surely followed.

But although the faithful butler expected the worst of the Hulk, he was still caught by surprise when the great green monster ripped the Vision's arm from its socket.

"Good heavens!" Jarvis exclaimed. The teapot slipped from his fingers, landing in a clatter upon the kitchen floor. Telephoto lenses caught an unmistakably human expression of agony upon the synthezoid's sculpted features. A shower of sparks erupted from the Vision's right shoulder. Oily lubricants and hydraulic fluid sprayed from severed tubing as the Vision's head jerked spastically. The amber jewel embedded in his forehead flashed on and off, the solar glow within the gem flickering weakly. Crimson lips whispered some plaintive plea or warning, but all Jarvis could hear was the roar of the Falls and the breathless commentary of the stunned newspersons.

He watched in horrified silence as the Hulk callously discarded the Vision's crudely amputated limb, hurling it over the edge of the Falls. Then the Hulk shoved the Vision and the tottering synthezoid followed his severed arm over the Falls. Jarvis prayed that the Vision would save himself by taking flight, reducing his artificial body's density until it was lighter than air, but instead the camera tracked his terrifying plunge until the android Avenger vanished into the swirling mists at the bottom. Could even the Vision survive such a precipitous drop? Jarvis hoped for the best, but decided to have the engineering laboratories in the Mansion's sub-basement up and running by the time the Avengers returned. *Perhaps I should alert Dr. Pym as well,* Jarvis thought, *and warn him to be on call.* The brilliant scientist, now a reserve member of the Avengers, probably understood the Vision's construction better than any other human on Earth.

With the maiming of the Vision, the ominous stand-off between the assorted heroes escalated into a veritable battle royal, fought on the land, the water, and the air. As the X-Men inexplicably came to the Hulk's aid, for reasons Jarvis could not begin to imagine, the two teams came to blows. Darting TV cameras were hard-pressed to keep up with the conflict while the worried butler struggled to identify the principals and track the course of the skirmish. The silver teapot, now dented on one side, lay forgotten at his feet.

Iron Man was the first who sought to avenge the Vision by taking arms against the Hulk. Jetting above the Falls, he

SEARCH AND RESCUE

subjected the defiant green behemoth to a barrage of repulsor rays, until struck from behind by an unexpected lightning bolt. The jagged electrical spear came from a flying woman whom Jarvis swiftly identified as Storm, one of the X-Men's leaders. Her tempestuous *nom de guerre* proved uncomfortably apt as she and Iron Man conducted an aerial dogfight that reminded Jarvis of the Battle of Britain, except that these flying aces jousted with beams of incandescent energy and electricity instead of old-fashioned machine guns. They proved well-matched in maneuverability and speed, although the female mutant had so far managed to keep one step ahead of her armored adversary, swooping and banking through morning skies that grew increasingly gray and thundery. Was the latter Storm's doing? The butler suspected as much. The once-blue skies soon looked as dark and forbidding as the Hulk's disposition.

The cameras quickly lost Storm and Iron Man amidst the roiling clouds, so the view switched to Goat Island, a small, wooded wedge of land nestled between the American and Canadian Falls. At the rocky tip of the island, the surrounding greenery laid waste earlier by the Hulk's rampage, Captain America faced off against Cyclops, the grim X-Man known for his devastating eyebeams, which were even now directed against the Avenger's stalwart leader. Cap (as his friends called him) blocked the crimson ray with his unbreakable metal shield, deflecting the attack back at Cyclops, who responded in turn by intercepting the returning beams with fresh blasts of ocular energy before unleashing new beams at whatever portion of Captain America's anatomy appeared unshielded, only to have each new attack parried deftly by the agile Avenger. It hurt Jarvis's eyes just to watch the coruscating beams bounce back and forth between the two rivals; it looked like some sort of newfangled videogame of the sort his nieces and nephews played, and each player seemed at the top of his game. The butler knew how skillfully Captain America could wield his shield, but he was surprised to see that the slender young X-Man seemed to be able to target his beams with equal precision and dexterity. *What if he succeeds in getting past Captain America's guard?* he worried. He had heard that Cyclops's eyebeams packed quite a punch. What's more, he could not help noticing that one of the decorative eagle wings adorning Captain America's blue cowl had already gone missing, no doubt the victim of a distressingly close call with a crimson beam. *Master Rogers has a sturdy constitution, but he is not invulnerable. That's why he carries a shield.*

With the dueling heroes deadlocked for the nonce, the camera zoomed in on a faint blue figure lying in the background, where the desolate wasteland left behind by the Hulk surrendered to the encroaching woods. "My word!" Jarvis gasped, stricken by the distressing sight of former Avenger Hank McCoy, alias the usually ebullient Beast, trapped beneath the trunk of a fallen maple tree. The shaggy, blue-furred mutant lay sprawled upon his back, the substantial tree trunk stretched across his torso. A heart-wrenching close-up revealed that the Beast looked dazed and only semi-conscious. His eyelids flickered and his thick, mud-covered indigo pelt was soaked. *Dear me,* Jarvis thought, *I hope Master McCoy has not been seriously injured.* The Beast had once been a cheerful and welcome presence within the stately walls of Avengers Mansion, before he chose to return to his roots as a charter member of the X-Men. *What a shame as well,* the butler reflected, *that the Beast should be incapacitated at so crucial a juncture;* as a trusted member of both teams, Henry McCoy alone stood the best chance of bringing about a timely cease-fire between the two teams.

SEARCH AND RESCUE

But could any individual, no matter how charming and sincere, quell the unquenchable fury of the Hulk? Before the loyal manservant's anxious eyes, the Hulk leaped from the crest of the Falls, his unbelievably powerful leg muscles propelling him high into the sky before landing on the island, dramatically interrupting the duel between Cyclops and Captain America. Even the anonymous cameraman on the shore was rocked by the impact of the Hulk's meteoric arrival on the island, as evidenced by the way the picture on the TV screen lurched awkwardly soon after the Hulk hit the ground. Jarvis well remembered all of Avengers Mansion shaking the same way whenever the Hulk threw a tantrum—which he did pretty much throughout his short-lived stint as an Avenger.

The Hulk's crash landing carved a crater in the soil of Goat Island, from which he emerged unscathed. His troglodyte-like visage filled the TV screen, conveying so much primordial menace that Jarvis stepped backward involuntarily, almost stumbling over the dented teapot. The Hulk glared malevolently at the world, baring jagged teeth the size of slates, and the camera itself retreated, drawing back to capture as well the more heroic figures of Captain America and Cyclops, who broke off their own contest to eye the Hulk uneasily. Their wary stances bespoke what Jarvis considered a prudent caution in the Hulk's presence. *I suppose it's too much to hope,* he thought wryly, *that the Hulk simply wants to break up the fight between Cyclops and the Captain.*

Not exactly. The other heroes' apprehensions proved justified when the savage green gargantua lunged first at Cyclops, then Captain America. A single swipe from the Hulk's huge hand downed the X-Man, forcing Captain America to come to the defense of his own opponent from moments before. The valiant Avenger fared little better than

Cyclops; although even the Hulk's fantastic strength was not enough to bend Captain America's indestructible shield, the monster took out his anger on the Captain's more fragile human body. One gamma-powered blow sent Captain America skidding backward across the island and, before the groggy hero could recover, the Hulk seized him with both hands. Triumphantly, the Hulk raised his unconscious foe above his misshapen head, then flung Captain America over the American Falls.

Jarvis gasped in fear. He had once visited Niagara on holiday and well-remembered how dangerous those particular Falls were. Unlike the adjacent Canadian Falls, which emptied into a deep pool from which brazen daredevils were occasionally fished, the American Falls fell directly upon a shelf of deadly and unforgiving rocks. No one had *ever* survived a trip over that lethal cataract. No one could.

Not even Captain America.

Chapter One

Five thousand feet above Niagara Falls, Iron Man pursued Storm through black, swollen thunderclouds. All his attention was focused on the task of catching the mutant weather-witch within the purple radiance of his tractor beam, yet the female X-Man was proving devilishly hard to snare. *I thought my armor was the latest thing in aerodynamic maneuverability,* he thought, *but Storm rides the winds like they belong to her, which, in a way, I guess they do.* There was no question that her elemental ability to control the weather gave her a distinct advantage in this airborne chase; Storm literally had the wind at her back at every instance, while the armored Avenger was forever flying into the face of an opposing gale. *Fortunately, I built this metal suit strong enough to ride out a hurricane.*

Encased in gleaming gold and crimson steel, Iron Man zoomed through the sky like a humanoid missile. Powerful boot-jets kept him aloft as he searched the turbulent atmosphere for the attractive but elusive X-Man. He had lost visual contact with his target, who had vanished into the foggy terrain of her "pet" clouds, but kept track of her via his radar and other long-range sensors. Unfortunately, the dense nimbostratus clouds provided Storm an arsenal of sorts, as demonstrated by the bolt of lightning that suddenly struck his armor, producing a shower of sparks.

"Sorry, lady," Iron Man muttered, "but you're going

SEARCH AND RESCUE

to have to do better than that." Insulation within his armor protected Tony Stark from electrocution while the built-in energy conversion system absorbed the bulk of the thunderbolt's voltage, channeling it into Iron Man's own power reserves. Storm's first few lightning blasts had thrown him for a loop, but now that he was ready for her, she was just feeding him more power. In fact, judging from the current readings, projected directly onto his retinas by virtual imaging units in his eyepieces, he was beginning to exceed capacity. *At this rate,* he thought, *I'm going to have to start firing plasma blasts at random just to discharge the excess energy.*

Perhaps realizing that her galvanic assault had lost its effectiveness, the unseen mutant crusader abruptly switched her tactics. Without warning, Iron Man found himself pelting with sleet, hail, and freezing winds. Fist-sized chunks of frozen rain pinged against his armor, already dented by a bumpy trip over the Canadian Falls, and ice began to form over his armor, including his boot-jets. The bitter cold penetrated sixteen layers of tesselated metal fabric, raising goosebumps on his skin. *Brrr,* he thought, cybernetically channeling some of that excess electricity to heat up the exterior of his armor.

The frosty coating melted away, but the instigator of the hailstorm remained out of sight, hidden behind billowing banks of fog. Iron Man felt like he was up against the meteorological equivalent of guerrilla warfare, with Storm free to strike out at him from the relative concealment of the cloud cover. *Too bad Thor's off on his own quest right now,* he thought. *We could use our own Thunder God at the moment.*

Almost as elusive as Storm herself were the nagging questions behind the dogfight. Why had Storm come to the Hulk's defense after he mutilated the Vision? What did the

X-Men have to do with Wanda's abduction? Granted, the Scarlet Witch was the only daughter of the X-Men's greatest enemy, Magneto, but Xavier's mutant strike force had never held that against her before. The unsolved mysteries preyed on Iron Man's mind; all his high-tech sensors and computer capacity could not illuminate *why* the X-Men and the Avengers were now at odds. Only by apprehending Storm and her companions, including the Hulk, did they stand any chance of finding out what had happened to the Scarlet Witch.

Peering through two rectangular slits in his gilded faceplate, he searched the churning mists for a glimpse of Storm. He tried to lock onto her body heat, and scan the skies with his sonar, but the icy winds and pounding thunder interfered with his sensors. *She's got to be here somewhere,* he realized. *I know it.*

Eyes searching for Storm, the last thing he expected to see was Captain America's shield, rocketing upward at, according to his radar, upward of fifty miles per hour. "What in the world . . . ?" he asked aloud, quickly guessing that the Hulk was responsible. Who else could throw the shield this high? Then the full implications struck home: If his shield was way up here, what had happened to Cap?

Iron Man deftly snagged the ascendant shield with his tractor beam, catching the historic weapon before it went into orbit. The magnetic ray drew the shield closer to the armored Avenger, who grabbed it with one gauntlet, then interrupted his pursuit of Storm to check on his fellow Avenger. *Not Cap, too,* he prayed, remembering the Hulk's brutal treatment of the Vision. He dived out of the clouds, just in time to see the Hulk, standing defiantly upon Goat Island, hurl a patriotically-garbed figure over the crest of the American Falls.

"No!" Iron Man gasped. He had already survived his

own spectacular tumble over the Falls, but Cap wasn't wearing an invulnerable suit of body armor. He had to catch Cap before he hit bottom, or the world would lose a living legend. The Golden Avenger went into a power dive, pushing his jets to the maximum, but wasn't sure he could reach the falling hero in time. *Blast it,* he thought anxiously. *This is going to be close....*

The wind rushing against his face, plus the cooling spray of the Falls, woke Captain America, who discovered at once that he was in freefall. He reached instinctively for his shield, only to find it missing. *That's right,* he remembered. *The Hulk threw it into the sky when he couldn't break it, then he—* Cap winced at the memory of the Hulk's mighty fist barreling at him with the force of an express train. *How long was I out?*

There was no time to worry about that. Well-trained reflexes responded to danger and he strove to control his fall, assuming a diving position, his arms spread out to slow his descent as much as possible. The wind whistled past his ears, merging with the roar of thousands of gallons of plunging water.

Every second counts, he realized, spying the daunting pile of rocks at the Fall's base. He didn't think his momentum could carry him past that lethal landing pad, but he owed it to himself, his teammates, and his country to try. *Never give up,* he resolved. *That's what America is all about.*

A familiar thrumming sound made itself heard and Cap glanced back over his shoulder to see the shining figure of Iron Man swooping toward him, rockets blazing. A purple glow suffused the triangular beam projector at the center of his crimson chestplate, and Captain America felt a faint tug upward, but Iron Man was still too far away for his magnetic ray to do more than slow Cap's descent; in the contest to decide the plummeting Avenger's fate, gravity was definitely winning. Cap found himself wishing that his traditional uniform included a cape, just so he could try using it as a parachute.

How much longer until he hit the ground? Cap stared straight down, willing his eyes to stay open despite the damp air rushing against his face. The craggy rocks below looked like they were growing faster than Giant-Man on a tear, expanding upward at him, and Cap suddenly wondered if his entire life was going to pass before his eyes or just the post-World War II years? There was an awful lot of personal history to go through in the next split-second or two. *If this is the end,* he thought, *at least I'm checking out on American soil, if only by a few hundred feet or so!*

Then, only heartbeats before Cap's flesh and bone collided with the stationary rocks, an unexpected gust of wind took hold of his body, lifting him up and away from the perilous rockpile. The powerful updraft seemed to come from nowhere, until Cap looked up to see Storm's statuesque figure silhouetted against flashes of blue-white lightning. "Of course," he murmured, grateful for the timely assist, "I should have guessed."

Intent on rescuing Cap, Iron Man appeared oblivious to Storm's presence in the skies above him. *Nice to know the X-Men still draw the line at murder,* Captain America thought, *with the possible exception of Wolverine, and even he seldom kills without provocation.* The life-saving zephyr held him aloft long enough for Iron Man's tractor beam to latch onto him more firmly. A purple radiance enveloped Cap as he found himself suspended in the air, the magnetic ray tugging on the chain mail links in his lightweight metal tunic. A tingling sensation rushed over his skin, which he decided was vastly preferable to feeling battered and broken atop the rocks.

Let's hear it for the miracle of American technology, he thought, *not to mention the divine intervention of a certain mutant weather goddess.*

"You okay, Cap?" Iron Man asked. Tony Stark's usually urbane voice was amplified and electronically distorted by the mouthpiece in his steel helmet. Doubtful that Iron Man could hear him over the tumult of the Falls, Cap gave him an encouraging thumbs-up sign. He was relieved to see his faithful shield safe in the other Avenger's iron grip. *So far, so good,* he thought optimistically. *Now if we can only call off this senseless fight . . . !*

Unfortunately, that meant calming down the Hulk, which made that a very big "if."

For a terrifying second, Hank McCoy thought the Juggernaut was sitting on his chest. "Kindly elevate your Brobdingnagian bulk from my hirsute and tortured torso," he declaimed. Then the Beast opened his eyes and saw he was talking to a tree. "I stand corrected," he said to the downed maple weighing heavily upon his ribs, "proverbially, if not literally."

In fact, he was not standing at all, but rather lying flat on his back in the mud, with a rather sizable piece of lumber holding him down. His dark blue fur was soaked and plastered to his skin. Sniffing, he discovered that the wet fur was more than a little pungent. He blinked and shook his head, trying to remember how exactly he had come to abide in this supine and decidedly uncomfortable situation.

Thunder reverberated far overhead, reminding him of another explosion in the recent past, one far too close for comfort. *Artillery?* his muddled brain prompted and his memory began to reconstruct itself, picking up just before that exceptionally alarming dream about the none too jocular Juggernaut. *Artillery it was,* he recalled. The armies assembled on either shore of the Niagara River had opened fire on the Hulk, catching the X-Men in the crossfire. He had been helping a stunned Storm make her way to the shelter of the surviving woods when a shell detonated nearby and this very tree fell on top of him. After that, his recollections got a lot fuzzier; he must have segued in and out of consciousness, although he had vague memories of Storm coming to his aid, and of being drenched by an enormous wave of water.

Since when did the majestic Niagara fall up? he wondered.

His pointed blue ears perked up, the guns on the shore seemed to have fallen silent, although the pealing storm clouds above him more than made up the difference as far as ambient noise was concerned.

"Thank providence for diminutive dispensations," he pronounced, anxious to determine the whereabouts and status of his esteemed fellow X-Men. He tried to look about him, but, pinned thus to the ground, all he could see was the blustery sky looming above him. The continued absence of both Storm and Cyclops while he lay incapacitated did not bode well for their quest to solicit the Hulk's aid in finding Rogue, missing in action since yesterday afternoon. *Something has gone amiss,* he deduced, *else I would not be left to my own devices.*

Getting out from beneath the insistent weight of the fallen tree was clearly the first order of business. Still feeling a tad woozy, he braced his hairy palms against the bark-covered underside of the toppled maple and labored to lift the massive encumbrance off his somewhat squashed physiognomy.

This shouldn't be too hard, he thought; his brute strength was nowhere near the Hulk's class, but he was certainly stronger than the average beast. Straining his genetically-enhanced muscles, he managed to lift the dripping timber a few inches away from his chest, giving his half-crushed lungs a chance to expand. But he wasn't able to slide out from underneath the tree and hold it aloft at the same time. Leafy branches scratched against his face and chest while rivulets of chilly water streamed down on him, making a difficult task even more unpleasant.

Just how, pray tell, did everything get so soggy and saturated anyway? he wondered. *Did I miss a tsunami or two while I was* hors de combat?

The Beast was beginning to wonder whether even Harry Houdini could have liberated himself from this particular predicament when he heard Cyclops call to him from several yards away. "Watch your head!" The Beast promptly sank the back of his head into the cold, squishy mud and covered his eyes with both hands. Even with his eyelids squeezed shut, a bright crimson glow suddenly lit up his view and he heard the heavy log shatter into splinters, the ill-fated target of Cyke's attention. Just as suddenly the ruby radiance departed, as did the oppressive weight upon his body.

"Abundant thanks!" the Beast exclaimed, springing at once to his feet. Oversized toes sank into the liquified earth and his head spun momentarily before a preternatural sense of balance reasserted itself. "Your dynamic assistance is most enthusiastically appreciated!"

But the X-Men's conscientious co-leader was in no position to acknowledge the Beast's effusively-expressed gratitude. The soaked, soggy mutant was chagrined to discover that Cyclops was under attack by none other than the intractable Hulk himself.

"Get ready to take the big plunge, Red-Eyes," the Hulk

bellowed at Cyclops. "I'm going to do to you just what I did to that star-spangled nuisance before!"

Star-spangled? The reference caught the Beast by surprise, until he remembered hearing Captain America's voice shortly before the military bombardment of the island.

What is Cap doing here? he wondered. *And what precisely is the Hulk claiming to have done to that most venerable of Avengers?* The Beast almost didn't want to find out.

Meanwhile, Cyclops had turned his fluorescent eyebeams against the advancing monster. The crimson rays, capable of punching through solid steel, broke against the Hulk's broad chest like waves lapping upon an unyielding granite promontory. The concussive force of the beam only slowed the Hulk's inexorable approach. His pitiless sneer only reinforced the menace inherent in his colossal fists.

Would that the Hulk were content to rebuff our entreaty with a mere exclamation in the negative, the Beast thought. Rather than providing the X-Men with valuable information and insights concerning Rogue's unexplained disappearance, the jade titan seemed more intent on pummeling Cyclops within an inch of his life—or closer. The Beast prepared to spring to his friend's defense, even while privately wondering what good his characteristic acrobatics and agility could do against so indomitable a foe. *Ah, for the halcyon days of yore when all we had to sally forth against was the Toad or maybe the Blob....*

Before his coiled leg muscles could propel him into the fray, however, the Hulk came under attack from another quarter. From above, coruscating orange rays, as resplendent in their own way as Cyclops's eyebeams, slammed into the Hulk's head and shoulders. "Arrgh!" the behemoth growled, sounding more surprised than stunned. A

SEARCH AND RESCUE

scowl announced his displeasure. "What now?"

The answer came zooming out of the sky, wearing a one-of-a-kind suit of invincible armor. "Time for round two, Hulk," Iron Man said, his amplified voice carrying over the din. Repulsor rays glowed from his gauntlets. Jets flared from the soles of his boots. "We're not finished yet."

Nor was the Golden Avenger alone. Shield in hand, Captain America came charging across the island, only a few yards behind Iron Man.

Hail, hail, the gang's all here, the Beast thought, wondering exactly how many Avengers had accompanied Cap and Shellhead on this particular mission. His spirits lifted; with reinforcements such as these, he and Cyke no longer seemed quite so overmatched. *Between the X-Men and the Avengers, the Hulk may actually have a fight on his hands,* he thought.

But the Beast's optimistic hopes were dashed when, rather than joining forces against the berserk Hulk, the newly-arrived Avengers took on the X-Men as well. His iconic shield held high, Captain America barrelled into Cyclops, knocking the slender X-Man off his feet, only to be driven back by a sizzling bolt of lightning that struck the ground between Cap and his downed adversary, the crackling thunderbolt turning a muddy puddle into a charred, steaming crater. The Beast looked up to see an ascendant Storm reigning over the tempestuous sky, her eyes glowing with elemental power. More than any expert meteorological report, he knew, those seething, incandescent eyes forecast dire weather ahead.

Never make Ororo mad, the Beast reminded himself, *unless you're ready for an honest-to-goodness hurricane.*

Distracted by Iron Man's repulsor rays, the Hulk forgot about Cyclops and turned his perennially hostile intentions toward the armored Avenger. His subsequent leap into the sky, catapulting himself fists first at Iron Man, made the Beast's own prodigious bouncing look like baby steps. The bounding green monstrosity and the soaring ironclad hero collided in midair, with Iron Man getting the worst of the head-on encounter. The force and momentum behind the Hulk's rock-hard knuckles sent Iron Man careening backward into the clouds, dozens of feet below Storm, who, though distant from the fray was far from detached from it. She flung raw electricity against Captain America, the Hulk, and Iron Man simultaneously, lighting up the heavens with constant flashes of jagged lightning. Thunder, incessant and deafening, gave voice to Storm's unleashed ire and refusal to surrender.

No question, the Beast thought, aghast at the dismaying spectacle of a three-way battle between the Hulk, the X-Men, and the Avengers, *I most indubitably missed something.* What could have brought the two teams to blows like this? Having served under both banners in his time, he knew that neither group was predisposed toward senseless and unprovoked aggression, unlike, say, the Hulk. "Wait!" he shouted. "Kindly abandon this unseemly altercation!"

Sadly, his earnest effort at peacemaking could not be heard over the combined hubbub of Falls, tempest, and super-powered strife. Cyclops's eyebeam ricocheted off the convex surface of Captain America's shield, barely missing the Beast, who had to cartwheel out of the way so that the beam struck instead the river behind him, briefly parting the waters.

Quelling this cacophonous imbroglio with naught but softly-spoken words of sweet reason, he realized, *may prove easier said than done.* To his surprise, another voice, coming from the American side of the river, intruded upon the ear-bruising racket:

"This is Colonel Lopez of the U.S. Army, addressing

SEARCH AND RESCUE

the Hulk and the X-Men! Stand down at once, or we will take Goat Island by force. You have five minutes to surrender."

The Beast recognized the amplified echo of an on-shore megaphone. "That is categorically what the physician prescribed," he mused aloud. Glancing to the east, he contemplated the khaki-colored troops lined up along the far side of the cascading Niagara River.

I need to get over there posthaste, but how? he thought. The breadth of the roiling water exceeded his ability to transverse in a single leap. Here and there, the tips of a few defiant stones protruded above the foaming white water, offering a tantalizing, if potentially treacherous, route across the river, but the Beast hesitated before committing himself to that daunting choice. Jumping from rock to slippery rock only a few yards upstream of one of the world's most impressive waterfalls would be a challenge even for him, with the consequences of a single slip inextricably terminal.

There was always the Blackbird, he recalled. Yet by the time he returned to the X-Men's personal aircraft, parked elsewhere on the island, lifted off, then landed somewhere on the opposing shore, the heated struggle upon and above Goat Island might well have escalated to nigh-apocalyptic proportions, especially with powerhouses like the Hulk and Iron Man involved.

No, he concluded, *there is not time enow for detours.* He needed to get across that river and he needed to do so with all deliberate speed.

Gazing speculatively, and with no little trepidation, at the nearest shard of exposed rock, he almost bounded from the island, when another idea occurred to him, one sparked by something he had witnessed mere moments before.

"Eureka!" he exclaimed, bushy blue eyebrows rising to

commemorate his brainstorm. *Like the proverbial crazy idea, that just might work!*

Simian-like fingers dug into the battle-ravaged landscape and plucked a rounded pebble from the earth. Looking past the embattled Cyclops, the Beast observed that Captain America was, at least for the moment, fully occupied fending off Storm's ground-seeking thunderbolts, giving the X-Men's other leader a momentary breather.

Perfect timing, the Beast decided. A second later, the tiny stone bounced off the back of Cyclops's head. Cyclops spun around. To the anthropoid X-Man's relief, Cyke chose to determine the identity of the pebble-thrower before shooting.

The Beast didn't waste time trying to vocalize his intentions over the sounds of rushing water and fierce battle. Instead he resorted to sign language, pointing first at himself, then at the troops across the river, and finally at Cyclops's dormant visor. The crimson glow concealing Cyke's eyes made it hard to read his expression, but the Beast hoped that years of teamwork, both in the Danger Room and in the field, would let him and Cyclops communicate silently, without need for a more extensive and elaborate round of Charades.

Why is there never a telepath around when you need one? the Beast lamented; regretfully, neither Professor X nor Jean Grey had accompanied them on this mission. When last heard from, both psychic prodigies were engaged in a vital expedition to the Savage Island, along with several more of their fellow X-Men. *Perhaps it is just as well,* the Beast thought. *Too many X-Men, and several more Avengers, may have only added to the cataclysmic chaos of this free-for-all. Just imagine Wolverine or the mighty Thor adding their combustible tempers to the equation!*

Right now, all he needed was Cyclops, provided the

SEARCH AND RESCUE

X-Men's most serious and sober soldier-in-arms deduced what the Beast had in mind. After a moment's silence, Cyke nodded and gestured for the Beast to step aside. He pointed his visor at the turbulent river and raised the inner lens all the way open.

A wide red beam ploughed through the river, clearing a path all the way across to the other side. "Shades of Cecil B. DeMille!" the Beast enthused. "Not to mention that Dreamworks cartoon a few months back!" Cyclops had well and truly parted the waters before him.

Now came the uncomfortable part. Taking a deep breath to steady his nerves, the Beast hurled himself bodily into the path of the awe-inspiring beam. Countless newtons of force immediately slammed into his back, pushing him forward at breathtaking speed. It was like sitting in the driver's seat of a Saturn rocket at liftoff. *I'm going to be black and blue after this stunt,* he thought, grimacing, *not that anyone will be able to tell....*

The intense pressure lasted only an instant. But, as he had hoped, the Beast found himself prone upon a grassy lawn overlooking the river. Several feet behind him, a protective metal railing had been bisected by Cyclops's initial blast, leaving behind a ragged gap. Further back, in the river itself, the water filled the channel that Cyke had briefly carved through the flowing torrent.

Nice of him to clear the way before I jumped aboard the Eyebeam Express, the Beast thought, wincing as he sought to mobilize his badly-abused body. His entire back felt as though it had been pounded upon repeatedly by the Absorbing Man's ball and chain.

He lifted his face from the damp, dewy grass to find a half dozen automatic rifles aimed at his head; the Beast suddenly envied Iron Man his impervious helmet. A squadron of nervous-looking soldiers peered down the sights of their M-16s, surrounding the Beast and leading him to hope, for his sake, that there were no trigger-happy mutant-haters among the assembled troopers, many of whom were staring at his bristling blue countenance as if he had just arrived from Mars.

"Er, take me to your leader?" he said weakly.

They didn't have to. His rank announced by the black colonel's eagles on his battle-dress uniform, their commanding officer came stomping across the lawn, a megaphone in one hand and a two-way radio in the other. Anxious subordinates, clutching charts and binoculars, trailed after him like a film star's entourage.

Just the individual that I wished to behold, the Beast thought, encouraged despite the battery of automatic rifles aimed at his unusually well-educated brain.

"Colonel Lopez, I presume?" the Beast started to stand up, only to hear a dozen firearms lock and load. *On second thought,* he reconsidered, *maybe I'll stay right where I am for the time being.* He entertained the notion of giving the soldiers a friendly smile, then realized that his bared fangs might be misinterpreted. *Little do they know that I prefer a good salad to raw meat.*

The Colonel shouldered his way through the crowd of young recruits. His lean face had been permanently furrowed by the responsibilities of command. "Identify yourself," he barked at the Beast. "Are you with the X-Men or the Avengers?"

"Both, actually," the Beast responded, more or less accurately. To be fair, he hadn't enjoyed active status among the Avengers since that time-warping contretemps with Morgan Le Fey a few months back, but now did not strike him as the most politic occasion at which to point out that particular distinction. "You could check with the appropriate authorities regarding my various clearances and cre-

SEARCH AND RESCUE

dentials, but I fear that we have precious little time to spare, Colonel, and I could definitely use your assistance."

The scowling officer mulled the matter for only a few moments before nodding in the Beast's direction. "I remember now. I saw you and the other Avengers fight Graviton in Times Square, back when I was just a private." Following their commander's lead, the uniformed riflemen backed away from the Beast, although a few of the more wary soldiers kept the Beast in their sights until the Colonel directed them to lower their weapons. "What can I do for you?" he asked the prostrate X-Man.

A couple of aspirin would be appreciated, the Beast thought. Slowly, keeping one eye on the potentially over-eager troopers, he lifted his aching body from the grass, leaving a squashed, Beast-shaped impression in the lawn. Grass stains streaked his blue fur. "In fact," he explained, "I am desirous of requisitioning an item of communications technology. That megaphone, to be precise." He pointed at the funnel-like apparatus gripped in the Colonel's left hand.

"Go ahead," Colonel Lopez said, handing the device to the Beast. "Lord knows it hasn't done me a bit of good."

The Beast sympathized with the man's frustration. There wasn't much conventional armed forces could do against the X-Men, let alone the Hulk. *Let us now ascertain whether my own powers of persuasion are sufficient to the task of restoring some degree of tranquility to Niagara.* The Beast was by no means Killgrave the Purple Man, whose every utterance compelled obedience, but he might be Niagara's last, best hope for peace. *With apologies to a certain TV space station,* he amended.

"Cap! Iron Man! Storm! Cyclops!" he called out, holding the megaphone before his lips. "This is your mutual acquaintance, the beneficent Beast. I believe an immediate truce is in order, the better to resolve whatever differences may have arisen. Allow me to offer myself as mediator, if such is required. I trust that will be acceptable to all concerned."

Except the Hulk, mayhap, he thought. Still, it seemed Storm's all-shaking thunder had lessened in volume and Iron Man's fiery repulsor rays no longer glowed like bright orange neon against the angry clouds. Then abruptly, they ceased. His gaze switched to the embattled island and the tiny figures on it. "Your binoculars, please," he requested from one of Colonel Lopez's lieutenants.

Had Cap and Cyke acknowledged his plea as well? Resting the borrowed binoculars upon the bridge of his nose, the Beast spun the lenses until the tip of the island came into focus. To his relief, he saw Captain America cautiously lowering his shield even as Cyclops held back his trademark eyebeams behind his visor. "Peace hath her victories, no less renowned than war," the Beast rejoiced in relief, quoting Milton.

"Huh?" the lieutenant asked, bewildered. Colonel Lopez gave the Beast a puzzled look as well.

Before the hirsute X-Man could helpfully attribute the quotation, an angry green figure shot like a cannonball away from the island, arcing across the sky until it landed with an earth-rattling thud only a few yards away from the Beast. The manicured lawn trembled beneath the mutant hero's bare feet.

"Spoilsport!" the Hulk accused, shaking an enormous fist at the Beast. "Killjoy! Who gave you the right to play Mother Teresa at my brawl?" He stalked toward the Beast, glaring murderously at the X-Man. "As far as I'm concerned, this little donnybrook's just getting started!"

The Beast gulped. The musclebound monster had crossed the river in a single leap. The Beast had known he would have to soon deal with the Hulk, but he hadn't ex-

SEARCH AND RESCUE

actly planned on facing the Hulk quite so up close and personal, at least not right away. *Oh my stars and garters!* he thought. The herculean Hulk was even bigger and more intimidating than he remembered. *He makes Colossus look positively ectomorphic.*

The surrounding soldiers opened fire on the gigantic green ogre, determined to defend the park and themselves from the gamma-spawned gargantua. Automatic rifles rat-a-tatted and the smell of gunpowder filled the air as the frightened troopers fired clip after clip against one solitary figure, who laughed sarcastically at the fusillade.

"Mediate this, party pooper!" he challenged the Beast, sweeping aside a row of armed soldiers with one back-handed blow. Bullets literally bounced off the Hulk's burly chest without leaving so much as a bruise.

"Cease fire!" the Beast shouted through the megaphone, making his voice heard over the blaring gunfire. He fretted for a second about usurping the Colonel's authority, but the ricocheting bullets were more likely to hurt someone else than the Hulk. There was no point in endangering the soldiers' lives, not when it was him the Hulk was after. "Lower your weapons," he ordered. "Let me talk to him."

Did I really say that? the Beast thought incredulously. *I must be out of my famously learned head.*

Confused soldiers looked to their commander for confirmation. "Fall back!" Colonel Lopez instructed his troops. "Let the Avenger see what he can do." As his soldiers retreated toward the north end of the park, the Colonel gave the Beast a worried look. *I hope you know what you're doing,* his eyes seemed to say.

No less than I do, the Beast thought as the Hulk approached, each step leaving enormous tracks in the ground. Arms as wide as telephone poles swung at his side. Faced with this brutish goliath, the Beast felt like David, *sans* sling.

"You want to talk?" the Hulk said skeptically. "Yeah, right."

The Beast's simian posture made him look shorter than he was, but the Hulk would have loomed over the beleaguered mutant even if he had stood as straight as the Washington Monument.

"So, what've you got to say?" the Hulk demanded. He looked more than ready to make the Beast eat his own words, one syllable at a time. "This better be good," he dared.

Well, McCoy, the Beast asked himself, *how do you get through to the Hulk?* His mouth went dry while his brain raced faster than Quicksilver. *Think! Put your intellect and erudition to work!* He was hardly Doc Samson, the recognized shrink of choice to the superhero set, but he had reviewed much of the scientific and psychological literature concerning Bruce Banner's metamorphic transformations. Current wisdom, he recalled, had it that the "Hulk" persona somehow provided an outlet for Banner's repressed aggression. The Hulk thus embodied—and then some—Banner's most primeval instincts. By that reasoning, threats, challenges, and ultimatums would only reinforce the Hulk persona and escalate the likelihood of violent confrontation. The trick, perhaps, was to reach the brain behind the bravado....

"Yes, perhaps, you can assist me with something that's been bothering me," the Beast suggested, swallowing hard to moisten his throat. "What precisely is the isotopic coefficient of a controlled gamma reaction under standard atmospheric conditions?"

Hostile green eyes blinked, caught off guard by the abstruse scientific question. The Hulk's acromegalic fists, poised to pound the Beast into the ground, hesitated as the unexpected query circulated through his testosterone-swamped synapses. "What the heck—?"

Taking swift advantage of the Hulk's momentary confusion, the Beast pressed ahead with his mind-tweaking gambit. "Think about it," he urged. "If the ratio of the half-life to the atomic weight is directly proportional to the photonic energy emissions, then how do you factor in the quantum fluctuations caused by electromagnetic phase shifts? Especially when you initiate the chain reaction by bombarding processed vibranium with unstable molecules?"

"No, no!" the Hulk said impatiently. "You have to isolate the vibranium inside the magnetic constrictors first. Then you can worry about the quantum emissions!"

Despite his surly tone, the Hulk's arms gradually dropped to his sides. *It's working!* the Beast thought. Now if he could keep coming up with genuine scientific conundrums relating to Bruce Banner's field of expertise. It wasn't enough to simply snow the Hulk with a blizzard of scientific queries; he had to stimulate the mind of the brilliant physicist trapped inside the Hulk's grotesquely distorted body and psyche. "But are we talking about Wakandan vibranium or the Savage Land variety? As I understand it, the fundamental properties of each isotope differ significantly," the Beast said.

As he posed this new dilemma, a metallic glint in the sky caught the Beast's eye. He glanced up discreetly to see both Storm and Iron Man hovering overhead, ready to intervene should the Hulk lose all patience with his furry interrogator. For the time being, though, they seemed content to watch from above, waiting to see if the Beast could succeed in soothing the raging Hulk with nothing more than words. *If not,* he thought anxiously, *there's not likely to be much left of Niagara when the fighting's over.*

"Different isotopes, sure," the Hulk agreed grudgingly, "but the variation in atomic weights cancels out when you get rid of all those stupid neutrons." He scratched his unkempt emerald hair with one hand. "You don't really need to mess with the coefficient until after the nuclei collapse, if that's what's bothering you."

The Beast wasn't sure, but he could have sworn that the Hulk's chartreuse flesh was starting to look a little pinker. Could it be that his improvised talking cure was bearing fruit?

Then again, the Beast thought, *maybe all the Hulk really needs is a gallon-sized Prozac.* He was tempted to address Banner by name, but, no, the Hulk might perceive that as an attack on his own identity and react accordingly. *We definitely don't want that,* the Beast decided. Better to sneak up on Banner's submerged personality by way of his copious scientific knowledge and insights.

"I see," he conceded readily, "but doesn't the nearly infinitesimal mass of the discarded neutrons contribute to an accumulation of dark matter at the reaction site? According to Reed Richard's most recent paper on the effects of the Negative Zone on subatomic bonding...."

"The Negative Zone has nothing to do with it, not on a macroscopic scale!" the Hulk insisted, suddenly more interested in convincing the Beast than crushing him. "We're talking about a strictly exothermic fusion reaction, yielding a geometrical increase in gamma radiation by several orders of magnitude. The neutrons don't mean jack." The Hulk leaned forward, thrusting his glowering face at the Beast. "Got that?"

"Got it," the Beast said hastily. On closer inspection, the Hulk didn't look like he was likely to change all the

SEARCH AND RESCUE

way back to Banner anytime soon. Perhaps they might have to settle for a slightly calmer Hulk.

I can live with that, the Beast thought. Come to think of it, Doc Samson's recent clinical studies suggested that the distinction between the Hulk and Banner had blurred over the years, evolving from the bad old days when they represented two diametrically opposed personalities. *Maybe I've managed to drag just enough of Banner to the surface to make the Hulk think first and smash later. Much later, preferably.*

Certainly, the Hulk looked less malevolent than a few moments ago. As the Beast held his breath, the volatile titan peered down at the comparatively puny X-Man, then shrugged his enormous shoulders. "What's this all about anyway?" he asked reasonably. "Don't tell me you and your mutant bodies came all this way just to quiz me on the finer points of gamma radiation?"

"As a matter of fact," the Beast assured him, "we did."

The stately Colonial manor on Graymalkin Lane looked innocuous enough. Sturdy red brick walls rose to meet gabled rooftops. Darkened windows looked out over a freshly trimmed lawn. Matching three-story wings flanked the large central building, from which a domed belltower provided an excellent view of the surrounding estate which included an Olympic-sized swimming pool, several acres of pristine woodlands, and a three-mile stretch of shore along Breakstone Lake. Nestled in the sylvan suburbia of Westchester County, the Xavier Institute for Higher Learning looked exactly like the ritzy private academy it was supposed to be.

Appearances can be deceptive, Nick Fury thought. The executive director of S.H.I.E.L.D., the Strategic Hazard Intervention Espionage Logistic Directorate, knew for a fact that the venerable edifice ahead also housed the—for the most part—secret headquarters of the X-Men. He doubted if the townsfolk in neighboring Salem Center realized they were harboring a mutant hangout in their vicinity, but S.H.I.E.L.D. had known where Xavier's super-powered proteges hung their hats for over a decade now. Fury had just never seen fit to crash the X-Men's HQ—until now.

"Well?" he asked. "Anybody home?" Together with an elite team of agents, he crouched in the shrubbery outside a heavy iron gate that guarded the front drive. Beside him, clad in a regulation dark blue S.H.I.E.L.D. uniform, Agent 146, Matthew Bradley, scanned the mansion with a handheld motion detector. Five more agents, all level 4 or higher, kept low behind Fury and Bradley, sticking tight to the shade trees lining the road. A little further down the road, an armored van, camouflaged as an ordinary moving truck, contained their heavy artillery. Just in case.

"I'm afraid I can't tell, sir," Bradley reported. Stubbornly, he fiddled with the controls of the flashlight-sized instrument, only to shake his head in frustration. "I keep running into some sort of interference, jamming me on every frequency. I don't know what it is; it's like nothing I've ever seen before."

"Figures," Fury said. His stubble-covered jaws clenched down on the stub of an unlit cigar. A simple black patch covered his left eye, but his healthy right eye showed no sign of surprise. "Reliable intel suggests that the X-Men have access to all sorts of advanced alien technology, specifically from the Shi'ar Empire. Probably rigged up something to shield the house from prying eyes, electronic or otherwise."

I should have known this wouldn't be easy, Fury thought. Not that he had much choice; the X-Men's raid on the Helicarrier yesterday cried out for rapid retaliation, especially since the mutants made off with the experimental prototypes of what the lab boys and girls were calling the Gamma Sentinels.

I still don't get it, Fury thought. *Why did the X-Men resort to a commando-style assault against S.H.I.E.L.D. in the first place?*

Fury didn't expect them to approve of anything involving Sentinels, but why hadn't the X-Men at least consulted with him first, before staging a preemptive strike in his own backyard? He and the X-Men had always managed to work things out "under the table" so far, like that time in Nebraska a few months back, when he looked the other way while the X-Men reined in that mutant firebug, Pyro. If he had been informed that S.H.I.E.L.D. scientists had been roped into another blasted anti-mutant research project, then maybe he could have nipped the whole dirty business in the bud. Before it came to this.

All in all, Fury thought, *I'd rather be hassling Hydra, but sometimes you don't get to pick your battles. And the X-Men started this one.* Maybe he'd get some answers after he took them into custody, even though he hardly expected the X-Men to surrender without a fight.

"What's next, sir?" Bradley asked. He replaced the motion detector in one pouch of his dark red supply belt, then drew a 5mm plasma beam projector from his side holster. "How're we going in?"

"Hard and fast," Fury answered. The more he thought about it, there was little point in trying to sneak up on the mansion, even if no activity could be glimpsed through the house's windows. With all the enemies they had, the X-Men had surely wired the entire grounds with every type of security measure known to humanity—and a few more besides. A quick, surgical strike was the only way they were going to claim any tiny element of surprise, provided the X-Men didn't already know they had company. "Alpha team ready to knock on the front door," he whispered into a secure radio link. "All other teams hold their positions." Taking no chances, he had agents stationed all around the estate, including underneath the surface of the lake, in the event that the X-Men tried to make a break for it.

"All right, you goldbricks," he barked to the agents under the trees. "Here's where you earn your combat pay." He drew his own plasma beam handgun and stood up in front of the gate. Stiff legs gratefully stretched to their full height. Adrenalin rushed through his system, mixing with the Infinity Formula that had kept him relatively youthful for the last five decades. "Ready . . . GO!"

Fury obliterated the lock on the iron gate with his blaster, then kicked the gate open with the heel of his boot. He led the charge across the spacious lawn toward the front of the mansion. No vehicles were parked in the driveway, he noted, but that didn't prove anything. Rumor was there was a lot more underneath the mansion than anyone might expect; the X-Men probably had all kinds of facilities down there, including an underground garage or two. Maybe even a complete set of Gamma Sentinels, too.

Only if I'm lucky, he thought. Multiple footsteps pounded behind him as he raced up the front steps, past elegant Doric columns, to the entrance of the main house. A marble portico provided him with cover as he disintegrated the doorknob with another blast of hot plasma. "This is S.H.I.E.L.D.!" he shouted to whomever might be listening indoors. "Open up or we're coming in!"

No answer came within the next five seconds, so Fury blasted open the solid oak door and stepped indoors. Bradley and the other agents poured past him, taking up strategic positions at every interior doorway. Despite the speed and efficiency of the operation, there was no way anyone in-

SEARCH AND RESCUE

habiting the house could not have heard the S.H.I.E.L.D. agents invade the mansion. A strident alarm sounded the minute Fury stepped across the threshold into the foyer. The harsh, high-pitched buzz hurt Fury's ears, until Agent 132 swiftly located the security controls and silenced the alarm. He gave her a nod of approval even as he braced himself for the opening salvo in the X-Men's defense: a bolt of lightning maybe, or a freezing spray of ice. His shoulder still stung where one of Archangel's metal feathers had sliced into it the day before. *How come nobody's ever born with harmless mutant powers?* he griped silently.

Several seconds passed, however, bringing no sign of resistance. His finger poised on the trigger of his blaster, Fury inspected his surroundings. From what he could see, the ground floor of the mansion perpetuated the illusion of genteel normalcy put forth by the Institute's conservative facade. A crystal chandelier hung over the tiled floor of the foyer, which led to a wide stairway whose polished mahogany balustrade curved gracefully up to the floors above. Side doors led to a library, a study, and, near the back, a good-sized dining room and kitchen, all apparently devoid of habitation at the moment. To Fury's immediate right, a display case in the entrance hall exhibited an assortment of academic awards and graduation photos dating back to the Institute's early years as "Professor Xavier's School for Gifted Youngsters." Fury snorted; sounded like the Professor could teach government bureaucrats a thing or two about coming up with convenient euphemisms for awkward truths.

Whitewashed or otherwise, the X-Men's home base was starting to look like it might actually be deserted, which wasn't going to make finding the Gamma Sentinels any easier. "Fan out," he ordered his team, taking a second to light his cigar. If Xavier or his students had any objection to him smoking indoors, Fury figured, then they'd darn well have to show up in person to complain. "Search everywhere, but remember, keep your weapons on stun. We want answers, not dead X-Men."

Fury waited downstairs in the foyer, while his agents explored the upper floors. *Blast it,* he thought, frustrated by the X-Men's seeming no-show. He wasn't eager to return to the Helicarrier empty-handed. He had left Contessa Valentina de Allegra de Fontaine, sub-director of internal operations, in charge of S.H.I.E.L.D.'s flying headquarters; hopefully, her on-site inspection of the evidence left behind when the X-Men raided the Helicarrier was yielding better results than his own fruitless search.

"Colonel Fury," Bradley spoke up, one hand over the communications plug in his ear. "We have reports that a group of X-Men have been sighted at Niagara Falls. They appear to be engaged in combat with both the Avengers *and* the Hulk."

Niagara? Fury chomped on his cigar as he digested Bradley's unexpected news bulletin. *What the devil were the X-Men doing in Niagara, close to three hundred miles from here? There was nothing up there but honeymooners and a whole lot of falling wet stuff.*

"The Avengers, too, you say? That's something, I guess," he muttered to Bradley. *Sounds like Cap and his costumed cutups are on top of things even if I'm cooling my heels here, getting nowhere fast.*

He was tempted to leave the mansion and haul his butt toward the border as quickly as possible, but he doubted he could get to Niagara Falls in time to make any difference in the superhuman fracas going on there right now. For better or for worse, that was the Avengers' show; the best thing he could do was finish sweeping the Institute for whatever clues might turn up. From the looks of things, he

SEARCH AND RESCUE

wouldn't be getting up close and personal with the X-Men for now, anyway.

The crystal chandelier shuddered. Fury glanced quickly at the ceiling overhead; somehow he didn't think any of his own expensively-trained people could be lead-footed enough to set the chandelier quivering. "Bradley?" he asked, but the younger agent was way ahead of him, his portable motion detector already aimed at the ceiling.

"I'm picking up an extra body," he confirmed; apparently, the jamming field did not function indoors. "In the attic, I think."

That was good enough for Fury. "Let's go!" he shouted. He ran up the stairs, taking the steps two at a time. Drawn by his pounding footsteps, the additional agents joined him on the second and third floors, falling into line behind him as he reached the top of the stairs, where a simple wooden door barricaded his path. Fury checked the knob and found the door unlocked. Looking back over his shoulder, he shot Bradley a glance. Agent 146 pointed his motion-sensitive instrument at the door, then nodded his head. Their quarry was just beyond the door.

Doublechecking to make sure his plasma weapon was set on stun, he kicked open the door and pulled the trigger almost simultaneously. A blazing stream of ionized gas preceded Fury into the attic and he listened in vain for the sound of a body hitting the floor. No such luck; he didn't even hear a single grunt of pain as he rushed through the door. His single eye swept the room from left to right, searching for a potential threat.

All he saw was green. Stepping from the stairwell into the attic was like leading a safari into a verdant jungle. Lush, abundant foliage surrounded him; the entire attic had been converted into an extravagant garden. Leafy fronds and blooming flowers lined every wall, vines and creepers spilling onto the wooden planks of the floor. More plant life sprouted from hanging flowerpots, suspended beneath sloping skylights that let in generous quantities of afternoon sunshine. The hothouse atmosphere within the garden was warm and humid; the fragrance of dozens of competing blossoms filled the air, to an almost overwhelming degree.

"Great, just great," Fury groused. Trying to find a human target in this botanical explosion was going to be like looking for a pine needle in a rain forest. *That's the problem with jungles,* he thought, remembering long-ago missions in the Pacific. *They're great for ambushes.* Despite his annoyance, he was still impressed by the sheer accumulation of thriving flora packed into the attic. Somebody in the X-Men had a real green thumb, and he didn't mean like the Hulk's. *Maybe that X-Men member, Ororo,* he speculated; he seemed to remember something in her file about a fondness for gardening.

Bradley followed him into the lush attic, his eyes glued to the display panel on his motion detector. He shook his head. "No good. If he's here, he—or she—isn't moving a muscle," he added, shrugging. Like Fury, he had his blaster ready.

S.H.I.E.L.D.'s executive director brushed a thorny branch away from his face as he advanced into the garden. Looking up, he spotted an open window among the glass skylights comprising the ceiling. Had Storm or some other airborne mutant flown in—or out—of the attic? His shoulder itched again where the high-flying Archangel had wounded him. Sunfire, Banshee, and Phoenix could also fly, and they had all been among the mutant strike force that had absconded with the top-secret Gamma Sentinels. "Head's up, people," Fury instructed his agents as they spread out through the densely-planted nursery. "Chances are, we ain't alone."

SEARCH AND RESCUE

His opening plasma blast had left a horizontal trail of charred leaves, denuded branches, and other telltale residue. *Tough*, Fury thought coldly. He had more important things to worry about than a bunch of pulverized posies, like just who might be hiding behind the next stand of ferns. His gut feeling told him that their unidentified quarry had not yet flown the coop. He could practically feel hostile eyes scoping him out, but from what direction?

Wait! What's that?

Fury couldn't be sure, but he could have sworn he saw a slight rustling behind a thick assortment of rose bushes. Red, yellow, blue, and violet petals drifted slowly to the floor in the wake of an almost imperceptible disturbance. Fury silently signalled Bradley, then nodded at the roses. Agent 146 dutifully swung his sensitive electronics toward the bushes Fury had singled out. "I think you've got something, sir," Bradley whispered. "I'm definitely picking up—"

Before he could finish, a compact figure sprang from the flowering shrubbery.

SNIKT!

Gleaming metal claws swiped at Bradley, slicing his handheld device in half. Another half an inch and the agent would have lost several fingers as well.

"Wolverine!" Fury shouted. The exposed X-Man wore a mask over his face, but Fury would know Logan anywhere. The short, scrappy Canadian had paid his dues in the spy game long before defecting to the superhero biz. Fury had worked with Logan plenty of times, and felt he could reason with the man, as long as the feral mutant wasn't in one of his patented berserker furies. Then there was no getting through to him until blood was shed. "Back off, Logan!" he ordered. "Let's talk."

Wolverine crouched at the back of the greenhouse, adamantium claws extended from the backs of his hands. His yellow and blue uniform had blended effectively with the multi-colored roses. The letter "X" adorned the buckle of a pale red belt, advertising his current group affiliation. Fury knew that the twin blue peaks rising from his cowl concealed equally spiky hair, one of the outward signs of the X-Man's animalistic nature. Right now, though, he needed to talk to the man, not the bloodthirsty beast he was capable of becoming. "Logan," Fury urged him, "you know you can talk straight with me. You may be in a heap of trouble, but I'm willing to hear your side of the story."

But Wolverine was in no mood to talk. His only reply a savage snarl, he lunged at Fury, razor-sharp claws slicing through the hot, muggy air. Fury threw himself backward barely in time to avoid being disemboweled; even still, the claws left three parallel tears through the Kevlar fabric of Fury's suit. Blood from a trio of superficial scratches dripped through the rips. *He's playing for keeps!* Fury realized. "Open fire!" he commanded the other agents.

Wolverine's superhuman reflexes were fast, but S.H.I.E.L.D. agents weren't exactly slowpokes either. A barrage of stun beams chased the mutant as he ducked and weaved past a half dozen agents as he bolted for the stairs. Leaves and flowers bit the dust by the score as blazing streams of plasma crisscrossed the attic; Fury figured it would be a miracle if they didn't set the whole place on fire. Shrugging off the blasts as if he scarcely felt them, Wolverine almost made it to the door, but, at the last minute, Agents 132 and 278 set up a crossfire that effectively sealed off the doorway behind a wall of searing energy that not even Wolverine could brave. *Good work,* Fury thought.

Unable to make it to the stairs, Wolverine leaped straight up instead, his claws digging into the vine-covered walls of the attic as he climbed toward the glass ceiling like a short, stocky Spider-Man. Stun beams slammed into Wolverine's back and shoulders, but his inhuman endurance protected him from the worst of their effects.

Blast that mutant healing factor of his, Fury thought; it always had given Logan an unfair advantage.

Time to call in the big guns. Fury grabbed a communicator from his supply belt and barked his orders into it: "Omicron Team, mobilize at once. Converge on residence immediately. Target: Logan, codename Wolverine."

"Acknowledged," a voice responded crisply. "Omicron Team, out."

So much for that, Fury thought, snapping the communicator back into place upon his belt. Determined to pursue Wolverine, he looked around quickly for a ladder, then realized that a gravity-defying gardener like Storm hardly needed one. "Fine," he muttered. Wolverine had left him all the ladder he needed, in the form of deep incisions cut into the wall by the mutant's thrusting claws.

Shoving his gun into his holster, Fury took off after Wolverine, using the hand and footholds that Logan had carved out. He climbed rapidly, keeping his eyes on the retreating soles of Wolverine's blue boots. The X-Man had a good lead on him, but Fury gambled that the plasma blasts had to be slowing him down some.

You're not getting away from me, Logan, he vowed, *not until I get some answers.*

Wolverine reached the ceiling and smashed straight through the pane of skylight glass. Shards rained down on Fury, who ducked to protect himself. "Watch out below!" he hollered. Bradley and the other agents scattered away from the falling fragments.

Once he was sure that the shower of glass had run its course, Fury clambered hastily up the wall. He fired his blaster through the shattered skylight to discourage any ambush attempts, then he pulled himself onto the roof, his heels finding precarious purchase on the sloping slate shingles that ran around the edges of the skylights.

Thank goodness it hadn't rained earlier; the shingles are slippery enough as is," he thought.

Fury looked around. The view from atop the main building was just as impressive as he had imagined earlier. Looking north toward Graymalkin Lane, he was gratified to see his secret weapons marching from the van to the manor at a rapid clip: three S.H.I.E.L.D. commandoes in deluxe Mandroid body armor. Each over seven feet tall, the Mandroids stomped across the lawn, their gleaming gold surfaces reflecting the sunlight beating down on them. Flexible power conduits linked their polished gauntlets and boots to the powerful thermoelectric generators built into the bulky shoulderpieces. There were no neckpieces as such; the mound-shaped helmets merged smoothly into the shoulders, giving each Mandroid an almost headless appearance. Only a narrow eyeslit, about six inches below the top of the mound, hinted at the presence of the human operator inside each Mandroid.

Just what the doctor ordered, Fury thought approvingly; the Mandroid suits had been designed by Tony Stark himself, specifically for operations against superhuman opponents. Three of them might be just enough to subdue Wolverine—if they were lucky.

"Over here!" he shouted to the Mandroids. He waved his arms and fired his blaster into the air to make sure he got their attention. The Mandroids responded by staking out positions at both ends of the mansion and right before the front entrance. *Blast!* Fury cursed. He could have used one more Mandroid to cover the back of the mansion. It was too late to do anything about that now, though. He'd have to make do with the mechanized reinforcements he had on hand.

SEARCH AND RESCUE

But where *was* Wolverine? To his left and right, the rooftop sloped away towards empty air, but Fury couldn't spot the X-Men's halfpint hellion. Brick chimneys rose at regular intervals atop the Institute, but offered little in the way of shelter from Fury's inspection. Where could he have gone in the few moments Fury lost sight of him? Logan was the best there was at what he did, Fury knew, but that didn't include flying.

Fury's gaze focused on the domed belltower jutting above the north end of the roof. The ornate cupola was not exactly the Washington Monument, but it was large enough to hide a grown man, especially a sawed-off runt like Wolverine. Walking a tightrope along the peak of the gabled rooftop, Fury stalked toward the tower.

"Give it up, Logan," he called to his unseen quarry. He ground out the end of his cigar on the top of a chimney, then dropped the stogie down the smokestack. "You're not getting away from here until I get some answers. Where are your mutant buddies? And what did they do with those Sentinels?"

Not a peep emerged from the other side of the tower, which puzzled Fury to a degree. Logan could be stealthy when he had to be, but Fury had never known the hot-tempered Canadian to run from a fight once his cover had been exposed. Right now, though, Fury couldn't even hear Wolverine's characteristic growl. *What's up with him?* he wondered.

Firing a warning shot around the southeast corner of the tower, Fury stepped carefully onto the righthand side of the roof, holding onto the tower's wooden base with one hand while hefting his handgun in the other. The roof angled steeply beneath him. A loose shingle slipped under his feet and he almost lost his balance. *I'm getting too old for this high-wire garbage,* he grouched privately. *Let Cap and Daredevil keep the whole running-around-on-rooftops routine.*

Rounding the next corner, after prudently preceding his

arrival with a burst of hot plasma, Fury saw evidence of Wolverine's recent passing. Chips of broken glass and fallen flower petals seconded the message left behind by a fresh-looking scuff mark. Logan had definitely been here. Most likely, he was circling the tower in synch with Fury, keeping the ostentatious structure between them. "C'mon, you stubborn Canuck," he said irritably, "let's get this over with. I've got better things to do than ring-around-the-rosie with you the whole blamed afternoon."

Fury eased cautiously around the next corner, bringing him right back to where he started, facing the rear of the tower. He listened carefully for any reply from the elusive mutant. At first he didn't hear anything, but then, just in time, he heard something scraping against the copper dome of the tower. His gaze shot up and he saw Wolverine spring from the top of the cupola, claws extended.

"Holy cow!" There was no time to fire off a shot, but Fury managed to block the descending talons with his blaster. Shining silver adamantium sliced through the muzzle of Fury's gun, which nonetheless deflected the claws enough to save him from turning into a S.H.I.E.L.D. shish-kabob. The force of Wolverine's leap knocked Fury onto his back and, grappling with the homicidal mutant, he rolled down the side of the roof toward the ledge. Letting the truncated gun fall, Fury locked his hands around Wolverine's wrists, in a desperate effort to keep those lethal claws at bay, while he dug in with his heels to slow his descent across the shingles.

Holding back the claws wasn't easy; Fury had forgotten how strong Logan was. Fortunately, Wolverine couldn't get much leverage while they were tumbling. Charting their downward transit out of the corner of his eye, Fury held onto Wolverine's gloved wrists until the two men reached the bottom of the roof and were about to go over the edge.

SEARCH AND RESCUE

Then he shoved the X-Man away with all his strength and reached out for the rain gutters running along the ledge. His fingers clamped around the side of the gutter, bringing his fall to a jarring halt. His legs dangling above the lawn two stories below, the flimsy metal of the gutter creaking unnervingly, Fury hastily pulled himself up onto the roof once more. Deep creases in the underside of his fingers stung painfully as he shook some circulation back into them and looked out over the last row of shingles, hoping to see Wolverine's stunned body sprawled out on the grass below.

Ain't no way a little fall like that's going to take Logan out of the game for good, but maybe it knocked the fight out of him, Fury thought.

To his surprise and extreme disappointment, the only one he saw below was Agent 132, Sumi Lee, looking up at him with an expression of concern on her face. Heck, there wasn't even a Logan-shaped depression in the lawn. "Where the devil is he?" Fury demanded. Lee pointed back up at him in time-honored he-went-thataway fashion.

Leather soles slapped against the shingles to his left. Fury looked south and saw Wolverine running, with astonishing confidence in his balance, toward the back of the roof. He couldn't begin to guess how Wolverine had gotten back on the roof after going over the edge, but there was no time to figure it out. Snatching his communicator from his belt, Fury barked an order into the miniaturized mike. "Target is heading south on top of the central building. All teams converge on the rear of the house. Repeat, head for the backyard . . . pronto!"

Leaving his bisected gun lying in the gutter, Fury took off after Wolverine, but the agile mutant had too much of a head start, and too much preternatural dexterity. "Logan, stop!" Fury shouted, only seconds before Wolverine flung himself off the back of the roof. A blur of yellow and blue hung in the air for an instant before dropping quickly out of sight. Fury knew better than to think, even for a heartbeat, that the aggravatingly resourceful X-Man was committing suicide. Sure enough, a second later, Fury heard a resounding splash from the back yard.

That doggone Canucklehead dived all the way from the roof to the swimming pool. That's one heckuva jump, Fury thought, impressed, and not one he'd want to attempt unless he absolutely had to. Fury knew he was in good shape for a man his age, or even any age, but he never forgot that he was still only human after all. Unlike some people.

Reaching the far end of the roof, Fury saw Wolverine rising from the deep end of the pool. The blue, chlorinated water sparkled beneath the noontime sun. *I'm surprised he can float at all,* Fury thought, *with all that adamantium in him.*

"Too bad," Fury muttered, watching glumly as Wolverine paddled to the side of the pool. Fury saw Logan was heading toward several acres of dense woodlands that seemed to beckon from across the spacious back lawn.

He's going to break for the woods, Fury knew with utter certainty, and there was no way Fury could stop him, at least not personally.

But maybe he didn't have to.

A pair of Mandroids advanced on the pool from opposite ends of the estate. Whirring servomotors carried their armored limbs swiftly across the grass until they reached the concrete walkway outlining the pool. By now, Wolverine had completely emerged from the pool and stood, dripping, on the sidewalk between the two Mandroids. His feral gaze darted from right to left, taking in both steel-jacketed titans. "Surrender and you will not be harmed," one of the Mandroids announced. His electronically amplified voice held no trace of doubt or apprehension. "Don't make us resort to force."

Fury could have told the agent inside the bulky armor that he was wasting his breath, but couldn't fault the man for following procedure, even if all his warning did was provoke Wolverine into striking first. The Mandroid stood more than a yard taller than the diminutive X-Man, yet you wouldn't know it from the way Wolverine charged fearlessly at one of S.H.I.E.L.D.'s state-of-the-art technological enforcers. Although he could not see Wolverine's masked face from where he was standing, Fury could easily imagine the crazed, bloodshot ferocity in Logan's eyes.

The Mandroid's right arm swiveled upward so that the handmounted stun cannon in his metal mitt pointed at the onrushing mutant. The cannon emitted a high-frequency neuronic burst that struck Wolverine head on. An agonized howl escaped the X-Man's lips, but he kept on coming, slashing out with his claws at the power cable connecting his target's right gauntlet to the central chassis of the Mandroid's armor. Sparks erupted as the adamantium razors severed the cable, cutting off the flow of power to the stun cannon. Fury grimaced and rummaged in his pockets for a fresh cigar, which he figured he was going to need. With one blow, Wolverine had already eliminated one of the Mandroid's major weapons.

But that didn't mean the armored agent was down for the count. His left arm swung like a mace and knocked Wolverine onto the cement near the elevated diving board. But Logan sprang up again almost instantly. The Mandroid swung with his right arm, but Wolverine ducked beneath the blow. Instead the Mandroid's reinforced steel arm smashed through the lightweight aluminum ladder supporting the diving board. Metal screeched in protest as the entire platform toppled forward into the pool.

Wolverine lashed out at the Mandroid's legs. His claws grazed the omnium steel outer layer of the armor until the besieged operator activated his protective force field. Portable generators located in the Mandroid's hip pods produced an intense electro-gravitic shield that deflected Wolverine's claws before they could do too much damage. A shimmering purple aura outlined the Mandroid's golden armor as Wolverine continued to flail away at his opponent, however, trying to overcome its defenses through sheer, savage persistence. Luminous blue flashes crackled wherever his claws came into contact with the glowing barrier protecting his foe.

Crouching on the rooftop, Fury struck a match against a slate shingle and lit his cigar. He took a deep puff to take the edge off his frustration at being stuck on the sidelines. He felt like an athletic coach forced to fight his battles from the bleachers. *At least I've got a front-row seat,* he thought as the fumes from his cigar filled his lungs; one of the distinct advantages of immortality was not having to worry about carcinogens. *Let's hope those Mandroids are worth everything we paid for them.*

The force field could also be used as a tractor beam, as demonstrated by the second Mandroid, who, standing astride the hot tub at the shallow end of the pool, directed a ray of purple energy at the frenzied mutant. The beam, capable of lifting nearly a thousand pounds, seized hold of Wolverine and hoisted him into the air in front of the first Mandroid, who diverted his own force field to offensive purposes, catching the struggling X-Man in a crossfire of opposing tractor beams. Squeezed between glimmering rays of force, Wolverine was carried out above the center of the pool. He hovered several feet above the sparkling surface of the blue water, kicking and thrashing violently, but seemingly unable to break free from the high-tech trap. His claws couldn't do him much good, Fury noted, if Logan couldn't reach anything with them.

The third and final Mandroid, the one who had originally been stationed at the front of the mansion, stomped onto the scene, but it was starting to look like the extra man-machine might not be needed. "We've got you now," the second Mandroid informed Wolverine, her voice revealing that there was a female agent inside that particular suit of armor. "You might as well stop fighting us. Resistance is futile."

Somebody's been watching too much Star Trek, Fury thought. Not that he cared much; the Mandroid operator could spend her free time vegging out on *Teletubbies* as long as she got the job done. He stood up, stretching his legs, and looked around for the best way down from the roof. The sooner he pried some answers out of Wolverine, the better.

Then, just when he thought the time-consuming conflict was finally over, something strange happened. Before his puzzled eye, the purple beams snaring Wolverine pulsed in a way he didn't recognize. Peculiar ripples seemed to radiate from Logan's trapped figure, flowing outward along the tractor beams toward the victorious Mandroids, who were now being pulled forward toward Wolverine. Immense metal feet scraped against cement as the Mandroids were dragged against their will toward the edges of the pool, leaving deep skid marks in the concrete behind them. Both Mandroids tried to cut off the beams at their source, but it was too late. Wolverine's levitating form suddenly plunged into the water below, dragging both Mandroids with him. Seven hundred pounds of omnium steel alloys, not to mention two flesh-and-blood S.H.I.E.L.D. agents, crashed facefirst into the pool. The Mandroid at the deep end immediately sank to the bottom while the one at the shallow end smacked against the concrete floor of the pool.

Fury wasn't sure which Mandroid had it better, but he hoped for their sakes that there was plenty of padding under the steel skin. Wolverine himself vanished beneath the frothing waves stirred up by the Mandroids' spectacular splash landings.

That left one Mandroid up and about. The other S.H.I.E.L.D. agents dashed out of the rear of the house and joined the Mandroid around the rectangular basin. If nothing else, they had Wolverine surrounded. There was no way he could exit the pool without having to get by Fury's dedicated people. Unfortunately, knowing Logan, he was perfectly capable of hacking his way to freedom through the mangled bodies of even the best trained field agents.

There was only one thing to do. "Boil him!" Fury barked into his communicator, and the remaining Mandroid responded. The Mandroid fired at the pool with a high-powered, 250 watt laser torch. The incandescent red beam raised the temperature of the pool to boiling point in a matter of seconds. Billowing clouds of steam rose from the pool, obscuring Fury's view of the scene and forcing the non-armored agents to back away from the bubbling cauldron the pool had become. Fury could hear the agitated water seething from three stories away.

"C'mon, Logan," he muttered. "Give it up." He wasn't worried about the two submerged agents. The Mandroid suits came complete with their own internal air supply and enough insulation and shielding to withstand extreme high temperatures and radiation.

Logan was another story. Not even that scrappy survivor could last long in that overheated stew. Fury peered through the rising mist, expecting to see a scalded figure leap, crawl, or scurry from the boiling water. Wolverine's mutant healing factor was going to get a real workout here, but Fury knew that the X-Man stood a better than even chance of

SEARCH AND RESCUE

recovering from his injuries; he just hoped Logan would stay conscious long enough to cough up some solid info on what the X-Men were up to.

But what was taking so darn long? As two full minutes passed, Fury grew uneasy. He had wanted to drive Wolverine out of the pool and into his assault team's clutches, not cook Logan within an inch of his life. Heck, judging from the quantities of steam spilling into air, there couldn't be that much water left in the pool.

"That's enough," he ordered into his communicator. "Let's see what we've got."

The Mandroid promptly shut off its laser and stepped back from the pool. Tiny drops of condensation beaded all over the golden armor. Fury waited impatiently for the mist to clear, grinding his cigar between clenched teeth. As opaque clouds of steam thinned, he saw that close to two-thirds of the chlorinated blue water had evaporated, leaving barely enough to cover the bottom of the pool. Two overturned Mandroids lay amidst the shallow water, along with the torn and twisted remains of the diving platform. Sporadic bubbles percolated to the surface of the slowly-cooling water.

But Wolverine was not there.

"What in blue blazes—?" Fury exclaimed. His gaze swept the pool from the deep end to the shallow, but located no trace of the indomitable X-Man. He saw the agents below shake their heads in confusion as they rapidly came to the same conclusion: their quarry had gone missing.

Where did he go? Fury wondered. *And, more importantly,* how?

Logan was a crafty devil, with lots of hidden talents, but disappearing into thin air wasn't one of them. It was like Wolverine had evaporated along with the liquid contents of the X-Men's recreational reservoir, which was flat-out impossible. *For that matter,* Fury recalled, *how had Wolverine kept from falling off the roof earlier? And how did he pull that stunt with the tractor beams? Since when has Logan been able to manipulate force fields?*

"I don't get it," Fury muttered. "Something doesn't add up." He watched unhappily as the agents below checked on the fallen Mandroids, not even smiling when Agent Lee gave him the thumbs-up sign. Nobody had gotten hurt, but, even outnumbered and outgunned, Wolverine had given them all the slip, leaving behind only still more unanswerable questions.

"All right," he barked to his team, "let's keep searching this building. Look under every ashtray, rug, and mutant thingamajig. These are classified weapons we're looking for, everyone, so I'm not leaving until we've checked out every square inch of this place."

Ashes from his cigar dropped onto the shingled roof and Fury ground the smoldering embers out with his heel. Deep down inside, he guessed they wouldn't find anything. The X-Men were long gone, and so were his hopes of easily recovering the lost Gamma Sentinels.

Fury turned north—toward Niagara Falls. He crossed his fingers and hoped that, whatever trouble they had gotten into, Captain America and his Avenger pals were getting closer to the truth than he was.

Chapter Two

"Och, 'tis about right, Bobby. Can ye lower the temperature a wee bit more?"

Dr. Moira MacTaggert, director and founder of the Genetic Research Centre, peered into the binocular lenses of an electron microscope whilst across the laboratory Bobby Drake, the mutant known as Iceman, laid his hand atop a sealed, transparent cylinder containing an open petrie dish. Waves of intense cold radiated from Bobby's palm, frosting the exterior of the plexiglass cylinder. "How's that?" he asked cheerfully.

"Perfect," Moira replied, not lifting her eyes from her microscope, which was connected by hidden cables to the lighted platform on which the cylinder rested. Her voice held a distinct Scottish brogue. A brown-haired woman in her early forties, she wore a pristine white labcoat over her everyday attire. A pair of horn-rimmed reading glasses hung on a chain around her neck. "By coolin' the sample to near absolute zero, you've slowed the chemical reactions to a point where I can actually watch the virus mutate."

Bobby shrugged; the slim American youth was no scientist. "Whatever you say, doc. I'm just glad I could help." He wore a two-toned blue uniform that left his head and short brown hair exposed. A crystalline layer of ice covered his right hand, extending partway up his wrist, but he didn't look at all uncomfortable. He wasn't even shivering.

SEARCH AND RESCUE

"I don't know how I'd manage without ye," Moira insisted. "Your innate ability to generate cold lets me control the temperature of this experiment to an astoundingly fine degree. None of my very expensive refrigeration equipment is anywhere near as precise." She looked up from her work to smile in Bobby's direction. "Thanks so much for flyin' all the way from New York to assist me like this."

"No problem," Bobby said amiably. "I know how important your work is, trying to cure the Legacy Virus and all. I'm always happy to drop by." He took a bite from the blueberry popsicle in his free hand; not surprisingly, Iceman had a weakness for frozen deserts. "What's a little jet lag between friends?"

My sentiments exactly, Kurt Wagner thought, watching the scene from above. He hung by his prehensile tail from one of several sturdy metal rings he had personally installed in the lab's ceiling several years ago, just to indulge his acrobatic proclivities. Moira's research complex, located on scenic Muir Island, off the coast of Scotland, had been his home for many years, although he had recently moved back to the X-Men's headquarters in America. His own mutant talents were not particularly required for Moira's latest round of experiments, but he needed little excuse to visit an old friend and familiar haunts.

Somebody *had to keep Bobby company on the flight over, after all,* he thought. *Too bad Kitty and Peter couldn't make it.*

At the west end of the laboratory, beyond the banks of monitors and computerized controls, a large plate glass window looked out on the island and the sea beyond. Kurt twirled beneath the hoop, twisting his pointed tail, the better to savor the breathtaking view afforded by the window. The entire research complex was built atop a steep cliff overlooking Cape Wrath. From where Kurt hung, he saw a narrow strip of land extend for only a few paces past the base of the building before dropping off abruptly, falling dozens of meters to the rocky beach below. More cliffs flanked the harbor on both sides, their barren, gray faces hiding numerous small caves and crevices. Rolling green hills rose above the cliffs, dotted with abundant patches of violet heather and the occasional wandering sheep. In the distance, across the placid blue waters, Kurt could barely glimpse the Isle of Arran, their nearest geographical neighbor. Twilight gave the entire vista a rosy sheen. *What beautiful country this is,* he reflected. *Why exactly did I leave it again?*

He caught a glimpse of his own reflection in the huge pane of glass. Kurt Wagner's appearance was just as striking as the rugged scenery outside, albeit in a radically different fashion. A coating of fine indigo fur covered a decidedly demonic visage, complete with pointed ears and lambent yellow eyes. Ominous shadows clung to his brow and the planes of his face, seemingly independent of whatever light source might or might not be available. Nor did his physical irregularities end with his satanic countenance or even his highly conspicuous tail; spotless white boots and gloves seemed to accent the fact that he had merely three fingers on each hand and no more than two toes per foot. The latter characteristic increased his resemblance to hellspawn by lending his feet an unmistakably cloven aspect.

That's right, he thought wryly. *I'm a mutant, with an obligation to help make the world safe for mutants and humans alike.* And, as he had long ago discovered, there was no better place to do so than among his fellow X-Men, where he fought the good fight under the colorful alias of Nightcrawler.

"What about you, Kurt?" Moira called out, interrupting

his autobiographical musings. "Are ye gettin' bored yet?"

"*Nein,*" he insisted, his accent as German as his vocabulary. "I've been basking in the warm glow of nostalgia." Swinging back and forth with his tail, he worked up enough speed to send him somersaulting through the air above Moira's head. Just as gravity threatened to pull him down, he disappeared in cloud of billowing black smoke that seemed to materialize from nowhere. A sulfurous odor suffused the air-conditioned atmosphere of the lab.

BAMF!

A second burst of smoke exploded between Moira and Bobby, and Kurt emerged from the fumes about four meters below his previous location, stepping lightly onto the tile floor. Well accustomed to Nightcrawler's unique mode of teleportation, neither Moira nor Bobby appeared startled by his dramatic vanishing act, although Moira wrinkled her nose and fanned the acrid smoke away with her hand. "One of these days, Kurt Wagner," she declared, "I'm goin' to figure out why you leave such a bloody stink behind whenever you pull that stunt."

"All part of my theatrical flair," Kurt said, taking a bow. He had been a circus performer before he became a superhero, and some habits were hard to break. His dark blue uniform, similar in hue to his indigo fur, still sported flamboyant swatches of crimson better suited to life under the big top. "My apologies, though, for the pungent pyrotechnics. No doubt you've gotten used to a cleaner standard of breathing over the last few months."

In fact, the noisome fumes were already dissipating. "To tell ye the truth," Moira admitted with a smile, "I think I've actually missed the smell of brimstone in the air. The Centre has seemed awfully quiet and empty since Excalibur disbanded and you all went your separate ways. Brian and Meggan off being newlyweds, you folks back at Charles's

Institute... I have to admit the old place gets kind of lonely sometimes."

"All the more reason to make a habit of these little transatlantic jaunts," Kurt reassured her. "Have no fear, *meine freunde,* you couldn't cut yourself off from the X-Men if you tried."

Indeed, he recalled, Moira MacTaggert's involvement with Professor Xavier's crusade to make a better world for mutants predated the very creation of the X-Men. Her Genetic Research Centre had contributed greatly to modern science's understanding of the causes and effects of human mutation, or so he had been told. Personally, he was more of a swashbuckler than a scientist.

"Thank you, Kurt," Moira said, sounding slightly choked up. She dabbed at her eyes with the sleeve of her labcoat. "And you, too, Bobby. I cannae tell you how much ye all mean to me."

Especially now that you're dying of the Legacy Virus, Kurt thought, unwilling to spoil the moment by voicing so somber an issue. He could only hope that Moira's own unquestioned brilliance could find a cure before her time ran out.

An ear-piercing alarm interrupted their poignant reunion, causing all three of them to look up suddenly. *"Vas?"* Kurt asked. "A jailbreak?" At any given time, he knew, a variety of dangerous evil mutants like Spoor or Proteus were kept under observation in underground cells beneath the Centre. Could one or more of them have broken free?

"I don't think so," Moira stated, running to consult a computerized control panel next to the open entrance to the laboratory. "Most of the remaining felons were shipped to the appropriate authorities after Excalibur disbanded. Plus, all the containment cells are automatically flooded with tranquilizing gas at the first sign of a disturbance." She examined a lighted display and nodded her head knowingly. "Nae, 'tis an intruder alert." With the press of a button, she silenced the blaring alarm, then keyed in a series of preprogrammed security commands. A heavy metal door slammed into place, sealing the entrance, at the same time that clanking steel shutters descended over the large glass window. More commands caused a row of television monitors to light up along one stretch of the wall. Kurt stared at the screens, which showed only incomprehensible displays of electronic "snow."

"Who is it?" Bobby asked. "Magneto? Apocalypse?" Like the laboratory, he readied himself for action. The icy sheath covering his hand spread quickly over his entire body, as ordinary flesh and blood metamorphosed into translucent, blue-tinted ice that looked as though it had been sculpted into the semblance of a humanoid figure. Frozen spikes grew like stalagmites along his arms and spine, whilst the floor beneath his feet took on a frosty sheen. "I kind of hope it's the Brotherhood of Evil Mutants again," Iceman quipped. His voice, now issuing from a throat of ice, acquired a peculiar crystalline ring. "I haven't flash-frozen the Toad for ages."

Moira glared at the TV screens in frustration as her fingers worked the controls. "Bloody hell," she cursed. "Something's interferin' with the video transmissions from the security cameras." She scrutinized the readings on a lighted display panel and a puzzled look came over her face. "Gamma radiation? Where the devil is *that* coming from?"

Kurt peered over Moira's shoulder at the security panel. He couldn't make head nor tail out of the abstruse electromagnetic data, but he deciphered the primary security display easily enough; flashing red lights highlighted several locations on a mounted schematic diagram of the entire

Centre. "Looks like we have multiple intruders," he announced gravely, "including one directly below us, in the medlab."

As team leader of Excalibur, the X-Men's defunct European division, Nightcrawler had learned to make command decisions quickly. "Iceman," he instructed his refrigerated teammate, "you stay here and guard Moira." He breathed a sigh of relief that Rahne, Moira's adopted daughter, was visiting friends in Edinburgh; that was one less person to worry about. Rahne had her own lycanthropic abilities to protect her, but she was still only a teenager. "I'm going to investigate. We need to know who we're up against."

"Got it," Iceman agreed. His breath chilled the air as he spoke, producing hazy puffs of fog with every syllable. Technically, he had seniority over Nightcrawler, having been among Professor X's first generation of proteges, but he seemed content to let Nightcrawler take charge, perhaps recognizing Kurt's greater familiarity with the premises. "Take care of yourself, pal."

"*Danke*," Nightcrawler replied. Closing his eyes, he visualized the medical facility one floor below him and wished himself there. As usual, he experienced a momentary sensation of intense heat, as if briefly passing through some infernal other dimension. He opened his eyes to find swirling black smog obscuring his view, until he arrived in the medlab, accompanied by the inevitable burst of smoke and noisy *bamf*. He winced at the explosive and pungent nature of his advent. *So much for stealth*, he thought, wishing, not for the first time, that his 'ports were less attention-getting.

As the inky fumes cleared, he found himself standing at the foot of an empty sickbed in the Centre's main infirmary. A half dozen more beds were lined up in a row along the northern wall of the chamber. Sophisticated diagnostic equipment, looking like something out of *Star Trek,* was mounted over the head of each bed. Closed supply cabinets ran along the opposite wall, behind Nightcrawler, while the scuffed tile floor revealed the tracks of a rolling equipment cart now parked neatly between two parallel beds. Sterilized surgical tools and bandages, wrapped in sealed plastic bags, waited atop the cart, ready for immediate use.

Fortuitously, no patients currently resided in the medlab. A devout Catholic despite his diabolic form, Kurt prayed that the crisis at hand would not fill the empty beds with casualties. He helped himself to a scalpel from the equipment tray, wishing that it were a full-sized rapier instead. Alas, his favorite swords were all on the other side of the Atlantic at the moment, far beyond the range of his talent for teleportation. *Serves me right for traveling light,* he thought.

But where was the mysterious intruder? Scalpel in hand, Nightcrawler scanned the seemingly empty infirmary. With the overhead lights turned off to save electricity, the only illumination came from the open doorway to the hallway beyond, but the dim lighting posed no difficulty to Nightcrawler, whose yellow eyes easily penetrated the darkness. Yet the silent medlab looked as lifeless as a morgue.

Suddenly Nightcrawler heard the sound of heavy footsteps echoing from the corridor outside, heralding the unknown invader's return to the infirmary. *"Mein gott,"* Nightcrawler whispered to himself. The intruder sounded big, whoever he was. Feeling exposed and vulnerable, Nightcrawler leaped upward, attaching himself to the ceiling like a spider on a wall. His dexterous fingers and toes dug into the minute seams around a pair of dormant fluorescent lights while he gripped the scalpel between his fangs.

Hanging upside-down as he was gave him an inverted view of the doorway, so that the ominous figure who suddenly filled the entrance, silhouetted against the light of the hall, appeared to be standing on his head. At first, Nightcrawler thought the inhuman outline belonged to Ch'od, the huge reptilian humanoid who served among that band of roving space pirates who called themselves the Starjammers; like Ch'od, the figure was at least three meters tall, with flared, wing-like ears and the muscular build of a gladiator on steroids. Despite the glare from the door, Nightcrawler glimpsed a scaly green hide, a protruding brow, and a mouthful of jagged, shark-like teeth.

What on Earth is Ch'od doing here? Kurt wondered. Last he heard, the Starjammers were light-years away from Scotland, fighting for truth, justice, and plenty of plunder in the distant Shi'ar Galaxy.

It came as a relief to discover, however, that their unexpected visitors were old allies, as opposed to vile enemies bent on revenge. No doubt the additional intruders detected by Moira's security setup were Corsair, Raza, Hepzibah, and the other Starjammers. Kurt wondered if Cyclops knew his father was back in the Milky Way again; Nightcrawler himself had not seen Corsair and his valiant crew since Jean and Scott's wedding many months ago.

Nightcrawler's tail plucked the scalpel from his jaws. *"Wilkommen, mein freund,"* he called out, seeing little need for further discretion. Then the looming saurian figure stepped further into the medlab and Kurt realized he had made a dreadful mistake.

The silent newcomer bore a striking resemblance to Ch'od, it was true, but as Nightcrawler's eyes compensated for the glare from the hall, he discovered significant differences as well. The intruder's scales were darker than his alien friend's, more olive-green than chartreuse, while the creature's hairless skull was adorned by a plethora of bony knobs that Ch'od had never possessed. Even more significantly, the newcomer's hostile sneer and malevolent red eyes conveyed an essential animosity that Nightcrawler would have hardly expected from the good-natured Starjammer.

The immense, lizard-like biped locked its gaze on the imprudent X-Man. "Subject designate: Nightcrawler," the monster intoned. Its deep, gravelly voice had an oddly robotic cadence, at odds with its primeval appearance; it was as though the Creature from the Black Lagoon had spoken with the mechanical monotone of Robby the Robot—or a Sentinel. "Aggressive action is mandated to neutralize mutant interference."

Spoken like a Sentinel all right, Nightcrawler thought with a sickening sense of recognition. But why the organic-looking scales and fangs? Who was the Sentinel trying to fool, and what exactly was it pretending to be? Now that he could see past the creature's superficial resemblance to Ch'od, Kurt thought the Sentinel's reptilian facade looked vaguely familiar, but he couldn't remember from where. He looked a little like a Skrull, with the green skin and bulbous, segmented brows, yet Nightcrawler had never seen a Skrull so large and impressively muscled, nor was the invader clad in anything resembling a Skrull military uniform. Like the Beast, the hulking creature wore only a pair of drab blue shorts. *Not exactly standard attire for Sentinels,* he thought, *but, then again, neither are crocodile skin and teeth.*

The Sentinel (if that's what it truly was) gave him little time to search his memory. Clawed hands seized the foot of the nearest sickbed, wrenching the bedframe from the floor, then swung it like a gigantic flyswatter at Nightcrawler, who had to do a backflip across the ceiling to evade the blow. Missing the X-Man, the metal frame shattered the overhead light fixtures instead. Sparks flared briefly and bits of glass and plastic rained onto the floor. Nightcrawler hoped for a second that the Sentinel might electrocute himself, but no such luck; the mutant-hunting monster was better insulated than that. Fiery blue traceries ran down the length of the bedframe to the robot's clawed fists, yet the electricity sputtered impotently around the scaly green hands.

"Surrender, mutant," the Sentinel commanded. Sheets littered the floor, along with a thin foam mattress, as the swinging bedframe pursued Nightcrawler down the length of the infirmary. Hoof-like feet ground the discarded blankets beneath the Sentinel as it tromped across the floor. "Surrender, mutant," the behemoth commanded chillingly. "You cannot escape the Abomination."

The Abomination!

Suddenly, Nightcrawler remembered where he had seen this particular lizard-man before: in the Professor's comprehensive database of superhuman menaces, mutant or otherwise. The real Abomination, alias Emil Blonsky, was one of the Hulk's regular adversaries, another gamma-mutated monstrosity who was supposed to be just as strong as the Hulk and twice as ruthless. Nightcrawler had never met the Abomination personally, but the genuine article had nearly killed two of Kurt's fellow X-Men, Archangel and Marrow, less than a year ago, shortly before Nightcrawler rejoined the team. Kurt recalled Warren's account of that incident with a shudder; his high-flying friend had described the Abomination as a particularly vicious foe. If this robotic facsimile of the Abomination was even half as dangerous as its inspiration, then they were all in serious trouble.

The Sentinel swatted at Nightcrawler with the metal bed-

SEARCH AND RESCUE

frame, coming so close that Kurt felt the breeze generated by the makeshift weapon's passage. He found himself being driven back into the northwest corner of the medlab: a dead end that left him little room to maneuver. The end of his tail remained wrapped around the handle of the scalpel, but the surgical tool seemed hopelessly outmatched by the much larger bedframe. Nightcrawler realized he needed a brilliant tactical ploy—*schnell!*

His luminous eyes flicked toward the doorway at the opposite end of the infirmary, the only source of light within sight. "Dim lights. Corridors B1 through B12," he shouted past the ersatz Abomination. Voice-operated technology responded immediately, lowering the lights in the adjacent hallway and throwing the entire level into shadowy darkness.

Kurt could see perfectly well, of course. *They don't call me Nightcrawler for nothing,* he thought. Beyond that, the drastic reduction in illumination allowed him to take advantage of another of his natural talents: the ability to turn all but invisible in deep shadow.

Cloaked in darkness, he scurried on all fours across the ceiling and away from the corner. *I need to get to the Communications Suite,* he realized, *and summon reinforcements. Just what the world needed, a more brutal breed of Sentinel. God help us all if every one of the intruders is fashioned in the image of the Abomination, with Hulk-like strength at its disposal.*

Without warning, the saurian skull swiveled atop a nearly-nonexistent neck. Red eyes, now suffused with an unnatural red radiance, fixed with impossible accuracy upon the invisible mutant. "Infrared tracking initiated," the Sentinel announced. "Target located."

The bedframe crashed to the floor as, discarding its weapon, a scaly hand reached out for Nightcrawler with unexpected speed. Before Kurt had a chance to react, a vise-like grip closed around his ankle, squeezing his leg with bone-crushing force!

Something was scratching at the shutters. Something large and very persistent.

Perversely, the same opaque metal blinds that protected Moira and Bobby from whatever was outside the Centre also prevented them from seeing what exactly was trying to get at them. Considering that this particular lab was three stories above ground level, Moira MacTaggert realized, the would-be invader could either fly or was very, very tall. How else could it reach the now-barricaded window?

"What do you think it is, doc?" Iceman asked. Even though the temperature of the laboratory was a comfortable fifteen degrees Celsius, his crystalline anatomy showed no sign of melting. She found it vaguely unnerving that she could see all the way through his translucent skull and torso, unlike the old days when he simply coated his flesh-and-blood body with frost or snow. Recently, however, the youthful X-Man had mastered the trick of transmuting the whole of his organic substance to living ice. *A biological oxymoron if ever there was one,* she thought, her scientific curiosity intrigued despite their present peril.

"I cannae say," she answered him. "If only I can get these bloody monitors to work the way they're supposed to . . . !" Row upon row of empty screens, displaying nothing but static, frustrated her. Putting on her reading glasses to better see the display panels, she fiddled urgently with the controls to the security cameras, trying to compensate for the inexplicable burst of gamma radiation that had scrambled the cameras' transmissions. *If I reverse the polarity of the neutron flow,* she thought, *maybe I can filter*

SEARCH AND RESCUE

out of some of this electromagnetic rubbish. Lord knows it always worked on Doctor Who....

To her surprise and immense satisfaction, a few of the screens cleared at once, permitting her and Iceman a peek at what was going on beyond the besieged laboratory. The Centre's interior cameras were still thoroughly bollixed, but at least they could now see the grounds outside the building, including the region on the other side of the large, shuttered window. Her moment of triumph evaporated, however, once she got a look at the bizarre and frightening entity struggling to gain entrance to the lab.

The creature had the graceful head, shoulders, and arms of a beautiful woman, albeit one colored in various shades of green. Lustrous emerald tresses, abundant and unrestrained, framed an attractive face whose unblemished skin was tinted chartreuse, a few shades lighter than her jade-hued lips. If only her head and shoulders were seen, Moira decided, this barbaric-looking green beauty might easily be mistaken for Jennifer Walters, the celebrated She-Hulk. Below her bare shoulders, though, her womanly appearance gave way to the shape and semblance of an enormous bird of prey. Dark green feathers, the same hue as her flowing mane, covered a stout, avian body of roc-like proportions. Colossal wings, at least three meters across, flapped vigorously as the creature clawed at the metal shutters with the scaly talons of a colossal raptor. Verdant tailfeathers spread out nearly a full meter past the bird-woman's hindquarters. Sea-green eyes held a glassy, insane sheen. Sharpened canines jutted from beneath her chartreuse lips.

Having devoted her life to the study of human mutation, Dr. Moira MacTaggert, Ph.D., recognized the strange hybrid creature from her research. "Och," she exclaimed, " 'tis the Harpy!"

"Like on *Xena*?" Iceman asked, his gaze glued to the startling image on the security monitors.

Moira rolled her eyes. Trust an American to learn his classical mythology from a silly TV show! "Sort of, but this Harpy was born of gamma radiation, not Olympian mischief." The symptomatic green coloring was a dead giveaway. "Betty Ross Banner, the late wife of Bruce Banner, a.k.a. the incredible Hulk, was transformed into the Harpy several years ago, after similar exposure to concentrated gamma radiation. She was cured eventually, but the case is well-documented. I'd recognize her anywhere."

"*Late* wife?" Iceman asked, sounding understandably puzzled. He scratched his glacial skull, producing tiny shavings of ice that dusted his shoulders like dandruff.

Moira shrugged. "She's supposed to be dead."

"Yeah, aren't they all," Iceman remarked. Flippant as he was, the lad had a point, Moira conceded; if she had ten pence for every time a reportedly dead super-villain resurfaced, she could finance a chain of Genetic Research Centres throughout the British Isles and beyond.

None of which did anything to alleviate their current plight. Could the fearsome Harpy actually breach the lab's defenses? Moira was distressed to see the Harpy's talons digging deep scratches in the chrome steel shutters. How is that possible? she wondered. The shutters weren't adamantium, but they were the next best thing, and the Harpy was shredding them with nothing more than a pair of gamma-spawned chicken legs!

"That's not going to keep her out for long, doc," Iceman stated, reaching much the same conclusion as Moira. "Okay if I fortify things a bit? It might leave a bit of a mess to clean up later."

Moira winced at the thought of gallons of melting ice flooding her expensive laboratory equipment, then consid-

SEARCH AND RESCUE

ered what the ferocious Harpy might do to that same equipment. "Go ahead," she replied. Certainly, it wouldn't be the first time these facilities ended up the worse for wear after some heated hostilities. "Do whatever ye have to do."

"Thanks, doc," Iceman said. "You won't regret this." He slid across the floor atop a frictionless plane of ice that formed ahead of his path. Coming to a halt directly in front of the wide picture window, he placed his palms against the huge pane of glass. And just in time; even as fresh ice began to flow from his fingertips, spreading over the window like a protective glaze, the impact of the Harpy's assault on the metal shutters sent cracks racing through the thick glass. Iceman hurriedly shored up the splintered window by pouring on the ice. Moira felt the air within the lab grow dryer as the frozen X-Man drew the moisture from the atmosphere to construct his wintry bulwark. A thick layer of bluish ice formed over the entire window, muffling the grating sound of the Harpy's talons scraping against the disintegrating steel shutters. "There," Iceman said confidently, stepping back to admire his frigid handiwork. "That should do it."

"G-g-good work," Moira said, shivering. She drew her white labcoat closed and hugged herself to keep warm. The sheer accumulation of ice had turned the sealed laboratory into an oversized icebox. She envied the internal thermostat that rendered Iceman immune to the chilling effect of the environment he had created. *He must be very popular on hot days,* she thought, *not that we ever have any of those over here.*

She'd gladly suffer a little discomfort, though, if it meant keeping the Harpy safely outdoors. She looked away from the imposing wall of ice to check on the security monitors keeping watch over the fierce bird-woman's activities. Moira was pleasantly surprised to see the Harpy drawing back from the shuttered window, flapping her mighty wings as she hovered about a meter away from the shredded metal barricade, which now glistened with condensation brought about by the icy coating on the opposite side of the window.

Could it be, the Scottish scientist hoped, *that the Harpy was abandoning her efforts to gain access to the laboratory?*

Not in the slightest. Before Moira's horrified gaze, the bird-woman raised her slender arms and pointed her fingers at the fortified window. Blazing orange fire discharged from her hands, striking the Centre with the force of an exploding bomb. The blast could be heard and felt all the way through the steel, glass, and ice that stood (if not for much longer) between the flying monster and her potential victims. Great chunks of ice crashed onto the floor as fissures worked their way through Iceman's defensive wall. Streams of melting frost ran down the newly-formed crevices, pooling onto the floor before Iceman's feet. "Hey!" he protested loudly. "You didn't tell me she could do that!"

I forgot, Moira thought; after all, the Harpy had not been an active threat for several years. Now that the full particulars came back to her, however, she recalled that the Harpy's so-called "hellbolts" supposedly packed the explosive punch of several kilograms of TNT. According to the original report, the bird-woman's energy bursts had proved sufficient to subdue the Hulk. They had also destroyed an Air Force fighter jet, resulting in the death of the pilot.

I wonder how a hellbolt stacks up against Cyclops's eyebeams, Moira couldn't help speculating, even as she realized that anything that could knock out the Hulk was not going to be stopped by a sheet of ice, no matter how solid or self-sustaining.

SEARCH AND RESCUE

Nevertheless, Iceman worked hard to reinforce his arctic embankment, filling the cracks and crevices with fresh ice, even drawing on his own substance to hold the icewall together; the frozen spikes along his arms and spine dissolved away as Iceman sprayed the window with frigid mortar. "Step back, doc," he warned Moira. "I'm not sure how long this is going to hold."

Nodding, Moira gingerly dashed to the questionable safety of the far end of the laboratory. She had to watch her step to avoid slipping on any patches of frost left behind by Iceman's trek across the floor. Her gaze fell on the sample of Legacy Virus still resting inside the airtight containment cylinder.

I better put that someplace safe, she realized. The last thing she wanted was for Bobby to get infected with the lethal virus, which was typically more dangerous to mutants than to ordinary human beings. She grabbed the plexiglass cylinder, stamped with the universal symbol for biohazardous material, and ran toward a circular, cabinet-sized adamantium vault filled with several identical cylinders.

For that matter, she thought, *I don't want to infect the Harpy either.* She had no idea whether a gamma-irradiated entity like the Harpy would be vulnerable to the deadly virus, but she didn't want to find out the hard way; if this really was Betty Banner, somehow returned from the dead, then there was an innocent woman trapped inside the distorted body of a mythological monster.

Tucking the cylinder carefully beneath her arm, Moira lifted the lid of the vault, releasing a gust of frosty mist from its refrigerated interior. An empty slot awaited Sample #17/102. *Too bad there's no room for me in there,* she thought. She could use a protective vault right now.

Another explosive blast rocked the laboratory, sending bits of broken glass and ice flying like shrapnel. Iceman shielded them from the rocketing fragments with a hastily-erected iceshield, but the shock of the detonation knocked Moira off-balance. She clutched onto the rim of the vault to keep from falling, the cylinder slipping from beneath her arm. Moira's heart virtually stopped as she heard the vial crack upon the hard steel floor.

"Bobby!" she shouted frantically. "The virus!"

The urgency in her voice caught Iceman's attention. His translucent blue eyes widened as he spotted the fallen cylinder. Turning his back on the crumbling barricade, he threw out his arm toward the cracked vial. Gelid moisture jetted from his fingertips, encasing the compromised cylinder within a solid sheath of ice. "Thank heavens," Moira exclaimed. With any luck, Iceman had reacted swiftly enough to keep the virus from escaping into the atmosphere.

I should test Bobby anyway, just in case, she thought, *assuming the Harpy leaves any of us intact.*

Iceman spun back toward the rime-covered window, but the momentary distraction had critical consequences. The combined heat and force of the Harpy's hellbolts had reduced his icewall to an avalanche of slush. With an ear-piercing screech, the crazed bird-woman crashed through shutters, window, and ice alike, invading Moira's scientific sanctuary amidst a cacophony of shattering glass and cracking ice. Her outstretched talons struck Iceman in the chest, bowling him over before he had a chance to defend himself.

"Beware the Harpy!" she squawked. Her harsh, unpleasant voice sounded like a cross between the ravings of a madwoman and the caw of an angry crow. "Surrender or be eliminated."

Bobby Drake slid on his back across the debris-covered floor of the lab, the smooth planes of his body sending him

SEARCH AND RESCUE

sledding like a toboggan out of reach of the Harpy. Splinters of steel and jagged shards of ice and glass littered the floor, but Iceman didn't need to worry about getting sliced or stabbed as long as he maintained his ice-form. Ice doesn't bleed; one of the distinct advantages of a frozen body over ordinary flesh and blood.

Thank you, Emma, he thought with just a trace of bitterness; he had never understood the full potential of his mutant powers until a ruthless telepath named Emma Frost took over his body—and showed him how to convert that body into ice, through and through. Since then, physical injuries had held a lot less terror for him.

A bank of computers brought his unplanned slide to a jarring halt. Iceman sprang to his feet and glanced down at his chest; the Harpy's claws had left deep rents across the crystalline surface of his torso. *Ouch,* he thought, mostly from force of habit. With a thought, he repaired the wounds by constructing frosty scabs out of the ambient moisture.

Thus restored, he quickly scoped out the scene, just like Cyke had taught him. Moira had taken shelter behind the containment vault while the Harpy flapped overhead, her predatory gaze shifting from Moira to Iceman and back again. Obviously, his first priority was to distract the berserk bird-woman from the defenseless human scientist.

"Hey, Ms. Rodan," he taunted the Harpy, "over here!" A snowball formed within his grip. Iceman gave the icy sphere a second to get good and hard, then pitched the snowball at the airborne intruder. The missile smacked against the Harpy's chartreuse cheek, and her head swiveled toward the offending X-Man with a jerky, bird-like motion. He was disappointed to see that the rock-hard snowball had not so much as bruised the Harpy's deceptively elegant features; she was even tougher than she looked. *Oh well,* he thought, *at least I got her attention.*

"Identified: mutant designate: Iceman," she screeched. "Compensating for cryogenic interference."

Compensating how? he wondered. He took a second to further survey the scene. The sturdy ceiling, no more than fifteen feet high, hampered the Harpy's aerial abilities while a gaping hole in the demolished window let in a cool night breeze. *Good,* he thought approvingly; the great thing about the U.K. was that there was never any lack of moisture in the air, which meant he had plenty of ammo to draw upon. "Compensate for this!" he challenged the enraged bird-woman. A second snowball slammed into the Harpy's face, and she swooped at Iceman, talons extended.

Iceman skated out of the way, sliding atop a self-generated sheet of ice. *Better keep moving,* he decided, not wanting to present the Harpy with an easy target for those nasty energy blasts of hers. He'd seen what the Harpy's blazing bolts had done to his icewall, never mind the steel shutters, and reached the not-too-complicated conclusion that he'd just as soon not end up on the receiving end of her personal pyrotechnics. With that in mind, he picked up speed, almost but not quite outpacing the slick, blue track he projected before him. In a matter of minutes, the floor of the laboratory resembled a full-sized skating rink.

But the Harpy was surprisingly fast, too. Her claws raked his back as she dived from above, briefly intercepting Iceman's path, before ascending for another run. This time Iceman barely ducked beneath the slashing talons.

Hmm, he noted, *no more energy bolts.* Maybe she'd used up all her firepower breaking into the building? If so, he might never have a better time to go on the offensive. *Let's go for it,* he decided.

The tips of the Harpy's wings brushed the ceiling as she circled several yards above the ice-coated floor, apparently out of reach . . . or was she? His speed and efficiency honed by countless drills, plus plenty of genuine combat experience, Iceman instantly erected a frozen stairway that he ran up pretty much simultaneously, generating each new step only a moment before his crystalline feet came down upon it. "Surprise!" he shouted at his flying foe, who suddenly found herself eye-to-eye with the cocky, young X-Man. A second later, heavy sheets of blue-white ice formed over the Harpy's feathered wings and, unable to stay aloft, she plummeted to the floor, landing with a crash upon the ice.

"Hah!" Iceman laughed, pleased at the effectiveness of his ploy. *And why shouldn't it have worked?* he asked himself triumphantly. He had once grounded Sauron, the human pterodactyl, much the same way.

A convenient ice-slide delivered him promptly to the floor, where he confronted the downed Harpy, who glared at him with wide, unblinking eyes. Not about to take any chances with the dangerous mutation, Iceman encased the bird-woman within a solid block of ice that merged inextricably with the thick layer of frost upon the floor, leaving only the Harpy's head free of an artificial snowdrift. He didn't want her to suffocate, especially not if Moira was right and the Harpy was just an innocent victim of some kind of radiation accident. *What a shame,* he thought compassionately. With the bulk of her avian body obscured beneath the ice, it was easier to think of his captive as a woman and not a monster.

"All's clear," he called out to Moira, letting her know the worst was over. It occurred to him that Nightcrawler had been gone for awhile now without checking back in with them. *I hope he's okay,* Iceman thought. There was a person-to-person communicator built into his belt, but he'd have to unthaw to use it; at the moment, his uniform, constructed of unstable molecules designed by Reed Richards, was made of solid ice just like the rest of him. He was reluctant to de-ice, though, until he was sure the danger was completely over. Hadn't Kurt said something about multiple intruders?

As if on cue, something pounded at the entrance to the lab. A massive, armor-plated door had slid into place when Moira first sealed off the lab, but now the door shuddered in its frame with each heavy blow delivered against it from the other side. The impressions of mighty, clenched knuckles bulged outward from the steel plating.

No way is that Nightcrawler knocking to get in, Iceman realized. Colossus was the only X-Man he knew with powerhouse fists like that, and Peter Rasputin was, in theory, miles and miles away.

"Further adaptation to cryogenic disruption required," the Harpy squawked. "Activating thermal conduction units." A reddish glow began to emanate from deep within the enormous ice cube that contained the trapped birdwoman. Despite the cold, her fangs were conspicuously *not* chattering. "Beware the Harpy! Beware!"

"Huh?" Iceman blurted, his attention torn between the pummeling at the door and the Harpy's unquenched defiance. The latter's oddly robotic syntax puzzled him as well; it dawned on him that he and Moira may have completely misread the true identity of their winged assailant. What if *this* Harpy wasn't the late Betty Banner at all, but some kind of mechanical duplicate?

The volcanic radiance coming from the freeze-packed Harpy caught his eye, and he watched in alarm as the ice enclosing the bird-woman melted at an accelerated rate. Cold, clear water streamed from the sides of the makeshift prison, carrying with it great chunks of soggy slush. Iceman concentrated all his power on the receding snowdrift, trying his best to keep the hostile Harpy in cold storage, but his handmade ice was liquefying faster than he could refreeze it. He could feel the heat radiating from the encased bird-woman, an unnatural warmth that bore little resemblance to even the hottest of fevers. It was like there was a portable nuclear generator blazing inside her, throwing off wave after wave of incandescent heat. That wasn't plain old body heat, he understood. This was something different, something inhuman.

Oh geez, Iceman thought as the awful suspicion sunk in. *I bet she's a Sentinel!*

The Harpy did not wait until the ice was completely dissolved to free herself. Throwing out her enormous wings with tremendous force, she sent the remains of her frozen prison flying off in every direction. "None can cage the Harpy!" she cawed triumphantly and took to the air, displaying no visible signs of hypothermia or even frostbite. The wind from her wings blew powdered ice and snow against Iceman's face. "You cannot escape the Harpy!"

"Yeah, right," Iceman said skeptically. He wasn't buying that story anymore. The way he figured it, the disguised Sentinel—until he learned otherwise, he'd consider it a Sentinel—had been programmed with a limited repertoire of stock super-villain phrases, purely to mislead the opposition and whatever media might be paying attention.

Just like a talking parrot, he thought, which was kind of weirdly fitting. He wasn't sure *why* exactly someone wanted to pass off a Sentinel as a deceased bird-monster, but he could work that out later. All he knew now was that there was no more point in holding back; killing a living being was one thing, trashing another stinking Sentinel was something else entirely. "All right," Iceman said, sucking up all the free moisture at his command, "no more Mr. Nice Ice."

The Harpy wasn't pulling her punches either. "Targeting mutant designate: Iceman," she announced from above, only a nanosecond before a red-hot burst of flame erupted from her seemingly human hands. *Un-oh,* he thought, *looks like she's recharged.* Iceman dove out of the line of fire, onto a self-generated luge that carried him sliding on his stomach away from instant incineration. Even though the main thrust of the hellish bolt missed him, rendering a square foot of floorspace completely free of ice, the fearsome heat of its proximity melted away Iceman's legs all the way up to his knees, and he had to devote precious seconds to restoring his limbs to their original proportions.

That was close, he thought, shivering (and not from the cold). Theoretically, he could regenerate his entire body as long as some fraction of his awareness remained intact, but he didn't feel like experimenting along those lines at this particular moment. The booming pounding at the armored door still reverberated across the lab, reminding him that the Harpy-Sentinel wasn't their only problem. *Where on earth is that pointy-eared German elf?* he wondered desperately, hoping to hear a well-timed *bamf* any second now. From the sound of it, he was only moments away from being outnumbered.

A burst of orange fire exploded in his path. The Harpy was shrewdly firing her bolts at the luge as it formed in front of him. Iceman changed course at the last minute, creating a hitherto-nonexistent detour out of the chill Scottish air, then throwing in a series of zigzagging curves to keep his course unpredictable. Making sure he had built up enough momentum to carry him through, he executed a partial loop-the-loop that left him upright once more, sliding upon the slippery soles of his feet while making random turns every other second. He knew he was only buying time, though. A more ingenious tactic was called for, hopefully before whatever was outside the battered door broke all the way through.

SEARCH AND RESCUE

"Here goes nothing," he muttered, puffs of condensed vapor fogging the air beyond his lips. Spotting the horrible Harpy out of the corner of his eye, he hurled a stream of sleet at her face. The cold, congealing liquid formed an icy mask over her face, blinding her as efficaciously as the hood over a falconer's hunting bird. *Perfect,* Iceman thought. *Now I just need to work quickly....*

Her powerful pinions flapped angrily as the Harpy tore at the frigid mask with emerald nails. She managed to quickly scrape the ice away from her eyes, but when she searched the laboratory for her frosty foe, those eyes widened in confusion.

Iceman was everywhere. Several Icemen, at least a dozen, stood in a variety of poses all over the laboratory. The stationary figures, each sculpted from identical blue-white ice, populated the scene, some staring upward at the Harpy, some looking away nonchalantly. There was even an Iceman hanging from one of Nightcrawler's trapeze rings in the ceiling, his translucent knuckles wrapped around the metal hoop. Everywhere the Harpy-Sentinel looked, she saw another unmistakable specimen of the previously one-of-a-kind Iceman.

"Anomaly... anomaly," she squawked. Her face became immobile as her head jerked toward one humanoid ice sculpture after another. "Registering multiple coordinates for mutant designate: Iceman. Processing probability analysis...."

The feathered Sentinel hesitated, hovering in midair as its computerized synapses coped with this unanticipated occurrence. Then, abruptly, it unleashed a hellbolt at a motionless figure standing resolutely, arms akimbo, upon the floor. The destructive energy blast struck the figure dead-on, eliciting a horrified gasp from Moira MacTaggert as she peeked over the rim of the durable containment vault.

81

A crystalline body snapped and cracked loudly, and, when the blinding flare passed away, all that was left of *that* Iceman was a truncated pair of legs rooted to the frosted floor, standing forlornly like twin pillars left behind by some long-collapsed edifice.

"Feel the fury of the Harpy!" she announced before turning her attention to a nearly identical figure posing adjacent to the one she had devastated only seconds before. "Feel the fury of the Harpy!" she said again and launched a second blast that took the head off the next Iceman in the line. "Feel the fury of the Harpy! Feel the fury of the Harpy! Feel the fury of the Harpy . . . !"

Sounding very much like a broken record, the determined Harpy relentlessly and methodically picked off each of the apparent Icemen, one at a time. Hanging from the trapeze ring fifteen feet above the wintry carnage, the real Iceman resisted the temptation to nod in satisfaction. *That's right,* he thought, his icy fingers stuck to the cold metal of the hoop, *use up all your firepower on my handy-dandy, instant ice doubles.* The same trick had fooled that mutant-hating creep, Bastion, a few months back, and it looked like it was working like a charm this time around. Still, as he watched the massacre from on high, being careful not to move a single crystalline muscle, he had to admit that it was more than a little unnerving to watch the Harpy blow his various self-portraits apart. He tried not to flinch as a hellbolt split one of his clones right down the middle.

Creating all those ice doubles from scratch had taken a lot of concentration and energy. The really tricky part, though, had been creating that ice-ladder to the ceiling, climbing as quietly as he could, then dissolving it completely before the Harpy got rid of her frozen blindfold. Iceman was glad to have a few moments to recuperate

SEARCH AND RESCUE

while the feathered Sentinel took out her cybernetic frustration on his lifeless duplicates.

And, from the look of things, the Harpy's fiery blasts were losing their oomph. Instead of entirely decapitating the seventh frozen decoy, the sizzling hellbolt merely melted "Bobby's" head to the size of an ordinary ice cube. *Now there's a disturbing image,* he thought; he could just imagine the wisecracks the Beast might make about the double's now-diminutive "cranium."

He waited until the Harpy had expended her firepower on at least ten imitation Icemen. With only one decoy remaining between him and the Harpy's lethal attentions, he let go of the trapeze ring and dropped toward the floor. Before he could hit the ground, however, a triangular sail, just an inch-and-a-half thick, grew from his shoulders, slowing his fall. He used his freshly-created parasail to glide after the Harpy. His rock-hard feet slammed into her back at the very moment that she released a final, sputtering burst of fire at the last of the sculpted ice doubles. Her outraged squawk of surprise merged with the wet, splintery sound of the clone melting to pieces.

Iceman kicked off from the base of the creature's wings, catching an updraft to carry him up and away from his inhuman adversary. His own wingspan, he noted proudly, nearly equalled the Harpy's. He bombarded the flying Sentinel with a barrage of icy hail that dislodged a few of the Harpy's synthetic feathers. The emerald plumes fluttered gently to the floor even as their recent owner banked sharply upon the wind and climbed toward Iceman, slashing out once more with her long talons.

The airborne X-Man thought he was ready for the Harpy's attack. An instant ice-shield attached itself to his upper arm and he held it up to block the raking claws. But the Sentinel had another trick beneath her verdant feathers;

an aperture opened in the Harpy's chest, which fired like a cannon at the unsuspecting Iceman, who suddenly found himself snared in some sort of electrified net. Thin metal filaments, glowing with blistering energy, sliced off the tips of Iceman's improvised parasail, sending him spiraling toward the ice-glazed floor below. He landed in a heap, hard enough to knock the wind out of him, hopelessly tangled in the electrically charged netting, which began melting into the very substance of his crystalline body. Despairing, Iceman realized he had to shed his ice-form before he melted away entirely, even if that meant leaving himself vulnerable to physical attacks on his restored flesh and blood. Talk about your lose-lose situations!

The corrosive heat of the net made it hard to concentrate, but Iceman closed his eyes and forced himself to visualize his humanoid alter ego: brown hair, pink skin, meat and bone and gristle. Blood rushing through pulsing veins and arteries. A human heart beating in his chest. Through some bizarre alchemical process known only to his own mutant metabolism, solid ice transmuted into organic tissue, turning Iceman back into Bobby Drake, a slender young man in a light blue uniform, lying in a puddle upon the floor. His hair clung damply to his skull. Ice-cold water glistened upon his back.

Despite this miraculous transformation, Bobby's circumstances hardly improved. The wires no longer threatened to reduce his limbs to liquid, but his mortal flesh felt the stinging sensation of who knew how many volts running through his body; it was like getting the shock treatment from Storm during a Danger Room skirmish. *I'm sorry, doc,* he thought as he felt his consciousness slipping away. *I didn't want to let you down.*

The last thing he heard before passing out was the sound of a heavy iron door crashing to the floor.

SEARCH AND RESCUE

• • •

Peering over the edge of the containment vault, Moira MacTaggert inspected the frozen wasteland the laboratory had become; it looked like a new Ice Age had hit Scotland, and never mind global warming. But what else could you expect when someone called Iceman came to your defense? Shattered replicas of the frigid X-Man were scattered about the lab, whilst Iceman and the Harpy took their battle to the limited airspace of the lab. Moira just hoped she'd be around to mop the bloody place up once the fighting was over.

So far, at least, Bobby seemed to be holding his own against the Harpy, leaving Moira to wonder what had become of Nightcrawler. *Watch out, Kurt,* she thought. *If we have a gamma-mutated bird/woman hybrid up here, Lord only knows what's poking around downstairs.*

Pounding blows smashed against the sealed entrance, distracting her from the aerial battle being fought above her. "Now what?" she muttered, sounding more exasperated than alarmed. The emergency bulkhead was made of reinforced steel, yet the thick plates were already buckling beneath the relentless impact of whoever was trying to smash his or her way into the lab. Moira glanced hopefully at the security monitors, but the internal cameras were still on the fritz, providing her with no clue as to the identity of the apparently super-strong housebreaker. *Judging from the sheer power of the blows,* she thought, *I think we can safely rule out Jubilee.*

A high-tech bio-medical laboratory was no place to store weapons, but Moira found herself wishing she'd stashed an Uzi somewhere among the microscopes and petrie dishes. The middle-aged scientist was no shrinking violet, and considered that she could make a fair accounting for herself in any ordinary donnybrook. It didn't take a Ph.D. to comprehend, however, that she wouldn't last long in unarmed combat against any being capable of making it through that door. *Blast it,* she thought, *I'm a scientist, not a bloody super-heroine.*

With one final, tremendous heave, the armor-plated door gave way, falling forward onto the floor of the lab with a deafening clang that echoed through the entire icebound laboratory. Moira braced herself for whatever ghastly monstrosity might makes its way through the now-open entrance. Imagine her relief when she spied a respected colleague instead.

Dr. Leonard Samson, possibly the world's leading authority on the psychology of superhumans, and the Hulk's personal therapist, strode into the ice-bedecked chamber. Along with his impressive academic credentials, he had a muscular build worthy of Hercules or the mighty Thor. His long green hair, flowing freely over his shoulders, testified to the effects of gamma radiation on his own DNA, although he had obviously been spared a transformation as grotesque as either the Harpy's or the Hulk's; the unpredictable vagaries of gamma mutation had dealt with him much more generously, merely enhancing his physical strength to Hulk-like proportions whilst adding a greenish tint to his distinctive mane.

"Have no fear, Doc Samson is here," he declared, utilizing the colorful nickname the media had inevitably dubbed him with. He had clearly come dressed for action, clad in a red leather outfit consisting of a sleeveless vest, trousers, and boots. Fingerless red gloves protected his clenched fists. A handsome, intelligent face swept the lab with his gaze, looking surprisingly unsurprised by its arctic appearance.

"Leonard!" Moira called out, rising from behind the vault. She did not know Samson well, but they had met at the odd scientific conference over the years. She remembered being particularly impressed by his paper on *The Behavioral Dynamics of Human/Super-Human Relations*. No doubt he hoped to treat the unfortunate Ms. Banner once he apprehended the crazed creature she had become; Moira hoped he could cope with an energy-blasting Harpy as well as he'd handled that symposium in Anchorage a few years back.

Samson turned piercing green eyes toward her. "Identified: Dr. Moira MacTaggert. Human, female. Director and proprietor of targeted facility. Prepare for relocation to Gamma Base."

The voice, deep and authoritative, was as Moira remembered, but the words and their delivery did not sound like anything she ever expected Leonard Samson to say. If she heard him correctly, he was after her, not the Harpy! "What are ye talking about, Leonard?" she demanded. "What's this all about?"

Before he could answer, the brittle sound of Iceman crashing to earth attracted Moira's gaze and filled her heart with anxiety. Enmeshed in a crackling electronic net, Iceman lay sprawled upon the fractured ice whilst the Harpy cawed triumphantly above him. Moira watched in horror as the frozen X-Man reverted to plain old Bobby Drake. She felt both victory and safety slipping away, an impression confirmed when a powerful hand grabbed onto her throat and lifted her off the floor. "Apprehended: human designate: Moira MacTaggert," Doc Samson proclaimed, not a trace of human emotion in his voice. "No further resistance is anticipated."

Where are ye, Kurt? Moira wondered desperately. Samson's strength matched that of his Biblical namesake. No matter how she struggled, she could not escape from his steely grip. Unable to turn her head, she barely managed to glimpse Bobby collapsing unconscious onto the floor a few meters away. With Iceman down, and Samson and the Harpy running roughshod over the lab and its inhabitants, everything now depended on Nightcrawler.

If only she knew where he was . . . !

"Unglaublich!"

Nightcrawler cried out in both agony and amazement. Delicate bones in his ankle cracked as the pseudo-Abomination tightened his grip on the ceiling-crawling X-Man. Nightcrawler tried to yank his leg free, but the Sentinel held on to him as securely as a ball and chain. In desperation, Kurt used his tail to fling the borrowed scalpel at his foe. The blade struck the monster in the throat, where it bounced harmlessly off the Sentinel's synthetic scales. "Apprehended: mutant designate: Nightcrawler," the robot reported to itself. "Elimination of mutant imminent." The Sentinel pulled Nightcrawler down from the ceiling and, as his fingers and toes were forcibly torn from their gravity-defying holds on the ceiling, the tortured X-Man escaped the only way left to him.

BAMF!

With a flourish of smoke and brimstone, he teleported away from the mock Abomination's excruciating grasp. A split-second later, he arrived in the darkened hallway, gasping for breath. All this teleporting, on top of the shock induced by his broken ankle, left him weak and exhausted. *Ordinarily, I'd report to the medlab,* he thought, biting down on his lip to keep from yelping in pain, *but that's probably not the best idea at the moment, considering that I just left an annoyed and artificial Abomination there.*

Grimacing, he limped down the corridor toward the elevator. The Comm Suite, from which he could theoretically send for help, was two floors away and he was in no shape

SEARCH AND RESCUE

to *bamf* that far. Fractured ankle bones ground against each other, producing sharp, shooting pains that brought him close to fainting. His vision blurred and grew dark around the edges, while the floor seemed to sway dizzyingly beneath his feet. He couldn't pause for a moment's rest, though; he knew he had to keep going—for Iceman and Moira's sake. To take the pressure off his injured leg, he kicked off from the floor with his good leg, lifting his body above his head, and started walking on his hands. "*Jah*, he murmured weakly, "that's better. I think."

Even for a mutant as acrobatically gifted as Nightcrawler, hand-walking at an urgent clip was tiring work, almost as hard as teleporting from one end of the Research Centre to another. A cold sweat broke out beneath his red-and-blue uniform, leaving him feeling damp and clammy. Although suspended in the air, his broken ankle throbbed mercilessly, and he wished for some serious painkillers, plus maybe an attractive nurse or two. The elevator, less than twenty meters away, seemed light-years distant.

How are Moira and Bobby faring? he wondered, concerned for his friends despite his own grievous situation. Could Iceman withstand a full-fledged Sentinel assault on his own? In truth, Nightcrawler had seldom fought beside the frozen hero, simply because their terms as X-Men had so seldom overlapped, so he had only a limited sense of Bobby Drake's capabilities. Cyclops and the others spoke well of Iceman, though, which reassured Kurt somewhat. The refrigerated X-Man could have never survived against the likes of Magneto or Sauron, if he hadn't learned something from his sessions in the Danger Room. *Bobby can hold his own*, Nightcrawler decided. *I just need to have faith.*

A deafening crash interrupted his worried musings. Still standing on his head, Nightcrawler looked back the way he came—and saw the phony Abomination emerge from the medlab in an explosion of flying timbers and plaster. Eschewing the convenient exit, the Sentinel simply bulldozed through the wall and into the hall, less than fifteen meters behind the shocked X-Man. "Tracking mutant designate: Nightcrawler," it said. Infrared scanners glowed balefully from sockets beneath the robot's troglodyte brow. "Target sighted."

Instinctively, Nightcrawler cartwheeled forward onto his feet, then gasped out loud as his weight came down on his bad leg. Tears leaked from his eyes and he almost lost his balance. Half limping, half dragging his foot behind him, he lurched toward the elevator, all the time hearing the lumbering footsteps of the disguised Sentinel closing on him. As soon as the lift controls came within reach, he jabbed the UP button with his middle finger and waited for the metal door to slide open, which didn't happen nearly fast enough.

"Come on," he whispered impatiently. According to the display above the entrance, the lift was still among the Centre's sub-basements, working its way up, floor by floor. *"Schnell, schnell!"*

"Beware the Abomination," the Sentinel said mechanically, apparently programmed to perpetuate its fraudulent imposture for the benefit of whoever might be listening. "The Abomination cannot be thwarted."

Nightcrawler could not be fooled. He knew a Sentinel when he heard one. Glancing back over his shoulder, he saw that the relentless robot was only a few meters away. To his vast relief, the elevator chimed, announcing the lift's arrival. *And none too soon,* he thought, squeezing past the metal door as soon as it began to slide open. The point of his tail stabbed repeatedly at the CLOSE DOOR button inside the lift even as he blurted out his destination to the voice-

SEARCH AND RESCUE

activated elevator system. "The Comm Suite," he panted, breathing hard. "Now."

To his frustration, the elevator door took its own sweet time in closing, pausing patiently for any further passengers. Unfortunately for the debilitated X-Man, one such passenger was even now bearing down on the elevator, its greedy claws reaching out for Nightcrawler once more. The light from the open lift poured out into the corridor, exposing the pseudo-Abomination in all its reptilian hideousness. Kurt flattened himself against the back of the elevator, then glanced at the emergency hatch in the ceiling of the lift. A possible escape route?

At last, the door leisurely began to slide shut, but it was too late. Scaly fingers caught hold of the door's edge, halting its progress an instant before the entrance completely closed. With a harsh wrenching noise, the Abomination-Sentinel ripped the steel door from its tracks, then charged into the cramped confines of the lift, only to find its quarry missing. The escape hatch slammed shut above the robot's head, granting the Sentinel only a fleeting glimpse of a pronged tail chasing its owner out of the lift compartment.

Nightcrawler heard the *faux* Abomination claw through the roof of the elevator beneath him, metallic green talons rending the flimsy steel barrier between the Sentinel and its prey. Favoring his injured ankle, Nightcrawler climbed even faster up the greasy elevator cable, confident that the massive robot could not easily duplicate his own agile ascent, yet eager to increase his lead on his indomitable pursuer. He swiftly counted off the floors as he climbed.

One. As he passed the closed elevator doorway that led to the laboratory where he had left Iceman and Moira, he thought he heard the muffled pounding of hammers upon steel, along with the cawing of . . . an enormous bird? He was sorely tempted to make his way back into the lab, to add what was left of his strength to his friends', but, no, he realized, summoning reinforcements had to be his top priority. "Hang on, *mein freunds*," he whispered. "Help will be on its way soon."

Two. Moira's security lockdown had also sealed the entrance to the Comm Suite, but, thankfully, Nightcrawler still remembered the appropriate security codes. Using all three of the fingers of his right hand, he rapidly keyed the correct numeric sequence into an access panel mounted to the wall of the elevator shaft. With a hydraulic *whoosh*, redundant layers of steel shielding slide aside to permit him entry to the chamber beyond. He hopped awkwardly from the cable to the floor of the Comm Suite, sending an agonizing pang through his injured leg despite his best efforts to shield the tender limb from the impact. "*Mein gott*, that hurts!" he muttered, wiping his greasy hands on his trousers. If he'd been a telekinetic and not a teleporter, his angry thoughts at that moment might have been enough to reduce the ersatz Abomination to so many nuts and bolts. . . .

Faxes, modems, scanners, and other equipment filled the suite, all tied in to the high-powered satellite dish erected on the roof of the Centre. He limped over to the main communications console and gratefully dropped into a movable seat. His fingers danced over the control panel as he fired up the communications array and sent out a general SOS to the X-Men, X-Force, and even—*why not?*—Generation X's private academy in Massachusetts. "Attention, priority Alpha!" he stated crisply into the mike. "This is Nightcrawler calling from the Genetic Research Centre on Muir Island. We are under attack by Sentinels. Repeat: Sentinels. Assistance is required as quickly as possible. Please respond immediately."

Too bad they're all an ocean away, he thought, but the

SEARCH AND RESCUE

X-Men could travel with amazing speed when they had to. He placed a pair of headphones over his pointed ears, and waited anxiously to hear if anyone had received his message. *Just our luck if nobody's home to take the call.*

"C'mon, Ororo, Logan, Rogue, somebody. Let me know you're there."

The headphones muffled but hardly blocked out the startling sound of something crashing through the ceiling behind him. *"Vas?"* he asked out loud, rotating his seat to locate the source of the disturbance. Surely the "Abomination" had not climbed up the cables already, let alone taken a detour by way of the roof? That was impossible! Nonetheless, a gigantic green figure now stood between Nightcrawler and the open elevator shaft, casting an ominously large shadow over the surprised and crippled X-Man. Kurt Wagner gulped as he recognized the savage creature grabbing onto his chair and effortlessly throwing Nightcrawler across the room with just one hand.

It was *not* the Abomination.

It was the Hulk.

Chapter Three

This is more like it, Captain America decided. Now that the Beast had successfully called a truce between the various warring parties, the X-Men, the Avengers, and even the Hulk could work together to achieve a common goal. Hank McCoy definitely deserved a round of applause; as far as Cap was concerned, teamwork was always preferable to knocking heads together.

The assembled heroes had gathered upon the Rainbow Bridge spanning the Niagara River downstream of the Falls. Colonel Lopez and his Canadian counterpart guarded both ends of the bridge, blocking traffic and providing the heroes with a degree of privacy from curious sightseers and aggressive reporters. TV news copters, driven away by the Hulk earlier, had returned in force, however, circling low above the two-lane suspension bridge with their cameras aimed at what was undeniably an impressive collection of colorful individuals.

We're all of us looking a bit worse for wear, Cap reflected. With the notable exception of the Hulk, they were all soaked and more than a little banged up. One wing was missing from his own cowl and his sore jaw kept reminding him of its unfortunate collision with the Hulk's fist. *I'm lucky I still have all my teeth,* he thought; the Hulk must have been holding back some.

The X-Men had not fared much better. Cyclops's yellow

bandolier was torn and his lower lip looked swollen, while Storm's exposed arms and legs were marred by numerous nicks and scratches. The Beast's dense fur largely concealed his injuries, but Cap noticed that the agile former Avenger was moving a bit more stiffly than he usually did, a pained wince occasionally dimming his characteristic smile. *Poor Hank,* Cap thought. He didn't envy anyone who'd been on the receiving end of Cyclops's eyebeams.

Only the Hulk, standing at least a head taller than anyone else on the bridge, appeared unscathed by the recent violence. True, his faded purple jeans hung in ribbons below his knees, but that was pretty much standard attire for the Hulk. "So what are we waiting for?" he rumbled ominously. A sullen expression seemed to have taken up permanent residence upon his neanderthal features. "I said I'd answer your stupid questions if everyone left me alone, but that doesn't mean I've got all day. Let's get on with it."

Storm gave the Hulk a disapproving look. His bad attitude was getting on everyone's nerves, but, thankfully, no one felt inclined to start another fight. "Hold tight a few more minutes," Captain America instructed the Hulk in his most authoritative voice. Hopefully, his relative seniority would carry some weight with the impatient Hulk while they tended to a more urgent matter.

Cap leaned out over the pedestrian guardrail, searching the churning basin beneath the Horseshoe Falls. A foggy white mist concealed the surface of the pool, frustrating the Star-Spangled Avenger's efforts to see any sign of activity below the turbulent white water. A rainbow arced through the mist. The weather, he noted, had improved dramatically since Storm joined the cease-fire, gray and angry clouds giving way to open blue sky. He just hoped the rainbow would prove a positive omen.

"C'mon, Shellhead," he whispered to himself. "What's keeping you?"

Another long minute passed before he thought he saw something break the surface of the misty pool. "Look!" Cyclops called out, pointing toward the water below. Cap followed his gaze and was relieved to see a gleaming metal figure emerge from the river. Iron Man shone in the sunlight, as he rose into the sky, cradling the broken body of the Vision. He flew slowly toward the bridge, the seemingly inert synthezoid weighing him down like ballast, until Iron Man's boots touched down on the pavement near Cap and the others. Staggering beneath the obvious weight of his burden, he carefully lowered the Vision to the surface of the bridge. The android Avenger appeared lifeless except for a faint, intermittent flickering in the amber gem embedded in the Vision's forehead. Even though he had been warned in advance, Cap was still shocked to see the Vision's right arm lying separate from his body.

"Sorry for the delay," Iron Man apologized. He sounded slightly out of breath. "It's pretty murky down there. It took me awhile to find his arm. My spotlight was broken, so I had to rely on the sonar." Cap noticed that Iron Man's armor was dented in places and the beam projector in his chestplate cracked. *Did the Hulk do that or Storm?* he wondered.

The blacktop beneath the Vision cracked loudly, narrow fissures extending like spiderwebs through the pavement around the fallen synthezoid. "He's heavier than he looks," Iron Man explained, stretching his arms as much as his armor would allow. "He must have increased his density to its upper limit before he took the plunge from the Falls."

Storm felt compelled to apologize as well. "I'm so sorry, Iron Man. I had no idea what had happened to your teammate. No wonder you attacked the Hulk." She shook

SEARCH AND RESCUE

her head, no doubt recalling how she had rashly come to the Hulk's defense. "I was tired and wet and recovering from a severe psychic shock, but I should have realized you had been provoked."

All eyes gradually turned toward the Hulk. It was he, Iron Man had explained to the X-Men, who had torn the Vision asunder, then tossed both pieces over the Falls. Unrepentant, the green goliath glared back at them, his arms folded across his chest, the massive biceps bulging like overstuffed sandbags. "Hey, I warned him to leave me alone," he grumbled. "Can I help it if he can't take a hint?"

Cap clenched his teeth, biting back an angry retort. He couldn't expect the Hulk to show any remorse. Helping the Vision was what mattered now. "How is he?" he asked Iron Man. The Vision's plasticine body looked disturbingly still. Only the flashing gem in his forehead hinted at any degree of animation. *Was he alive or dead?* Cap wondered. *Or did those words mean anything at all where an artificial lifeform is involved?* The Vision's predecessor, the original android Human Torch, had "died" several times, but was currently up and running again. With any luck, the Vision was just as durable.

"I've seen him worse," Iron Man said bluntly. He had a point; Cap recalled at least two occasions on which the Vision had practically needed to be rebuilt from scratch. "His primary operating system has gone into emergency shutdown mode to conserve energy, but I should be able to reattach his arm back at the mansion, then reboot him with only minimal memory loss. If he's lucky, he won't even remember the accident."

Iron Man's hopeful diagnosis elicited a skeptical expression from Storm and Cyclops. Cap didn't blame them; the dismembered Vision sure looked like a seriously-wounded casualty of war. "Trust me," Iron Man informed them, "this isn't nearly as bad as the time the Feds completely disassembled him, or the time Morgan Le Fey blew him apart with a mystical blast. Now *that* required some major reconstruction work."

"That's our Vizh," the Beast remarked. He crouched ape-like, his knuckles grazing the pavement, and inspected the synthezoid's amputated arm. Unlike the rest of the Vision's body, the disconnected limb appeared lightweight and gelatinous in texture. "He takes a licking, and keeps on ticking."

"Fine," the Hulk snapped testily. "If Robby the Robot is going to be okay then, can we maybe get on with business? At this rate, my snazzy green hair's gonna go gray again before I get away from this overrated tourist trap."

Iron Man had heard enough. "Listen, Hulk," he barked. "I just spent fifteen minutes fishing your crummy handiwork off the floor of the river and the last thing I need is your lip." He took an angry step toward the Hulk, the servomotors in his armor whirring audibly, but Captain America laid a restraining hand upon the Golden Avenger's shoulder.

"Easy, old friend," Cap said. His crimson glove was almost the same color as Iron Man's shoulderplate. "That's not going to help the Vision—or Wanda."

"Aw, let him go," the Hulk urged, sounding disappointed by the Cap's diplomatic efforts. He flashed a wide, malicious grin. "I'll crack open that metal shell like a boiled lobster. It won't take long, I promise."

"No," Cyclops said firmly, stepping bravely between Iron Man and the Hulk. "We've wasted too much time already." He turned his visor toward the two surviving Avengers. "You mentioned the Scarlet Witch a moment ago. What sort of danger is she in?"

SEARCH AND RESCUE

There upon the bridge, flanked by watchful armies on both sides, the two teams compared notes, sharing with each other the bizarre and unsettling chain of events that had brought both mutants and human heroes to Niagara Falls in search of the Hulk. Captain America was not too surprised to discover that the X-Men's quest was very much like their own. *The pieces are coming together,* he thought, *even if we can't quite make out the big picture yet.*

"Sounds to me," Cyclops said, "like the Scarlet Witch was abducted not long before Rogue disappeared, and under similar circumstances."

"Living marionettes, animated tee-shirts... this just keeps getting stranger," Iron Man complained. He had earlier confided to Cap his concern that this case might end up involving sorcery, not exactly scientist Tony Stark's cup of tea. "The common link here, besides the suggestively analogous m.o.'s, is the presence of gamma radiation at both sites."

The mention of gamma rays caught the Hulk's attention. For the first time, he seemed more than grudgingly interested in what the costumed heroes had to say. "Gamma radiation, mysterious disappearances," he muttered, more to himself than to either the Avengers or the X-Men. His surly expression darkened further as he mulled over what he had just heard. "It can't be. Not *him* again."

"Do these clues mean something to you, Hulk?" Storm asked. Her striking blue eyes held a trace of hope. Perhaps their costly pursuit of the Hulk would prove worth the hardships they'd endured.

I hope so, too, Cap thought.

For once, the Hulk answered without argument and only a token amount of attitude. "Not all that weirdness about puppets and flying shirts," he said, "but the rest of it? Yeah, that rings some bells. The way I see it, your buddies got beamed out of there after the puppets and all put the kibosh on them. Problem is, there's only one slimeball I know who uses trans-mat technology powered by gamma energy: my old sparring partner, Samuel Sterns. Or, as he likes to call himself these days, the Leader."

The Leader! Cap didn't know whether to be relieved or appalled now that the Hulk had finally provided them with a suspect. The Avengers hadn't crossed swords with the Leader for years, not since that time the Leader tried to change history by travelling back to the dawn of human evolution, but Cap well remembered just how fiendishly brilliant that megalomaniacal mastermind could be. *If the Leader is responsible for kidnapping Wanda and Rogue, getting them back is not going to be easy.*

"I thought he was dead," Iron Man protested.

"Me too," the Hulk confirmed. "I messed him up pretty bad in Alberta awhile back, in this underground city of his. It looked like he'd finally kicked the bucket once and for all." He scowled and shrugged his ample shoulders. "You know super-villains, though. They keep coming back, like the flu."

Cap knew what he meant. He'd lost count of the number of times that the Red Skull or Baron Zemo had returned from the grave. But why would the Leader come after Wanda or Rogue? The Hulk was the usual target of his insane schemes of revenge.

"Forgive me," Storm interrupted, "but who is the Leader? I'm afraid I'm not familiar with this individual."

"Another singular product of gamma radiation," the Beast offered helpfully, "only this time the metamorphic effect went straight to his head, increasing the size and capacity of his cerebellum. Essentially, he ended up as awesomely intelligent as the Hulk is—"

"Watch it," the Hulk growled. His voluminous shadow

SEARCH AND RESCUE

fell over the hairy mutant, who flinched instinctively.

"—stronger than most," the Beast concluded tactfully. "Like so many other misguided prodigies of our acquaintance, he promptly set about to conquer the world. Absolute intelligence, alas, apparently corrupts just as absolutely as raw power." He glanced nervously at the Hulk. "Present company excluded, of course."

Cap decided to intervene before the Beast's loquacious ways got him deeper into trouble. "Thank you, Hulk. You've been very helpful." He held out his hand to shake the Hulk's immense green mitt. "You're free to go, provided you don't intend to create any further disturbances here. Our quinjet is parked not far from here. Perhaps we can drop you off someplace private and secluded?"

The North Pole, for instance? he thought. *After all, if it was good enough for the Frankenstein monster in the novel....*

"Forget it, yankee doodle." The Hulk ignored Cap's proffered hand. "If the Leader is involved in this shindig, then I'm coming with you. That big-brained *fuhrer* has been a pain in my posterior long before he messed with you and your missing gals. If he's going down, I'm going to be there, whether you want me or not." He looked the assembled heroes over dubiously. "Besides, I'm not sure any of you are up to it."

"What?" Iron Man answered indignantly. The motile metal of his gilded faceplate allowed some of his ire to show through. "Who invited you along?" Judging from the offended and/or dismayed expressions on the three mutants' faces, Iron Man wasn't the only one taken aback by the Hulk's brashness. "I can't speak for the X-Men, but I can tell here and now that the Avengers have been doing fine without you, Hulk, and against adversaries as dangerous as the Leader, if not more so."

"I'm coming with you," the Hulk insisted, hands on his hips. He towered over the armored Avenger. "You *got a problem with that,* tin man?"

"Maybe," Iron Man said, undeterred by the Hulk's looming presence. Even dented and dripping from his dive beneath the Fall, Iron Man's armor made him an imposing figure. Metal gauntlets were clenched; clearly what the Hulk had done to the Vision hadn't been set aside.

Captain America shared his sentiments, especially where their injured comrade was concerned, but felt obliged to play peacemaker once more. The lives of at least two women were at stake. "Stand down," he ordered Iron Man, and the Golden Avenger reluctantly complied, stepping back from the Hulk to join Captain America a few feet away. His armored fists remained tightly clenched.

Cap considered the Hulk carefully. The hot-tempered behemoth had served with the Avengers before, however briefly, and certainly there was no love lost between the Hulk and the Leader. The only thing that worried the veteran hero was whether or not the Hulk would place his anger against his old enemy over the safety of the hostages. What if his barbaric desire for revenge endangered Wanda or Rogue?

Somewhere inside that furious monstrosity is Bruce Banner, he reminded himself, *and Banner is a decent, honorable man.* He had to hope that, ultimately, some tiny portion of Banner would be enough to curb the Hulk's most crazed, counterproductive impulses. *Heaven help us if I'm wrong.*

"All right, Hulk," Cap said. "If the X-Men have no objections, you can join us on this mission. I'd rather have you fighting with us than against us." He looked at Storm and Cyclops, unsure which of them served as leader of their team. "Is that acceptable to you?"

SEARCH AND RESCUE

"Give us a moment, Captain," Storm requested. She and Cyclops conferred quietly, casting a few doubtful looks at the Hulk, then leaned over to whisper to the Beast. *Interesting,* Cap thought. From the looks of things, it appeared that the X-Men proceeded more through consensus than through an established chain of command. *Whatever works for them,* he decided.

Their huddle lasted for only a minute or two. Cyclops nodded at Cap and answered for his teammates. "We have no objections to working with the Hulk. The important thing is finding our people."

"I couldn't have put it better myself," Cap agreed. He glanced about the bridge. Overhead, the buzzing news copters were getting alarmingly closer. *For all we know, the Leader could be watching us on CNN right now,* he thought.

"I suggest we reconvene at Avengers Mansion, where we can take better advantage of our resources. I assume you X-Men have transportation of your own?" he asked.

"Our able and adaptable aircraft awaits on yonder isle," the Beast assured him, giving the Hulk a wide berth as he bounded toward the American end of the bridge. "Given the Hulk's esteemed status as a charter member of the Avengers, however, perhaps he would be most comfortable travelling with you?" He did little to conceal his eagerness to foist the irascible man-brute off on the Avengers.

Technically, Cap remembered, they had revoked the Hulk's membership years ago, but now was no time to mention that. "Good idea," he said firmly. "Hulk, you're with us."

"Terrific," Iron Man muttered sarcastically, low enough so that only Cap could hear. "This should be a fun flight."

At least we'll be able to keep an eye on the Hulk, Cap thought, despite sincerely mixed emotions over acquiring such an explosive loose cannon for their team. To his surprise, the Hulk voluntarily lifted the super-dense remains of the Vision, leaving Iron Man only the amputated arm to carry. Following after the Beast, Captain America led the others back toward American soil, only to be confronted by an armed battalion commanded by Colonel Arturo Lopez.

"I believe we've finished with our business here," Cap reported to the officer. "The Hulk is leaving with us, so there should be no further need for you and your troops."

"Not so fast," Lopez said sternly. His lean face was grim, like he had to do something he wasn't too happy about. "I appreciate your efforts here, Captain, but, with all due respect, I have standing orders to apprehend both the Hulk and the X-Men." He fixed a stony gaze on Cyclops and his team. "The X-Men, in particular, are wanted regarding an attack on a government installation less than twenty-four hours ago."

"What?" Cyclops objected, sounding genuinely surprised. The Beast and Storm looked equally perplexed. "What is he talking about?"

Cap held up his hand to still further argument. "Let me ask you something point blank," he said to Cyclops. "Did you or any of your team attack the S.H.I.E.L.D. Helicarrier yesterday?"

Cyclops shook his head. "No, this is the first I've heard of any attack. We've been searching for Rogue nonstop since she disappeared yesterday afternoon."

"And that search didn't include a raid on S.H.I.E.L.D.?" Iron Man pressed them.

"No, of course not," Storm insisted. "We have no grievances against that organization. To the contrary, Nicholas Fury is one of the few top-ranking officials in your government who has not supported any anti-mutant campaign."

SEARCH AND RESCUE

That's overstating things a bit, Cap thought. While he could not deny that the United States had sometimes sacrificed individual liberties on the altar of national security, he remained convinced that such excesses and extremism did not represent America as a whole. The mutant-haters and genetic segregationists were only one small part of the American reality. Still, Storm sounded sincere when she said the X-Men had no reason to suspect Nick Fury of foul play against them.

"What about the rest of your team?" Cap asked, recalling the classified security footage he had seen depicting various X-Men running amuck on the Helicarrier. He mentally compiled a list of the costumed mutants caught by the security cameras as they deployed their unearthly powers against Fury and his agents. "I don't see, for instance, Banshee, Sunfire, Iceman, or Marvel Girl."

"My wife goes by the codename 'Phoenix' now," Cyclops corrected him. "She's with the Professor and the rest of the team in Antarctica now. As for the others you mentioned, Banshee is semi-retired these days, teaching in Massachusetts, while Iceman is assisting a colleague of ours in Scotland. Sunfire hasn't fought beside the X-Men in years, but this doesn't sound like his style. Last I heard, he was still Japan's number one super hero."

"Not counting Astro Boy," the Beast quipped.

Who? Probably a contemporary pop culture reference, Cap guessed, although he didn't get it. His own tastes had been shaped in the Thirties and Forties, during the era of Bogart, Bing, and Abbott and Costello. For a second, he wondered idly if the Beast had even heard of Betty Grable. *I need to get out more,* he decided.

What Cyclops had told him more or less gibed, however, with his own knowledge of the individuals involved, although he'd been unaware until now that Cyclops and

Phoenix had gotten married. *Good for them,* he thought. He found himself leaning toward the idea that the oddball assortment of past and present X-Men who had attacked the Helicarrier were impostors of some sort. Lord knew it wouldn't be the first time unscrupulous pretenders trashed the reputations of otherwise upstanding heroes; Cap himself had been temporarily replaced by a disguised Skrull less than a year ago.

"That's what I figured," he told Cyclops, then turned to face Lopez. "Colonel, I have reason to believe that the X-Men are innocent of the charges against them. I'll vouch for them until we find evidence to the contrary." He nodded at the officer's two-way radio. "You can check with your superiors if you like, but I think you'll find my priority clearances in place."

Lopez scratched his chin, thinking it over. Cap could tell he wasn't looking forward to pitting his soldiers against a well-trained team of super-powered mutants. "No," the colonel decided, "your word's good enough for me. I'm satisfied to remand the X-Men into your custody." He squinted past the three mutants to the mountain of green muscle towering above them. "Um, what about the Hulk?"

"You can arrest me," the jade colossus said, not intimidated in the slightest by the poised guns of nearby troops, "if you think you can."

Cap didn't expect he'd have much trouble convincing the colonel to let him escort the Hulk away as well. He suspected that authorities on both sides of the border would be glad to see all of them go.

Too bad they couldn't expect the Leader to be so cooperative, if and when they finally tracked him down.

Chapter Four

The most annoying thing about being smarter, by several orders of magnitude, than anybody else was that the only person who could truly appreciate your genius was you.

The Leader sighed. Such was the cross he bore, by virtue of his magnificent, gamma-endowed brain. Even his partner in this latest enterprise, despite coming from an infinitely more advanced civilization than the one currently making a mess of the planet Earth, lacked any full understanding of the intricate nuances and subtleties that distinguished the Leader's every waking thought.

I am a prophet unrecognized in my own land, he thought, savoring a draught of delectable self-pity, although he intended to remedy that situation, once he had a world of his own to rule. Then the hapless subjects of his new dominion would have no choice but to acknowledge his transcendent superiority—or face immediate execution. After all, there would be no place in that brave new world for minds too feeble to grasp the utter primacy of the Leader's awesome intellect; it would be only common sense to cull the herd of those mental defectives oblivious to his grandeur.

Brahms' Symphony No. 4 in E minor, Op. 98, played softly in the background as the Leader sat at the nerve center of his spanking new base of operations, constructed

SEARCH AND RESCUE

in part with the resources and technology provided by his partner. His pale green fingers rested upon an ergonomic control panel of his own design, while his voluminous skull, housing a brain larger than any other, rested against the high, padded back of a futuristic stainless steel throne. The twin hemispheres of his fantastic cranium swelled like balloons above his contemplative brow, their complex convolutions barely covered by his hairless epidermis. His flesh, the faded green of some stubborn subterranean fungus, was largely covered by a simple orange jumpsuit, but the resplendent dome of his skull proclaimed the sublime nature of his historic transfiguration to any who might look upon him.

For now, though, Leader was alone, left to the profound privacy of his own meditations while his partner pursued their joint agenda elsewhere. He raised a Baccarat glass of wine—Chateau du Lac, 1934—to his thin lips as he effortlessly absorbed information from over three dozen video screens simultaneously. The screens were stacked, row upon row, directly in front of his throne so that he could inspect them all without having to move more than his eyeballs. Most of the high-definition color monitors were tuned to a variety of global news sources: CNN, MSNBC, the BBC, Video Free Latveria, and the strictly subscription-only Super-Villain Channel, among others. A select few, however, broadcast their images exclusively to the Leader, such as the video and audio feed coming straight from the sensory receptors of his newly-acquired Gamma Sentinels.

"Excellent," he murmured to himself as he in effect stared through the eyes of his pet Sentinels as they ransacked the offices and laboratories of the famed Genetic Research Centre on Muir Island. So far, the intimidating automatons had easily overcome whatever meager opposition the mutant defenders of the Centre had presented;

while the presence of Iceman and Nightcrawler at the Centre had not been anticipated, the Gamma Sentinels had made short work of the two callow X-Men. Now operative GS-3, cunningly crafted in the image of the hate-maddened Harpy, kept watch over the bound figure of Dr. Moira MacTaggert, the only inhabitant of the island who held any genuine interest to him. MacTaggert's work on the genetic transmission of specific mutant traits had been intriguing, even impressive for an unevolved human female; he looked forward to interrogating her at his leisure once she was safely transported to the base.

The Harpy herself could be seen via the eyes of GS-1, a better-than-passable simulacrum of that Freudian fool, Leonard Samson. The Leader had to applaud whatever faceless bureaucrat had come up with the deliciously droll idea of disguising their new robotic centurions as the Hulk and his bestial brethren; he supposed he should be offended that the techno-wizards at S.H.I.E.L.D. had not included an artificial "Leader" among their mechanical menagerie, but their short-sighted omission was merely more proof, as if any more were needed, of the way an unthinking world valued brute physical power over intelligence.

To be fair, the Leader granted, *it would hardly be possible to build a Sentinel that came close to duplicating my own brilliance;* even Omnivac, his most accomplished creation in the field of artificial intelligence, had been a mere shadow of its maker's unparalleled cognitive powers.

His mood darkened as he recalled how the barbaric Hulk, in company with the self-righteous Avengers, had destroyed Omnivac on the Leader's orbiting space station a few years ago, right before he himself had almost perished in a prehistoric volcano, thanks to Captain America, Iron Man, and, most especially, the Hulk. Putting down his wine, which had acquired an unwanted bitter aftertaste, he focused the majority of his consciousness on CNN, which was still broadcasting prerecorded news footage of the senseless tripartite battle between the X-Men, the Avengers, and the Hulk. He watched again as Iron Man and the Hulk, one-time allies against his own manifest destiny, expended their strength and energy in costly combat atop scenic Niagara Falls.

"Encore! Encore!" he urged sardonically. It soothed his soul to see his former enemies battling amongst themselves, thanks to his own machiavellian manipulations. That the strife had ultimately ended in an ignominious and personally inconvenient truce was of little import; his projections had predicted an 83 percent probability that the self-styled heroes would eventually join forces, even if he had held onto a wistful hope that the unreasoning fury of the Hulk might up the casualty rate a tad.

Call me an unrealistic, wild-eyed dreamer, he thought, sighing indulgently once more, *but, deep down inside, I really thought that the Hulk might kill a couple of X-Men or Avengers.*

But, alas, as so many times before, Banner and his wretched alter ego had foiled his fondest expectations. *One day I will make him pay for that,* he vowed, *and sooner than he thinks.*

By his advance calculations, the motley assortment of costumed crusaders must have converged by now for their most dire consultations, most likely at the Avenger's ostentatious townhouse in Manhattan. Unless the Hulk had grown significantly dimmer since their last encounter, always a possibility where Banner's endlessly mutable metamorphoses were concerned, he had to assume that his brutish nemesis had already detected the Leader's hand at work in the oh-so-distressing disappearances of the Scarlet Witch and Rogue, and shared that inevitable insight with both the X-Men and the Avengers. It was considerably *less* likely that the puzzled heroes had yet realized that Wolverine had been abducted as well, given that the feral X-Man had been snatched in the middle of his beloved wilderness, far from public view. That missing piece of data would cost all concerned dearly, particularly as his master plan continued to play out.

The Leader had no fear of immediate discovery. Correctly attributing their present difficulties to the Leader was one thing; finding him would pose a more challenging puzzle. To his certain knowledge, the only semi-sentient souls who knew of the location and existence of his current domicile were his militaristic partner and his loyal lieutenants. *And even should the united acumen of "Earth's mightiest heroes" bring them close to uncovering my new address,* the Leader recalled with smug satisfaction, *my partner will be waiting to strike at their ranks from within.*

A chime sounded from his control panel, reminding him that it was time to check on his involuntary guests. *How time flies,* he reflected, *when you're plotting the downfall of all you despise.* He pressed a lighted pad on the arm of his throne, and the entire seat rotated 180 degrees, bringing him around to face another set of controls, as well as a transparent pane of reinforced glass.

Through this picture window—in reality, the obliging side of a one-way mirror—he spied his unwilling test subjects: Wolverine, Rogue, and the Scarlet Witch. Shorn of the garish costumes they usually affected, the three captives wore matching orange jumpsuits, which looked rather more flattering on Rogue and the Witch than it did on their hirsute throwback of a companion. Each mutant specimen was confined to his or her own high-tech sarcophagus, lidless to permit easy inspection by the Leader from the adjacent control chamber. Wires and electrodes were connected to key junctures on their body, while I.V. lines provided them sufficient water and nutrition, along with medication as needed. The Leader was proud of the design of the containment sarcophagi, which had completely eliminated the risk of transporting the specimens from cells to lab and back again. Automated equipment provided him with the means to perform any experiment without ever leaving his chair, let alone having to deal with the predictably irate subjects in the flesh. He had heard enough defiant superhero rhetoric over the course of his career, and felt no need to subject himself to any more.

Per his meticulous estimations, his mutant guinea pigs had been allowed sufficient time to recuperate from the last round of admittedly demanding tests. Before commencing a new slate of experiments, the Leader decided to take a few moments to review the results of his findings to date.

It is always important to keep one's ultimate goals in view, he philosophized, *lest one lose sight of the vision amidst the vivisections.*

For many years now, his paramount objective—his utopian dream—had been to create a new race of gamma-mutated beings to populate a world of his own design, with himself reigning like a god over a more evolved species of human being. In the past, this had led to such ambitious endeavors as infecting New York City with a contagious gamma gene, detonating a stolen gamma bomb in a major population center, and even attempting to gamma-irradiate the primordial soup from which all terrestrial life would eventually evolve. As laudable as such enterprises had been, they had all suffered from the inherent randomness of genetic mutation. For all his unquestioned sagacity and expertise, he had thus far remained unable to predict whether any given specimen, exposed to sufficient quantities of gamma rays, would evolve into a being of superior intelligence and sensibilities—or a Hulk. The best he could do was irradiate a multitude of individuals and hope for one or two specimens whose mutant traits proved worth preserving. A rather time-consuming and inefficient procedure, to say the least.

These new test subjects, gathered by his partner's highly versatile lieutenants, potentially held the key to a better, more elegant way of achieving his aims. If his current experimental campaign bore fruit, he would soon acquire a power he had long desired: to induce specific genetic mutations at will. These captive mutants—in particular, the two female specimens—possessed a singularly tantalizing combination of innate talents, talents he hoped to combine and duplicate to great effect. Imagine! No more animalistic hulks, abominations, and harpies; instead he would engender a new breed of proud, green supermen and superwomen created in his own omnipotent image.

Consider: the ill-bred, backwater swamp trash known only as Rogue. Her unique mutant ability consisted of the power to absorb and assimilate the equally unique attributes of other mutants and mutated beings. In essence, she could somehow isolate the genetic template of any super-being and transfer the essential elements of that template to another specimen, namely herself. It required only the slightest of conceptual leaps to imagine refining this process in order to imprint a chosen mutant trait onto as many subjects as desired. True, at present, the "Rogue effect" tended to be temporary, except in rare instances, and had unfortunate negative effects on the original mutant donor. It also appeared that the process resulted in serious psychological trauma to the recipient of the trait selected. Still, the Leader was convinced that he could eliminate such unwanted limitations and side effects in time.

Who knows? he thought. It was even possible that the

data his Gamma Sentinels were now extracting from the Genetic Research Centre might hold the secret to bringing Rogue's "wild talent" under more precise and scientific control. A man could dream, couldn't he?

Consider also: Wanda Maximoff, popularly known as the Scarlet Witch. On a fundamental level, genetic mutation was a matter of probabilities, the random rearrangement of agitated chromosomes into new and potentially superior configurations, and probabilities were what the Scarlet Witch's notoriously ill-defined powers were said to control. Contrary to Einstein's famous aphorism, ultimately invalidated by the findings of modern quantum physics, God did indeed play dice with the universe, but the Scarlet Witch possessed a knack for weighting the dice. Her power alone, tamed and made to produce specific and reproducible results, could finally allow him to induce precisely the mutant characteristics he sought to instill in his followers, without relying on the fickle dispensations of chance.

A thrilling prospect, even if one as yet still beyond his reach. The Leader frowned, contemplatively stroking his bushy black mustache, the only trace of body hair remaining on his immaculate body. So far, if he was to be brutally honest with himself (and to whom else could he so candidly confide?), his tests upon the Scarlet Witch and her trademark "hexes" had produced conspicuously mixed results.

Hexes. The very word provoked a contemptuous scowl from the Leader. How could one expect to identify the scientific basis of the subject's enigmatic abilities when the entire world had conspired to swaddle the Scarlet Witch's genetic gifts within veils of superstitious hogwash? That there were mystical forces at work in the universe he could not deny, not in a space-time continuum that included such entities as Dr. Strange and the Asgardian gods, but there was mutation, and there was magic, and, in his experience, the one very seldom had much to do with the other. He had no doubt that there was an underlying scientific theory behind Wanda Maximoff's demonstrated capacity to manipulate the laws of probability, even if the subject herself seemed to take all this fuzzy-minded "witchcraft" business a little too seriously. But what could you expect from an ignorant gypsy raised in the backwards recesses of the Balkans?

With a tap of his finger, he called up a statistical breakdown of his experiments with the Scarlet Witch to date. The data was projected between him and the observation window by his own specially-designed holographic emitters. He shook his capacious head as he reviewed the statistics, which were just as he remembered: The Witch could affect probabilities, of that there was no doubt, but the effectiveness and reliability of her hexes varied significantly depending on her emotional and physical state. Even more discouraging, the results were even more erratic when her hex powers were transferred to Rogue via direct physical contact. Rogue was able to mimic Maximoff's tricks, but with less control and precision. It was as though some crucial component of the Scarlet Witch's powers remained ephemeral and impossible to quantify.

Magic? He resisted the notion with every fiber of his logic-loving being, but he was starting to wonder.

Still, such minor impediments and irritants were a small price to pay to acquire the god-like puissance he sought. Only by combining the harnessed powers of Rogue and the Scarlet Witch could he: a) produce the mutations he deemed worthwhile, and b) transfer those mutations from one subject to another.

That consummate facility would more than justify his time and trouble. Why, the creative potential was practically unlimited, nor need he limit himself to the near-infinite possibilities of the human genome. Soon, very soon, he aspired to mix and match the genetic characteristics of both human and alien donors. His gaze lingered on the Southern-born woman in the central sarcophagus, the one with a striking white streak running through the center of her copious brunette locks. How would Rogue's mutant physiology react to the absorption of extraterrestrial traits and abilities? He looked forward to conducting that very experiment in the near future, perhaps when the Leader's partner returned from his undercover assignment. *That,* he thought, quoting the estimable Bard, *is a consummation devoutly to be wished.*

But what of his third lab rat, the atavistic man-animal who went by the highly appropriate name of Wolverine? In truth, the pugnacious X-Man was less essential to the Leader's grand design than his female associates. His mutant healing factor, however, had intrigued the Leader for a number of reasons, chief among them its provocative similarity to the Hulk's own dismayingly remarkable regenerative powers. Too many times the Leader had personally witnessed the accursed jade goliath's near-instantaneous recovery from what should have been mortal injuries; it was his devout hope that, by subjecting Wolverine's healing factor to intensive scientific analysis, he might find some chink in the Hulk's all-encompassing immunity to physical harm. Moreover, even if this much longed for hope proved in vain, he might at least come away with some useful techniques he could employ to speed the recovery of future test subjects.

Hidden behind the reflective anonymity of the one-way mirror, the Leader watched his captives stir fitfully in their gleaming sarcophagi, as stimulants introduced to their I.V. lines roused them from exhausted repose. The trouble, he reflected, with conducting trial and error experimentation on fragile living beings was that they so seldom survived the experience.

"Gambit?"

Rogue awoke from Cajun-spiced dreams to find herself confined in the same cold steel casket she had been trapped in before. *Shoot!* she cursed inwardly. *Here I was hopin' this was all just a bad dream. No such luck, I guess.*

Groggily, she blinked the sleep from her eyes. Unfortunately, that didn't improve the view much; she was still staring at her reflection in the long horizontal mirror facing her, crammed like an Egyptian mummy into an upright coffin full of candy-colored wires and little blinky lights and other snazzy sci-fi gizmos, along with (how could she forget?) a hypodermic needle injected into her arm. Metal clamps, sturdy enough to resist her super-strength, held her flat within the casket, which was propped up at a forty-five degree angle to the floor. A clamp around her neck kept her from turning her head, but by moving her eyes from left to right she could spot the reflections of her two fellow prisoners, each stuck in an identical coffin on opposite sides of Rogue. She heard Wolverine breathing hoarsely a few feet to her left; to the right, the Scarlet Witch was silent, maybe even too silent.

Good thing Storm's not here with us, Rogue thought. With her claustrophobia, this would probably be Ororo's worst nightmare. *Not that the rest of us are having a grand old time, that is.*

She inspected herself in the mirror, not liking what she saw there. Dark, puffy circles ringed her tired brown eyes, giving her an uncomfortable resemblance to a raccoon. Greasy bangs, white in the middle and russet brown on the sides, dangled before her forehead. Her complexion, usually

SEARCH AND RESCUE

a picture of ruddy health, looked uncharacteristically pale and wan.

I look awful, she realized. Not too surprising, considering; getting poked and prodded like a New Orleans voodoo doll, while cooped up tighter than a heifer in a henhouse, wasn't exactly conducive to a gal's beauty sleep.

From the looks of them, her partners in captivity weren't doing any better. Wolverine growled in his sleep, his face twitching angrily, his jagged teeth grinding noisily together, almost drowning out the constant low thrumming of the machinery surrounding the prisoners on all sides. Silver claws *snikt'd* in and out of his clenched fists every few seconds, flashing strobe-like beneath the harsh overhead lights.

Rogue was getting worried about Logan. Wherever his head was now, it wasn't a good place to be. His personality had been regressing ever since they first woke up in this antiseptic hellhole, like he was losing his civilized inhibitions and reverting to the wild animal inside him. She knew why that was, of course; when their faceless tormentor forced her to absorb Wolvie's memories and powers, she'd gotten a real taste of what he was going through now. This whole setup was dragging up all his buried memories of that other time up in Canada, the original "Weapon X" experiments, when a bunch of no-good government scientists filled him full of adamantium, torturing him to the point of insanity. All those bad days, and the bad feelings they left burrowed in his soul, were coming back now, stronger than ever, and Rogue wasn't sure how much longer Logan would be able to hold it all together. She'd felt the unreasoning savagery, the sheer animal frenzy, building up inside him, and what scared her the most was just how irresistible and intoxicating that primal fury was.

How can Wolvie possibly keep that under control? I don't think I could.

She squirmed within her unyielding bonds. *How long have we been trapped here anyway?* she wondered. Prickly stubble carpeted Logan's cheeks, what looked like at least a days' worth, but who knew with that hyped-up metabolism of his? Rogue always figured he just shaved with his claws whenever he felt like it. Beyond that, the sterile chamber seemed locked out of time, with no way to tell day or night, let alone chart the passage of hours. Even the gravity felt funny, like she didn't weigh as much as she should. She glared at the translucent I.V. tube feeding into her elbow; the meals here weren't much to speak of, but she couldn't have lost that many pounds already, could she?

A soft groan came from the right. Rogue's gaze shifted to the captive reflected on the other side of her own coffin. She scowled in sympathy for the woman in the mirror; if anything, the Scarlet Witch had it worse than either she or Wolverine. Not only was she encased in the same sort of raised, lidless sarcophagus, Wanda was also blinded by an opaque metal visor, so as to keep her from focusing her witchie powers on their prison. Likewise, polished silver hemispheres covered her hands, trapping her fingers so that she couldn't begin to make anything resembling a mystical gesture.

Rogue knew from personal experience just how oppressive the blindfold and the metal mitts were. The sadistic mastermind behind their imprisonment had previously imposed the same restraints on Rogue, for as long as she had involuntarily possessed the Scarlet Witch's powers, although the visor and such had slid back into hidden recesses within the coffin once the transference had worn off.

Her cheeks flushed with shame as she remembered how she had been compelled against her will to sample Wanda's memories and abilities, the automated machinery pressing their uncovered hands together, the touch of skin on skin being all that was needed to effect the transference, draining the Scarlet Witch's most private thoughts and secrets as surely as a vampire sucked its victim's lifeblood. Rogue felt like a vampire, too, even if Wanda's essence had been forced upon her. Bad enough to inflict such an invasive personal violation on a friend like Logan, someone who already knew and trusted her; how much worse to impose so unwanted an intimacy on a woman she barely knew, a woman who didn't even like her.

There was bad blood between Rogue and the Scarlet Witch, dating back to the old days, years back, when Rogue ran with Mystique and her Brotherhood of Evil Mutants. Wanda Maximoff still blamed Rogue, with good reason, for what the young mutant outlaw had done to her close friend, Carol Danvers, the former Avenger once known as Ms. Marvel. On that one terrible occasion, Rogue's absorption of her opponent's mind and attributes had been permanent; it was Ms. Marvel's exceptional strength that still resided in Rogue's limbs, Ms. Marvel's defiance of gravity that granted Rogue the power of flight, and Ms. Marvel's memories that still lingered at the back of Rogue's mind. Carol Danvers, recently returned to the Avengers under the name of Warbird, had never been the same after her tragic encounter with Rogue, and the guilty X-Man doubted that Wanda Maximoff could ever forgive Rogue.

Especially now that I did to Wanda the same thing I did to Ms. Marvel, just less permanently.

The ironic thing was, Rogue mused, now that she'd melded with the Scarlet Witch's mind, experienced the world from her perspective, she was surprised to discover just how much she and the Avenger had in common. Although raised on opposite sides of the world, they had both suffered the early pain of being mutant outcasts, both had been lured into a life of crime by a villainous parent.

Heck, we both started out in the Brotherhood of Evil Mutants, Rogue realized, *before getting a fresh start in the Avengers or the X-Men.*

Even their love lives seemed similarly doomed from the start; was the Scarlet Witch's failed marriage (to an android, of all things!) any more hopeless than Rogue's own unfulfillable passion for a man she couldn't even touch? Rogue would have shook her head in amazement if not for the restrictive clamp around her throat. Who would have ever guessed that the Avenger and the X-Man, one respected, one feared, would turn out to be sisters under the skin?

Too bad the transference doesn't work both ways, she thought ruefully; *maybe then Wanda would finally realize that I'm truly sorry about what I did to Carol Danvers, that I never meant to rob her of everything.*

"RAWRR!"

With an angry roar, Wolverine came awake abruptly. Wild eyes opened, streaked with red. He fought and writhed against the clamps, straining frantically to free himself. His claws *snikt'd* impotently. Foam flecked his lips, and pulsing veins throbbed upon his brow as his fierce howl echoed within their prison.

"My God!" Wanda gasped, shocked to wakefulness by the deafening roar. "What is that?"

Rogue realized the blinded Witch had not guessed the source of the bestial tumult.

She probably thinks there's an enraged tiger loose in the lab, Rogue thought. But there was no time to explain; Rogue feared Wolverine would injure himself in his frenzied efforts to escape from the casket—and the memories it held. "Logan!" she shouted. Her throat was dry and

SEARCH AND RESCUE

hoarse, but she swallowed hard to work up enough saliva to speak. "Logan! Listen to me. You've gotta snap out of it!"

But he didn't seem to hear her. He looked like he didn't even know where—or who—he was. If Logan could have chewed his own arms off to escape, Rogue believed he would have done it. She had only seen him like this a few times before, usually right before somebody got sliced to shreds.

"Logan!" she tried again. "It's me, Rogue! Remember?!"

This time she seem to get through to him. "RRRR— Rogue?" A hint of sanity crept into his bloodshot eyes. His limbs ceased their convulsive thrashing, and his contorted face relaxed into something closer to calm. He searched the images in the mirror, as if grounding himself once more in this particular time and place. His eyes held a look of weary regret, and he took a deep breath before speaking again. "Sorry, darlin'. You didn't need to see that."

"It's okay, Wolvie," she assured him, her throat tightening with emotion. "I understand. You don't need to explain."

The Scarlet Witch, on the hand, was still in need of elucidation concerning what her startled ears had just heard. "*That* was Wolverine?" she asked incredulously.

"Yeah," Logan growled, sounding more like his old self. "You got a problem with that?"

Before Wanda could craft a reply, the rumble of moving machinery caught the attention of all three prisoners.

Oh no, Rogue thought. She didn't know exactly what was about to transpire, but she knew what the resumption of mechanical activity meant: another round of inhuman medical experiments was beginning.

"Here we go again," Wolverine snarled, and Rogue

thought she heard a heartrending groan from the Scarlet Witch. *What now?* Rogue wondered apprehensively. In some ways, the anticipation—and the uncertainty—was almost worse than the painful and degrading tests themselves; it was like sitting outside the doctor's office when you were little, worrying if you were going to get a shot and wondering how much it would hurt.

Previous experiments had tested the limits of their respective mutant powers, even subjecting Wolverine to a cruel variety of injuries just to see how quickly he healed. Rogue had gotten a spoonful of the same nasty medicine after getting Logan's healing factor forced on her in another experiment. Their anonymous persecutor, cowardly hiding his or her face behind what had to be a one-way mirror, was always thinking ahead; Rogue figured her coffin had been deliberately situated between Wolvie and the Witch to make it easier for her to touch either one of them.

There had also been a series of grueling examinations in which remote-controlled waldoes had extracted samples of blood, hair, skin, saliva, bone marrow, and even spinal fluid from Rogue and her fellow human guinea pigs. She tried not to think about the grisly procedures, performed largely without anesthesia, except to wonder what the robotic limbs would come for next. So far she had been allowed to keep all of her teeth, but she figured that was only a matter of time. *We've got to get out of here,* she resolved fiercely, *but how?* By now the X-Men, and probably the Avengers, had to be looking for them, but Rogue wasn't about to lay back and wait patiently for a rescue attempt. She tested the unbreakable steel clamps holding her in place, only to find them just as immovable as before.

Her casket, however, suddenly revealed itself to be surprisingly mobile. Unseen motors hummed as all three coffins began traveling along some kind of conveyor belt or tracks. Rogue felt like a prop in an old-fashioned shell game as the pinioned mutants were reassigned new positions before the mirror, with Wolverine now occupying the central berth between the two women.

So? Rogue asked silently, giving the mirror a dirty look she hoped penetrated through to the other side. *Was I just demoted or what?*

Not for the first time, she wondered who was hiding behind that silvered glass. Magneto? Bastion? The Hellfire Club? She wasn't sure why any of the X-Men's old enemies would bother to hide their identity like this. Heck, most of them could hardly resist a chance to gloat over a couple of captured X-Men. Mister Sinister, on the other hand, tended to be a bit more on the sneaky side; could they have fallen into the clutches of Gambit's unscrupulous old boss? These sick experiments seemed like the kind of thing Sinister would get off on.

Is that you, you diamond-headed dirtbag? she accused the mirror. *Killing all those innocent Morlocks wasn't enough, you had to come after us, too?*

No answers were forthcoming, only busy waldoes that swiftly and efficiently went to work reconfiguring the various lengths of plastic tubing flowing in and out of the punctured mutants. Wolverine grunted as a mechanical arm inserted another line into his left arm, stabbing a convenient vein right through the fabric of his orange jumpsuit. Multiple steel hemostats, mounted at the ends of articulated metal appendages, pinched the hollow tubes shut at strategic junctures. Rogue, whom as an X-Man had learned a thing or two about emergency medicine, could have sworn the waldoes were setting up some kind of complicated transfusion procedure.

Then a hemostat clicked open and the blood, dark and venous, began flowing from the flattened elbow of her right arm—straight into the tube newly inserted in Wolverine's left arm. *But that's crazy,* she thought in horror, eyes wide at the sight of her blood pouring into Logan's body. *We're not even the same blood type!*

Yet that wasn't the worst of it. Her shocked gaze swept across the face of the mirror until she saw an identical flow coursing from the Scarlet Witch to Wolverine.

"Ah don't believe it!" she exclaimed out loud, her Southern drawl in no way softening the desperate panic in her voice. Logan was receiving simultaneous transfusions from both her and Wanda, thus doubling his chances of a fatal hemolytic reaction. Could even Wolverine survive such a devastating shock to his system? That, she realized bitterly, had to be the blasted point of the experiment.

"Stop it!" she hollered at the mirror. "You're goin' to kill him!" She saw a look of confusion come over the bottom half of Wanda's face, the part not covered by the metal visor. Right now Rogue practically envied the Scarlet Witch; at least she couldn't see the barbaric atrocity being committed upon Wolverine's unsuspecting circulatory system.

Two, maybe three, incompatible blood types mixed in Logan's veins, producing an immediate adverse reaction. His entire body jerked uncontrollably and his eyes rolled up until only the whites could be seen. His face and hands turned blue, proof that the clash in his bloodstream had cut off the flow of oxygen to his cells. The paroxysm shook him violently; Rogue knew that he had to be suffering internal shock and hemorrhaging. "Stop it, you maniac!"

Not that she truly expected any mercy from their unknown captor. Instead she placed all her hopes in Logan's mutant immune system. In the past, it had saved him from any number of toxins and hostile organisms, even the implanted embryo of a sleazoid Brood warrior; now it was up to that same superhuman resilience to protect him from the hemolytic warfare tearing him apart from inside.

The automated hemostats cut off the flow of blood after a minute, but the damage had already been done. His corpse-like blue pallor increased and his breathing grew weak and ragged. The bone-shaking seizure ceased abruptly and Wolverine sagged within his restraints, his chin dipping as much as his neck-clamp permitted. Rogue couldn't hear any breathing, and her own heart skipped a beat. Had the unconquerable fighter, the best there was, finally met an enemy he couldn't defeat? If so, Rogue vowed that, one way or another, she would make someone pay for Wolverine's ugly death, even if she had to tear this miserable place down to the ground to find out who was responsible.

"What is it?" the Scarlet Witch asked anxiously, her blindfold sparing her the ghastly sight. "What's happening?"

Choking back angry sobs, her eyes tearing despite her best efforts to stay strong, the way Logan would have wanted her to, she wondered how to break the terrible news to Wanda. The Witch had not known Wolverine well, but she knew the heroic Avenger would mourn his death regardless. "It—it's Wolverine," she began haltingly. "He's—that is, I think—"

An explosive gasp broke the silence between the two women. Rogue's heart pounded as she saw Logan's body jolt back to life. The cyanotic blue tint of his oxygen-deprived flesh began to fade, supplanted by a healthy shade of pink. He coughed wetly and a trickle of black, clotted blood dribbled from his lips. Then his head lifted, and pained, exhausted eyes met Rogue's in the mirror. "Well, that was a ball and a half," he said gruffly.

Rogue couldn't contain her relief. "Oh, Wolvie!" she gushed. Logan had often warned her about wearing her emotions on her sleeve. "Ah wasn't sure you was goin' to make it."

"Tell you the truth, darlin'," he admitted. "Neither was I." He closed his eyes again, just to give them a moment's rest. When he spoke again, she could hear the simmering fury in his voice. "Whoever's behind this flamin' stab lab's got a really twisted idea of hospitality."

An impatient sigh emerged from the visually-deprived Avenger two caskets away from Rogue. "Good to hear you're still with us, Wolverine, whatever they did to you, but, if it's not too inconvenient, could someone *please* let me know what's going on."

A word that rhymed with "witch" briefly popped into Rogue's mind, but she realized that was unfair. *I'd be getting pretty fed up and frustrated, too, if I couldn't even see what all the shouting was about.* Rogue started to explain about the latest perverted experiment their jailer had devised when, with brisk proficiency and dexterity, the waldoes went to work again. Hemostats clicked and tiny plastic valves were opened and closed in careful sequence. Flowing saline flushed clean the lines connecting the three mutants.

For a second or two, Rogue feared that the same awful experiment was about to be repeated, subjecting Wolverine to another round of near-fatal agony. Then she realized that, no, something different was in store. The transfusions had resumed, but now the dark venous blood was streaming in one direction only, from the Scarlet Witch to Wolverine, *through* Wolverine, to Rogue herself. *Dear God, no!* she thought, overcome with dread as the mingled essences of both Logan and Wanda ran into her veins, bringing with them a flood of alien thoughts and sensations.

Blood-to-blood communion proved even more effective than mere skin-to-skin. In the space of a few frightened heartbeats, she lost all sense of her own identity. She was at once all three individuals: Rogue and Logan and Wanda. X-Man *and* Avenger. Donor *and* recipient. Brown eyes turned blue, then brown again, before splitting the difference somewhere in-between. Streaks of auburn colored the white swath running through her hair, while raw animal vitality, only slightly depleted by her/his/her recent brush with death, set her senses aflame. Fragments of fresh memories spun like a kaleidoscope within her roiling, disordered mind. Hand-carved marionettes attacked her in an empty museum gallery. Flying tee-shirts, inscribed with virulent anti-mutant slogans, wrapped themselves around her face and hands, suffocating her and cutting off her vision while, all around her, terrified fairgoers shrieked in panic. A family of shape-changing deer gored her with their antlers in the shade of a towering forest. "Gambit!" she cried out in torment. "Mariko! Vision!" Her mouth was full of unfamiliar fangs and languages. She screamed obscenities in English, Japanese, and Romany, then begged for relief. "Help me! Help us! Please!"

Then the pain hit her, twisting her insides so hard she could barely breathe. Part of her polyglot consciousness, the same part that suffused her with a ferocious hunger to strike back at her enemies, recognized the excruciating pangs wracking every organ in her body. The mismatched blood was clotting inside her, tearing her apart, starving her brain. Her head throbbed behind her eyes and darkness stole her sight. All she could hear, over the rapid-fire drumming of her heart, was an agonized howl that didn't sound remotely human.

That howl was her own.

Chapter Five

"There. That should do it."

Iron Man stepped back from the operating table, where he had just finished reconnecting the Vision's severed arm. A pen-sized laser wielder was gripped between the steel-sheathed fingers of his right gauntlet. Magnifying lenses, which had slid into place within his eye slits, receded now that the delicate work was completed. "I'm no Henry Pym," he announced, referring to the Avengers' premiere roboticist and the Vision's putative grandfather, "but I think he should be good as new."

The seemingly lifeless synthezoid rested atop a shining chromium operating table, located in a sub-basement of Avengers Mansion in Manhattan. The reattached arm remained softer and less incredibly dense than the rest of the android's body. Adamantium supports held the surgical platform intact despite the extreme weight of Iron Man's mechanical patient. An unlikely assortment of X-Men and Avengers looked on anxiously while the Golden Avenger waited to see if the Vision would spontaneously awaken now that he'd been repaired. Iron Man wished he could wipe the sweat from his brow, but he could hardly remove his helmet while the X-Men and the Hulk were present. *That's the problem with having company over,* he thought wryly.

Several seconds passed and the Vision remained as inert

as before. Only the Hulk appeared unconcerned; the green goliath slouched against the far wall, looking bored and impatient. He cracked his enormous knuckles noisily. "Aren't you done yet?" the Hulk rumbled. "For pete's sake, he's just a machine. Only you do-gooding Avengers could get this worked up over a piece of broken hardware."

Iron Man clenched his fists so hard the laser wielder crumpled within his grip. He started to reply angrily, but caught a warning look from Cap. Instead, to his surprise, Storm spoke up. "Our friend and ally Douglock is a machine as well," she rebuked the Hulk, "but we X-Men consider his life to be of no less value than our own."

"Then you're all a bunch of soft-hearted suckers," the Hulk retorted. He glowered at them from beneath a sloping brow. "Trust me, when you've trashed as many killer robots and mandroids as I have, you get a lot less squeamish where smashing wind-up people are concerned."

I've fought plenty of mechanical men, too, Iron Man thought indignantly. *Dreadnaught and adaptoids and so on. But that's no excuse for callous disregard toward a hero like a Vision.*

The android Avenger had proven his humanity and courage a hundred times over, no matter how cold and unfeeling he might seem to the outside world. *You'd think a misunderstand monster like the Hulk could appreciate that,* Iron Man thought.

Cyclops forestalled further debate by stepping between Storm and the Hulk. His glowing red visor and serious expression offered little hint of his own feelings on the subject. "How is your patient, Iron Man?" he asked. "When do you expect him to revive?"

"I was hoping that his cybernetic brain would reboot automatically once I restored his arm," Iron Man admitted, "but it's looking like I'm going to have to jumpstart his entire system. Fortunately, I think I know how."

Iron Man directed his chest projector at the Vision's brow. Replacing the lens broken at Niagara Falls had been easily accomplished once he picked up a spare at the Mansion; the modular design of his armor made such repairs a simple matter provided the right parts were available. If only the Vision could be fixed as readily.

Solar power, absorbed via the amber gem in his forehead, powered the Vision. The sun was already setting outside, but Iron Man figured he could provide an adequate substitute. Using the vari-beam projector in his chestplate, he aimed a beam of energized photons directly at the Vision's solar jewel. At first, nothing seemed to be happening, then the synthezoid's pliable right arm hardened visibly, achieving the same uniform density as his entire artificial body. "Look," he said, encouraged by this positive sign, "he's achieving equilibrium." According to gravimetric sensors built into the operating table itself, the Vision's intensely amplified weight was rapidly returning to normal parameters, somewhere between 150 to 200 pounds. "He's coming back on-line."

"Thank heavens," Captain America said.

"Praise the Goddess," Storm seconded.

"Most felicitous congratulations!" the Beast enthused, bounding across the lab for a better look. "Once again you have proven yourself a maestro mechanic of unparalleled skill and ingenuity."

Iron Man shook his head. "It's nothing any qualified technician couldn't handle," he insisted, motivated less by false modesty than by a vigorous desire to conceal his civilian identity. He cut off the photonic beam, convinced the concentrated radiant energy had done its work. "Working for Mr. Stark for so many years, you can't help picking up plenty of scientific know-how, especially when your life

SEARCH AND RESCUE

often depends on keeping a suit of complicated, high-tech armor up and running."

The gem in the Vision's brow flashed busily. Assuming a uniform density was just the first step in the Vision's warm-up procedure. A low electrical hum came from the synthezoid's supine body until, at last, red plastic eyelids flickered, exposing lighted amber orbs that stared with renewed intensity at the ceiling. The Vision sat up abruptly, provoking gasps of relief from the X-Men and his fellow Avengers.

The Hulk merely snorted and scratched himself rudely. "About time," he muttered, not caring who heard him.

Twenty minutes, and several much-needed showers, later, the various heroes reconvened in the Avenger's conference room. The Beast made himself at home, hopping over to the nearest communications console and tapping in instructions with both hands and most of his toes. The remaining X-Men stood around awkwardly, feeling distinctly out of place, until Captain America graciously insisted that both Cyclops and Storm take a seat at the round steel table in the center of the conference room. *I wonder if this is Wanda's chair?* Cyclops wondered as he sat down. Over the years, the Scarlet Witch had been both a foe and ally to the X-Men. Now it seemed that she and Rogue faced the same dire fate, most likely at the hands of the notorious Leader.

"So, Vizh," the Beast asked congenially, eyeing the once-more-intact synthezoid, "I'm curious. Now that you're in one piece again, are you left-handed or right-handed?"

"Neither," the Vision answered. He sat calmly at the conference table, apparently untraumatized by his recent brush with demolition. His canary-yellow cloak was draped over his shoulders. "My creator, the mad robot Ultron, saw no functional purpose in the human preference for one side over another."

"I see," the Beast said. "You and I have ambidexterity in common then." He wiggled his furry fingers like a concert pianist, then pressed one final button with his big toe. "That's that," he proclaimed cheerfully as he left the communications station to join his comrades at the table. He nimbly perched atop the back of one of the silver egg-shaped chairs. His blue fur still looked slightly damp from the shower. "Mission accomplished. I have successfully set up a two-way link with our own computerized message center back at the Institute. Any incoming calls to our suburban domicile will be rerouted here and vice versa."

"Any word from the Professor and the others?" Cyclops asked urgently. Like Ororo, he wore a voluminous terry-cloth bathrobe while the Avengers' butler, Jarvis, generously restitched their torn and tattered uniforms. By contrast, Captain America had simply changed into a spare uniform. Cyclops suspected that Iron Man had done so as well; even though he couldn't tell if the Golden Avenger was wearing the same suit of armor as before, the dents he'd received during his battle with the Hulk were now missing.

"I'm afraid not," the Beast answered, "nor was there any recent communique from the perpetually peripatetic Wolverine."

Cyclops scowled. He hadn't really expected to hear from the Professor and the rest; their mission to the Savage Land had been of indeterminate length. He spared a second to hope that Jean was not in any danger, then worried about Wolverine. It bothered him that he had no idea where Logan might be, or when he intended to return. He could be anywhere from Madripoor to the Yukon. *That's just like him, though,* he recalled, sighing in resignation. Wolverine

SEARCH AND RESCUE

would turn up when he turned up; that was the most he could hope for.

"I do not suppose," Storm added, "that there was any ransom demand from Rogue's abductor?" She sipped from a mug of hot herbal tea, more evidence of the Avengers' hospitality.

"The Leader's not interested in any stupid ransom," the Hulk contributed roughly. Unlike the rest of the heroes, he had declined the Avengers' offer of a shower and smelled like it. Cyclops's nose wrinkled beneath his visor at the rank odor coming from the looming green gargantua. The Hulk still wore the same ragged jeans as well; Jarvis had bravely volunteered to provide the Hulk with a change of clothing, but the coarse monster had merely sneered at the suggestion. Now the Hulk lumbered about the conference room, too obstinate and antisocial to even consider sitting down at the same table with the other heroes.

And I thought Wolverine had a bad attitude, Cyclops marvelled.

"Sterns can get all the cash he wants, just by applying that swollen brain of his to the stock market, the races, lotteries, or whatever," the Hulk continued. His deep hatred of the Leader was evident in his tone, as well as in the smoldering fury in his eyes. "Whatever he snagged your pals for, it's not about money."

There are other kind of ransoms, Cyclops thought, but chose not to press the point; they had spent too much time sparring with the Hulk already.

"Tell me more about these Gamma Sentinels," Cyclops asked Captain America. The veteran hero sat across from Cyclops, between Iron Man and the Vision. "What makes them so special?"

Cap cradled a mug of hot coffee—black, with just a drop of milk—between his gloved hands. He nodded at Cyclops, looking like he appreciated Cyclops's efforts to keep the focus on the problems at hand. "According to Nick Fury, the idea was plausible deniability. Each Sentinel mimics the powers and appearance of a well-known product of gamma mutation: The Abomination, the Harpy, Doc Samson, even the Hulk. The devious minds behind the Gamma Sentinels wanted anti-mutant weapons that did not point back to them; the plan was to blame any 'necessary' anti-mutant offensives on freakish monstrosities with a reputation for wanton destruction." He paused to glance at the scowling Hulk. "No offense intended."

The Hulk looked more disgusted than affronted. "Let them blame their dirty tricks on me. Like I care what John Q. Public thinks of me." It occurred to Cyclops that the Hulk's reputation could hardly get worse; he had the all the infamy he deserved, and then some.

The X-Men's co-leader found Captain America's explanation regarding the Gamma Sentinels depressingly believable. Previous generations of Sentinels had always proved to be public relations disasters for the governments and corporations involved; he wasn't surprised to hear that a more covert pogrom was in the works.

"In any event," Cap continued, "since these new Sentinels are also powered by internal gamma reactors, any residual radiation serves to perpetuate the hoax. Heaven only knows, though, what the Leader intends to do with the Gamma Sentinels. Nothing good, that's for sure."

The existence of the Gamma Sentinels still didn't explain how or why Rogue and the Scarlet Witch were abducted, hours before the Sentinels were stolen from S.H.I.E.L.D., but it seemed safe to assume that the Leader was behind all three events. Finding the Hulk's superintelligent nemesis had to be their next move. "Hulk," Cyclops addressed the surly giant, "you said earlier that you

SEARCH AND RESCUE

last encountered the Leader in Alberta. What else can you tell us about that incident?"

The Hulk frowned at the memory. "Big-Brain had a whole underground city there, called Freehold, buried beneath the Columbia ice fields. He'd packed the place with gamma-powered super-types he'd created himself, along with lots of desperate humans he promised a better world to. Eventually, there was this big fracas between him, me, and some invading Hydra storm troopers. In the process, the Leader got shot full of holes, then blew up in the usual cataclysmic explosion. Like I said, he's supposed to be dead, but I'll believe that when I've crushed his wormy skull between my own bare hands." He smiled vindictively at that image, then shrugged his colossal shoulders. "The city's still there. Some wannabe Leader named Omnibus is running the show now."

"I remember reading something about that very same subterranean sanctuary," the Beast commented, "but I thought the whole kit-and-kaboodle was destroyed a few months ago."

"That was merely a rumor," the Vision stated, presumably calling up the relevant data from his own memory banks. Cyclops noted that the impassive android seemed to bear no animus toward the Hulk despite the Vision's recent (if short-lived) mutilation, nor did he display any trace of discomfort in the man-brute's presence. "The alleged destruction of Freehold was never sufficiently confirmed."

"Sounds like that's the place to start if we want to track down the Leader and our missing teammates," Cyclops declared, anxious to get on the move.

"I agree," Storm assented promptly. Given her deep-rooted claustrophobia, Cyclops knew she could not be feeling enthusiastic about visiting any sort of underground stronghold; he admired her unhesitant willingness to brave her fears for the sake of Rogue and Wanda.

"It's settled then," Captain America said, rising from his seat and strapping his famous shield onto his back. "Vision, are you positive you're up to this? There's no shame if you need more time to recover from your injuries."

"Your offer is generous but unnecessary," the synthezoid answered. Cyclops was struck once more by the eerie coldness of his voice; he'd met Sentinels with warmer personalities. "Unlike organic tissue, my artificial flesh does not require time to reknit itself. Now that Iron Man has repaired any ruptured instrumentation, I am quite fit for the mission under discussion. In fact," he added, and here Cyclops thought he detected a hint of heat in the android's voice, "I must insist on taking part in any attempt to rescue the Scarlet Witch."

That's right, Cyclops recalled. Weren't the Vision and Wanda supposed to be an item of sorts, or was that over a long time ago? His memory on the subject was fairly fuzzy, but he could just imagine how irate he'd feel if someone tried to leave him behind while Jean was in danger, no matter what injuries he might have incurred. *Maybe the Vision isn't so inscrutable after all.*

"Very well," Captain America agreed. "Glad to have you aboard, Vision." He looked across the table at his mutant guests. "X-Men, I assume your aircraft can transport you to Alberta in a timely fashion. If not, you're welcome aboard our quinjet."

"That won't be necessary," Cyclops began. A high-pitched beep, coming from the comm station, broke into the discussion. All heads turned toward the console, where a flashing red light accompanied the audible beeping.

"Aha!" the Beast exclaimed with obvious satisfaction. "An incoming message, forwarded on from X-Men HQ."

SEARCH AND RESCUE

He loped over to the controls while Cyclops waited impatiently to discover who had contacted the Institute in their absence. It would be wonderful to hear that Rogue had somehow managed to rescue herself, but that was probably too much to hope for. Still, the call might be from Jean or the Professor, which would be good news in its own right. Between the Leader and the stolen Sentinels, he figured they were going to need all the help they could get. "Hold onto your proverbial hats, gentlemen and lady," the Beast instructed as he fiddled with the comm controls. "Permit me to take a fleeting moment to adjust the volume."

A second later, a familiar, German-tinged voice emanated from the speaker, causing Cyclops to leap from his chair in surprise:

"Attention, priority Alpha! This is Nightcrawler calling from the Genetic Research Centre on Muir Island. We are under attack by Sentinels. Repeat: Sentinels. Assistance is required as quickly as possible. Please respond immediately."

The Beast did his best to reply, instantly dropping his ebullient manner and manipulating the comm panel with focused speed and concentration. "Kurt! This is Beast. We're with the Avengers. What additional facts can you give us? Kurt? Kurt!"

The concerned X-Man tried restoring communication with Nightcrawler for what felt like an endless minute, then reluctantly gave up. He came away from the comm station, shaking his bushy head at the other heroes. "It's no good. The transmission has been terminated at the other end, which bodes ill for poor Kurt, not to mention Moira and Bobby, who should also be in residence."

"Iceman and a scientist we know," Cyclops translated, noting Captain America's puzzled expression. "They're with Nightcrawler on Muir Island, off the coast of Scotland."

"That would be Dr. Moira MacTaggert, I take it," Iron Man guessed correctly. "I'm familiar with her work, and her Centre, although I've never had occasion to visit that establishment." Cyclops was impressed. "Sounds like we've located our missing Sentinels."

"At the expense of our dear friends' well-being," Storm observed. She rose from her seat, tugging the bathrobe snugly around her. "We must go to their aid at once."

"Oh yeah, what about Alberta?" the Hulk protested belligerently. "I want the Leader, not a bunch of runaway robots."

"Those Sentinels are almost certainly doing the Leader's bidding," Cyclops pointed out. He was shocked that the Hulk wanted to place his own personal vendetta over the safety of Kurt and the others. *Then again,* he thought, *why should I be surprised? This is the Hulk we're dealing with.*

"Which means the Leader is sure to be thousands of miles away from the brouhaha in Scotland," the Hulk insisted. "That's the way he works, sitting on his sickly green butt far from the scene of the crime, while his pawns run around doing his dirty work." The lime-green titan slammed a fist into his palm, clearly wishing he could punch the Leader instead. "If you really want to find the Leader, Scotland's the last place to look for him."

"How can you be so heedless of our friends' plight?" Storm accused the Hulk. "Common decency compels us to render whatever assistance we can."

The Hulk just laughed at Ororo's passionate assertion. "Says the white-haired weather girl in the borrowed bathrobe. What you going to do, Stormy? *Rain* on my parade?"

Tension permeated the crowded conference room. The Hulk and the X-Men assumed body language better suited to a back alley brawl than the onset of a rescue mission. Storm faced the Hulk resolutely, undaunted by his sizable height advantage and menacing attitude. Cyclops stepped to one side, making sure he had a clear shot at the Hulk, just in case. Even Captain America, he noted, had one hand on his shield.

"Oh dear," whispered Jarvis, newly arrived to take away the empty cups and mugs.

The Beast sprang onto the conference table, taking them all by surprise. "At the risk of defusing what promises to be a truly explosive confrontation," he said, "might I point out that both locales demand our prompt attention. We must assume that Rogue and the Scarlet Witch are in no less danger than the luckless inhabitants of Muir Island, which makes trailing the Leader to his clandestine lair arguably as urgent as providing succor to Nightcrawler and company." The shaggy mutant searched the faces of the assembled heroes, looking for common ground, then held up two fingers. "I suggest we divide our forces evenly. Two teams, one to Alberta and one to Muir Island. Is that acceptable to all concerned?"

Sounds like a plan to me, Cyclops thought. Hank was certainly earning a merit badge in diplomacy during this crisis. He saw Storm, Captain America, and Iron Man nod their heads as well. But would the Hulk go along with the Beast's proposal? That was the big question.

"I can live with that, I suppose," the Hulk begrudged finally. "But I'm going to Alberta, after the Leader. The rest of you can split up however you like."

That's big of you, Iron Man thought sarcastically. From a strictly strategic point of view, he assessed, the Hulk's caveat left something to be desired. His brute strength could be more valuable in a clash with the Gamma Sentinels than wasted on a fact-finding mission to the Leader's last known address. Cap must have reached the same conclusion since a frown marred his chiseled, All-American features. *I don't know about Cap and the others,* Iron Man thought, *but I've had enough of the Hulk walking all over us.* He stomped across the room to stand head-to-head, more or less, with the recalcitrant giant. Even with his dense boots and armor, Iron Man still had to tilt his helmet back to look the Hulk in the eyes.

"Listen, Hulk," he said forcefully, just as he would at any board meeting. "Didn't you hear what Cap said? These Gamma Sentinels are robot duplicates of your old foes, even you yourself. We need you in Scotland, where your strength and experience can come in useful, not poking around for clues in Canada. Let somebody else handle that."

"What do I care what happens to those losers in Scotland?" the Hulk shot back. He shoved Iron Man roughly with one hand, hard enough to leave impressions of his fingertips on the Avenger's metallic chestplate. "That's not my problem."

Iron Man refused to give ground. With a single cybernetic command, he magnetized his boots to the floor. "Really?" he challenged the Hulk. "There wouldn't be any gamma reactors at all, let alone Gamma Sentinels, if not for Bruce Banner. That makes them as much your responsibility as anyone else's. Or don't you bother to clean up your own messes."

"I'm warning you," the Hulk snarled, shaking his fist in Iron Man's face. "Don't talk to me about Banner. Ever."

Looks like I hit a nerve, Tony Stark thought. *Good.* As an inventor himself, he knew all about the guilt a conscientious scientist could feel when his work was put to dubious purposes. Despite his best efforts, Stark had often suffered the anguish of knowing that technology he had created had been perverted to evil ends—and felt an obligation to do something about it. He had to assume that, somewhere deep inside the unfeeling monster that was the Hulk, Bruce Banner carried the same burden.

"Like it or not, Hulk, you and I both know that Banner is part of you, which makes you accountable, in part, for whatever atrocities the Gamma Sentinels commit." Iron Man kept his clenched fists at his side, relying on moral persuasion rather than threats to get through to the Hulk's buried conscience. "Now you can smash me into a paperweight if you think you can, but that doesn't change anything. And I'm betting that Banner understands that, even if you don't."

"Don't call me Banner!" the Hulk bellowed, loud enough to hurt Stark's ears even through multiple layers of armor. With a roar like a bull elephant, he raised his fists over his head, ready to bring them crashing down on the armored figure standing before him, who found himself privately wishing he were somewhere else, operating Iron Man's armor by remote control.

So much for my hardball negotiating tactics, Stark thought. *Remind me not to tell Donald Trump about this incident—after I get out of the hospital.*

Then, right as Iron Man braced himself for the mother of all headaches, something strange began to happen to Hulk. The color began to fade from his chartreuse skin, taking on a paler, pinker tint. Bulging muscles deflated, scaling down to less gigantic proportions. Emerald eyes turned brown, and his entire body shrank before the other heroes' eyes. Tan whiskers sprouted from a face that grew less bestial by the second, forming a neatly-trimmed beard that failed to conceal the identity of the slender, brown-haired man who had taken the Hulk's place.

How about that? Iron Man thought, letting out a sigh of relief through the vent in his faceplate. *I got through to Banner after all.*

The transformation clearly took a lot out of him. Banner's raised arms wilted to his sides while his bare chest heaved as though he had just run a marathon. After a few moments, though, he lifted his sagging head to glance around at his surroundings. Weary eyes took in the impressive assemblage of Avengers and X-Men who waited for him to regain his composure. "Somehow, Toto," he murmured, "I don't think we're in Niagara Falls anymore."

At least his sense of humor's intact, Iron Man observed. He sympathized with the man's disorientation; he remembered too well what it was like to find yourself somewhere with little or no idea how you got there. "Hello, Bruce," he said as gently as his electronically-distorted voice could manage, in case Hulk-outs left a hangover afterwards. "How much do you remember of what the Hulk's been up to?"

"Enough to know you're right, Iron Man," he answered, his voice growing stronger as his tumultuous metamorphosis faded into the past. Banner looked up at Iron Man, who now stood several inches taller than the scrawny scientist. "The Gamma Sentinels need to be stopped. If you need the Hulk in Scotland, I can get him there." He held on tightly to the waist of his now-oversized jeans, lest the baggy trousers drop to his ankles. "Er, perhaps someone can spare a belt?"

"Allow me to fetch a change of clothes, Dr. Banner," Jarvis volunteered. A couple of catastrophic clashes averted, the dutiful butler gathered up an assortment of used coffee cups. "Which reminds me, Master Cyclops, Mistress Storm, I've completed the repairs on your uniforms, which

SEARCH AND RESCUE

you'll find waiting for you in the guest rooms."

"Not bad service, sounds like. Don't forget to leave the old guy a tip, Cyke."

The unexpected voice came from the door, startling Jarvis so that he dropped his tray. Porcelain mugs shattered upon the steel floor of the conference. "My word!" the butler exclaimed, holding a hand to his chest. Iron Man spun around to see a short, stocky figure framed by the doorway. His blue-and-yellow uniform was instantly recognizable, but Cyclops identified him first....

"Wolverine!" Cyclops blurted. The missing X-Man had appeared without warning, taking them all by surprise.

Where in the world did he come from? Cyclops wondered. *And do I really want to know?*

Iron Man had another issue on his mind. "How did you get past our security systems and automatic defenses?" he demanded, sounding personally offended by the ease with which Wolverine had penetrated the Avengers' headquarters.

"This is me you're talkin' to," he reminded them. He leaned casually within the doorframe, picking at his teeth with a single adamantium claw. "I was sneakin' my way into tighter tins than this before Shellhead's fancy iron suit was even a gleam in Stark's eye." He strolled into the conference room as though he owned the place; Cyclops didn't know whether to be pleased or appalled by the rugged Canadian's confident attitude. "Caught the news about you folks teaming up at Niagara Falls, so I hot-footed it here, figurin' this is where you'd be heading." He cocked his head toward the silent communications console. "From what I've been hearin' the last few minutes, sounds like I got here just in time."

He nodded at Banner, still struggling to hold on to his

drooping trousers. "Hiya, doc. Give my regards to your hefty alter ego. We ain't had a good scrap in too long."

"Just where have you been, Wolverine?" Cyclops wanted to know. He hated demonstrating how little he had his team under control in front of Captain America and the other Avengers, but he also wanted to know why and where Logan had gone AWOL.

"That's none of your business, Cyke, but I'll tell you anyway." Wolverine sat down across from Cyclops, resting his heels upon the tabletop. "I was just payin' a visit to old Ma Nature, out by the Adirondacks. Plenty of untamed wilderness up there, just the place for heedin' the call of the wild, if you know what I mean."

"I'll take your word for it," Cyclops said brusquely. He had no reason to doubt Logan's explanation of his whereabouts; Wolverine had always felt most at home in the great outdoors. In the long run, Cyclops was just glad that Logan had shown up at all.

We may not know where Rogue or the Scarlet Witch are, but at least Wolverine is accounted for.

Chapter Six

Wolverine was growling like an animal again, making Wanda almost glad that he was locked up like the rest of them. Not even Tigra the Were-Woman, possibly the Avengers' most feral alumnus, had ever sounded so wild and untamed.

As berserk as he sounds right now, she thought, *I'm not sure he could even distinguish friend from foe, not that I've ever been particularly friendly with most of the X-Men.*

She could hear Rogue, two coffins away from Wanda, murmuring softly to her fellow X-Man, trying unsuccessfully to soothe the savage beast who no longer seemed to answer to the name of Logan. *Maybe he's just hungry for something besides an intravenous drip,* Wanda thought. *Too bad we can't throw him a raw steak.*

A mild headache weighed upon Wanda's brain, making it hard to concentrate. Was it a hangover left over from whatever drugs their nameless jailer had pumped into her, or a lingering side-effect of Rogue's vampire-like power? The last thing she remembered, before waking once to the perpetual darkness of her blind captivity, was the awful sensation of the X-Man's southern belle draining her mind and energy again, this time out through Wanda's veins. Rogue had barely begun to explain about the involuntary transfusions before her voracious talent had sapped Wanda's awareness, thrusting the Scarlet Witch into a

SEARCH AND RESCUE

dreamless coma from which she had only just emerged.

What's the point of these debilitating tests? she wondered angrily. If the idea was to uncover how their various mutant powers worked, she wished the unseen experimenters luck; she had devoted much of her adult life to trying to make sense of her peculiar abilities, with notably mixed results. Only months ago, in fact, the aged sorceress Agatha Harkness had presented the Scarlet Witch with yet another "explanation" of Wanda's powers.

The venerable enchantress had told her one-time disciple that Wanda's mutant heritage, a legacy of her father Magneto, the X-Men's oldest and most personal enemy, had been imbued at birth with the primal magic of Chthon, an ancient mystical entity bound to the very mountain upon which Wanda was born. Had it not been for Chthon, the Scarlet Witch would have developed relatively straightforward energy-based powers like her father and any number of other mutants; instead she had been granted a subconscious link to the underlying mystical energy suffusing all living things.

"Chaos magic," Agatha called it. Wild magic. Nature magic.

Wanda had only just begun to learn how to master her chthonic gifts, yet she couldn't help wondering: was there any way she could exploit her new understanding of her powers to liberate herself from her present entrapment? Judging from the sterile scientific ambience of her stay here, she doubted her mysterious captor(s) were prepared to cope with genuine magic. Even when those animated marionettes had attacked her at the folk art museum, she had sensed no supernatural energies at work. It seemed safe to assume the forces arrayed against her now were strictly those of science and technology.

But how, in such a cold, lifeless environment, could she

call upon Nature to deliver her? She sensed no green growing things, no blowing wind nor freely running water, anywhere around her. The air she breathed was antiseptic in the extreme, completely devoid of free-floating microorganisms. Though she tried, she could not even establish any sort of bond with the Earth itself; its nuturing soil and seething, volcanic heart felt impossibly far away. Aside from herself, the only living creatures she was at all aware of were the two captive X-Men, cut off from her by their own entombment in this mechanized mausoleum.

Wait, she thought. *As much as I resented it, couldn't Rogue's usurpation of my mind and powers, through the mingling of our blood, have forged a link of sorts between us? Perhaps, rather than letting my anger over that violation divide us, I can use that enforced affinity to create a bridge between our minds.*

Blood to blood, heart to heart, soul to soul. "Sympathetic magic" it was called. Nature magic. And what could be more natural, more primal, than a bond of blood?

Although already shrouded in darkness, Wanda closed her eyes and visualized her own lifeforce flowing into Rogue. *The blood is the life,* so the Bible taught, and the Scarlet Witch held that image in her mind as she reached out across psychic and physical barriers to the X-Men's empathic soulsucker. She had never tried anything like this before, Wanda knew, and the odds were against her succeeding. Then again, her mutant hex power had always been about skewing the odds and making the most unlikely of possibilities inevitable. *Anything is possible,* she thought, *even if it only happens once in a thousand chances.*

A familiar scarlet luminescence filled the empty blackness before her cloistered eyes and she felt her consciousness shift perceptibly. When the effulgent red glow faded, she discovered to her delight that she could see again—through the eyes of Rogue!

By shifting Rogue's gaze to the right, Wanda could see her own imprisoned body, garbed in an unflattering orange jumpsuit, like a convict on a chain gang might wear, and blinded by a polished metal visor. *No more,* she vowed confidently, smiling grimly inside Rogue's head. She felt her magic tingling within the X-Man's fingers.

"Hey, what's happenin'?" Rogue blurted as, to the female X-Man's surprise, her fingers assumed arcane configurations, making occult gestures that meant absolutely nothing to Rogue. Wanda derived a tiny bit of satisfaction from the X-Man's confusion.

For once, she thought, for the first time since coming to within the lightless sarcophagus, *I'm not the one in the dark.*

Calling upon her own mystical knowledge, and the faint echoes of her power still residing within Rogue, the Scarlet Witch hurled a shimmering hex sphere at her own reflection in the mirror, and was gratified to see sparks fly from the mechanisms embedded in the shining silver sarcophagus.

An unexpected power surge fried the intricate circuitry controlling her high-tech coffin. Wanda's own eyes snapped open at the sounds, bringing her at once back to her own body. She tugged on the metal clamps confining her wrists, finding them loose and unlocked.

Thank you, Agatha, she murmured fervently, *for every hour you spent to make me the witch I am today.*

She worked her hands free from the clamps, then gladly pushed the metal visor away from her face. The harsh, fluorescent light of the testing chamber made her eyes water after so many hours in the dark, but she brushed the tears away with the back of her hand and quickly went about liberating the rest of her body from its entanglement within the coffin. She yanked adhesively-placed electrodes from her brow and elsewhere, then carefully withdrew the intravenous needle from her left arm, putting pressure on the site for a few seconds to make sure it wouldn't bleed. The I.V. line dangled along the side of the sarcophagus, leaking saline onto the floor.

In less than a minute, she was no longer pinioned within the futuristic iron maiden that had held her for longer than she wanted to consider. Her bare feet dropped onto the cold metal floor. After so many hours of compulsory inactivity, her legs felt weak and rubbery. Her head swam dizzily and the entire chamber seemed to spin around her, but she soon regained her balance. *I still feel light-headed,* she thought, *not to mention light in general.* Was there something odd about the gravity . . . ?

Sweeping a lock of auburn hair away from her eyes, she cast an anxious look at the long horizontal mirror running along one entire wall of the testing chamber. Was anyone viewing her escape from the other side of the glass? She realized she had to hurry, before an enemy could arrive to nip her breakout in the bud. For all she knew, the entire Kree army was already on its way.

"Oh mah goodness!" a baffled-looking Rogue exclaimed, staring wide-eyed from the confines of her own sarcophagus. "How did you do that? *What* did you do?"

"Magic," Wanda answered tersely. There was no time to give Rogue a fuller explanation, even had the Avenger felt predisposed to doing so. *I may have helped myself to her eyes and hands,* she thought, *but I don't owe Rogue anything, not after what she did to Carol—and me. She should just be thankful I'm not about to leave either her or Wolverine trapped in this unholy place.*

The Scarlet Witch considered the shackled X-Men. Wolverine was nearest, so she stepped toward his coffin, only to jump backwards, heart pounding, when he suddenly snapped and growled at her like a rabid dog, one she found herself none to eager to unchain. Staring cautiously into his blood-streaked brown eyes, she discerned no light of sanity or recognition. He glowered at her like a caged animal, eager to rip out her throat the moment he got a chance.

Rogue first, she decided.

Freeing the young mutant renegade was child's play compared to the improbabilities required by Wanda's own escape. "Get ready," she warned Rogue before she gestured at the other woman's sarcophagus. A radiant hex sphere, which the Scarlet Witch now understood to be a sort of "chaos grenade," enveloped the incarcerated X-Man, causing every one of the casket's locking mechanisms to disengage simultaneously. "There. You're free," Wanda stated. "Careful of the I.V."

Biting down on her lower lip in impatience, Rogue hurriedly untangled herself from the wires and tubing, wincing as she pulled the hypodermic needle from her arm. *They must have employed an adamantium needle,* it occurred to Wanda, *in order to penetrate Rogue's invulnerable skin.*

"Thanks, sugah!" Rogue drawled as she flew free of the sarcophagus. Wearing an identical orange jumpsuit, she touched down on the floor beside Wanda, reeling a little as she did so.

"Are you all right?" the Scarlet Witch asked, worried despite her longstanding grievances with this woman. Rogue looked a bit shaky.

"Yeah," the X-Man said unconvincingly. Swaying slightly, she wiped her brow, then massaged her temples with her fingers. "Wolverine's healing factor got me through that transfusion reaction, just like it did him, but it's not somethin' ah want to go through again anytime soon." She made an effort to straighten her posture, then looked down at her bare hands. "Ah don't s'pose you got a pair of gloves on ya? Ah feel kinda naked without 'em." A rueful smile saddened her expression. " 'Sides, it's safer that way."

I suppose it is, the Scarlet Witch thought. The potential drawbacks of Rogue's vampire-like power had never really dawned on her before. *She can't touch anyone . . . ever?* Wanda was surprised to feel a twinge of sympathy for the younger woman.

Meanwhile, Rogue regarded the trapped Wolverine with a mixture of pity and indignation. "Well?" she asked Wanda eagerly. "Go ahead. Cut him loose."

Wanda eyed the atavistic X-Man, who appeared to have regressed beyond the point of reason. The mindless intensity of his gaze made her flinch when her wary eyes met his. "If you say so," she said dubiously, not entirely convinced this was a good idea.

Another hex sphere unbolted the locks restraining Wolverine. Not pausing to remove the medical accouterments still attached to his body, he lunged from the middle sarcophagus, snarling like a maddened wolf—or wolverine. His powerful leap tore the I.V. lines from both his arms; the plastic tubing whipped about like miniature firehoses, spraying the floor with a mixture of blood and saline. Knife-edged claws came at Wanda, as she realized in horror that the crazed X-Man had perceived her hex sphere as an attack. She threw herself out of the way barely in time to avoid the slashing claws, grateful that Wolverine had been hobbled in part by his long internment inside the steel coffin. As is, the edge of one blade sliced through her left sleeve, right below her shoulder, nicking the tender skin beneath.

Ouch!

Wanda raised her hands to defend herself, but Rogue

tackled her unhinged teammate first, pulling his arms back with her superior strength and placing him in a full nelson. Wanda noted that Rogue took care not to touch Wolverine's bare skin, just the fabric of his prison garb.

"Logan!" she shouted urgently. "It's me, Rogue! You have to calm down!" Heedless of her words, Wolverine strained to free himself from her unbreakable hold. His eyes were wild and dilated. Foam sprayed from his lips. Looking on, aghast, Wanda was reminded of Tiger Shark, a card-carrying Master of Evil, in one of his bloodthirsty feeding frenzies, not of a veteran superhero respected by the likes of Captain America and the Black Widow. She had never seen Wolverine like this before.

For a long moment, she feared that they would have to render Wolverine unconscious to get him away from here, but Rogue refused to give up on her snarling comrade. "Logan! Listen to me! We're not your enemies." Despite her justifiable prejudice against the woman, Wanda had to admire Rogue's determination, as well as her loyalty to her friend. "Snap out of it, Logan! We need you!"

To Wanda's surprise and relief, Rogue's heartfelt pleas had an effect. The unreasoning fury dimmed in Wolverine's eyes and he seemed to come to his senses. His straining limbs relaxed, to a degree, and he looked on Wanda with cooler, less ravening eyes. A look of regret joined a frown upon his face as his searching gaze fell upon the gash in Wanda's sleeve—and the shallow cut in her arm. "It's all right," he said hoarsely. "You can let go of me now, darlin'. I ain't going to hurt nobody who doesn't deserve it."

Rogue released her hold on Wolverine, who stretched his arms experimentally. The silver claws retracted into metal shunts embedded in the back of his hands. Wanda felt significantly safer now that the deadly blades were safely out of sight, at least for the time being. "Sorry about the scratch," he told her. "I'm sure it must have seemed like a good idea at the time."

Wanda accepted his apology, gruff as it was. "This," she assured him, placing a hand over the minor injury, which smarted when she thought about it, "is the least of our problems. I suggest we find a way out of here as quickly as possible."

"You'll get no argument from me, witchie," Wolverine agreed. He glanced around at the antiseptic white wall that curved around the back of the test chamber. The wall appeared completely seamless, with nary a door in sight. "I don't know about you two, but I don't see no flamin' EXIT signs."

"No problem," Rogue chirped, drawing back her fist in front of the wall-length mirror. Impervious knuckles smashed through the silvered glass, showering the floor with shattered fragments—and revealing the control room on the other side. Rogue grinned devilishly. "Ah've been wantin' to do that since we got here."

She scraped away the remaining shards of glass with her bare hands, then clambered into the chamber beyond. Stepping carefully to avoid the jagged fragments on the floor, Wolverine and Wanda followed after her.

The control room was unoccupied, their anonymous torturer apparently taking a break from his or her heartless experimentation. Obviously intended to be operated by one person, the room barely held two X-Men and an Avenger, even though none of them were built like Thor or Giant-Man. Shaped like a semicircle, approximately six yards in diameter, the control chamber was built around a single steel throne, capable of rotating 360 degrees. Control panels circled the throne, except for a single wedge-shaped exit. Although the empty throne now faced the shattered one-way mirror, the curved wall behind the chair contained row upon row of active video monitors, each turned to a different broadcast. *Whoever works here,* Wanda deduced, *likes to keep well-informed.*

Unfortunately, that description applied to just about every megalomaniacal control freak from Dr. Doom to Ultron to the High Evolutionary. They would have to look harder to find out who had abducted them.

"Wait a sec," Rogue said, pointing at the bottom row of screens. "Isn't that Moira's lab on Muir Island?"

Muir Island? Wanda thought quizzically. *Isn't that somewhere near Scotland?* She followed Rogue's line of sight and her eyes widened in surprise when she saw, on four separate screens, what seemed to be live images of the Hulk, the Abomination, the Harpy, and Doc Samson, all apparently searching some kind of scientific facility.

There's something wrong here, Wanda thought, her brow furrowing as she tried to make sense of the startling images. For one thing, Leonard Samson was a hero, not a pillaging villain. Plus, didn't the Hulk and the Abomination hate each other, and wasn't the Harpy supposed to be dead? So what were they all doing there on those screens, seemingly working together to raid someone's lab? A name popped into her head, heard somewhere sometime before. Could "Moira" be Moira MacTaggert, the famous geneticist?

"Looks like we're not the only ones this creep is interested in," Wolverine remarked. He looked around the control room for clues to their kidnapper's identity, then sniffed the air. "Don't recognize the scent."

Wanda started to admit that she was stumped, too, when her gaze was riveted by one of the upper screens, identified as belonging to CNN. There on the color monitor, caught by a telephoto camera, was the Vision, being torn apart by the Hulk! Wanda gasped and clutched her chest as the jade monster ripped the Vision's arm from its socket, then shoved the dismembered Avenger over the brink of a tremendous waterfall. As she kept on watching, unable to look away, the same footage was shown over and over, sometimes in slow-motion. A caption at the bottom of the screen identified the horrifying images as old news footage recorded the day before at Niagara Falls.

Wanda's throat tightened. Her legs felt boneless and she had to grab onto the silver throne to support herself. The Vision—destroyed? She didn't know what to think, let alone how to feel. Their marriage had been over for a long time, but he was still the man/android/whatever that she had loved longer than any other. He had even been the father of her children, when she still had children. . . .

Less emotionally affected by the shocking footage, Wolverine noticed something else. "Niagara Falls. Muir Island. The Hulk's gettin' around, if both of those really are the Hulk." He sounded suspicious, reminding Wanda of her own doubts concerning the footage from Scotland. There was more here than met the eye, she was sure of it. "Let's go," she said to the others. Her voice faltered just a little. "I—I've seen enough."

Did the X-Men recall, or even know, her history with the Vision? If so, neither Wolverine nor Rogue raised the subject, perhaps preoccupied by the evident danger to their friend Moira. Wanda didn't know whether to be hurt or relieved by their silence.

Unlike the test chamber holding their empty sarcophagi, the control room offered a way out. Wolverine led the way, sniffing for trouble ahead. Wanda exited last, preferring to have Rogue ahead of her rather than behind her.

Just to be safe, Wanda thought, feeling a bit guilty for her doubts concerning the young X-Man and her parasitic powers. *Maybe, when this is all over, I should talk to Rogue about that ugly business with Carol, give her a chance to explain her side of the story.*

The door from the control room opened onto what appeared to be a ring-shaped outer chamber that circled a central cylinder formed by both the control room and the test chamber. Possibly, Wanda guessed, the layout of this entire complex followed a concentric design, leading her to wonder how many rings there were in total. In contrast to the cold, clinical feel of the inner circle, this outer ring had been furnished with comfort in mind. Simulated walnut bookshelves, packed with leatherbound volumes on an eclectic variety of subjects, lined the curving walls of the ring. Plush, wingback chairs and overstuffed sofas offered a series of cozy venues for reading and relaxation, while a soft orange carpet provided a pleasant change from the glass-strewn steel floor they had left behind. A treadmill, positioned before a blank video screen, presented an opportunity for exercise. As the heroes hiked counter-clockwise through the ring, they even came upon an imitation fireplace whose holographic flames threw off real heat. What they *didn't* find, however, was a quick way out. Also conspicuously absent were windows onto the outside world—or any hints to the elusive resident of this hermetic world.

"This is gettin' us nowhere," Wolverine muttered. "For all we know, we're going in circles." Halting in his tracks, he released his claws and slashed a large letter "X" across the spines of a random shelf of books. "Basic woodcraft," he explained to his startled companions. "Always mark your trail."

Not a bad idea, Wanda thought, but before she could say so, a sarcastic voice boomed from on high, freezing them all in place and drawing their eyes to the ceiling:

"THOSE WERE FIRST EDITIONS, I'LL HAVE YOU

KNOW. I'M AFRAID THIS AMUSING LITTLE ESCAPE ATTEMPT HAS GONE FAR ENOUGH. SUCH VANDALISM CANNOT BE TOLERATED, AFTER ALL."

The snide, epicene voice, no doubt coming from hidden loudspeakers in the ceiling, sounded vaguely familiar to the Scarlet Witch, but the electronic amplification and distortion made it hard to identify. "I should have known this was going too easily," she said, shaking her head. "He—or she—has probably been onto us ever since we smashed that mirror."

Rogue looked about her warily, anticipating hostile action. "So how come he waited so long 'fore callin' in the guards?" she asked out loud.

Wanda shrugged. "Perhaps he wanted to get us safely away from all his expensive scientific equipment and monitors, so his fancy control room wouldn't get smashed up in the fighting." She raised her hands in front of her. An eldritch red glow surrounded her fingertips as she concocted a hex. "Or maybe he just wanted to see how far we'd get. Another blasted test."

"Fine with me," Wolverine growled. He crouched in a fighter's stance, his claws poised and ready. "Bring 'em on. I don't mind fightin' my way out."

But fighting whom? the Scarlet Witch wondered. Hired guns? Alien soldiers? Puppets? *We have to be ready for anything.*

Vents opened in the ceiling, spilling a fine pink powder into the furnished ring. She backed away from the powder instinctively, yet it didn't appear hazardous. Soon the powder had thoroughly dusted the carpet, making it impossible to avoid stepping on the minute particles. They felt dry and spongy beneath her feet, not corrosive at all. Pushing his luck, Wolverine scooped up a handful of the pink dust and sniffed it. "Nothing poisonous," he reported unequivocally. "Smells like finely-ground rubber."

"Rubber?" Rogue asked incredulously. The dust kept pouring from the ceiling until they were ankle-deep in the stuff. "What they tryin' to do, build a padded cell from the ground up?"

Not exactly, the Scarlet Witch thought. She had a sneaking suspicion she knew what was coming next. This trick with the powder rang almost-forgotten bells in her memory; she hadn't actually taken part in that adventure, years ago, but she'd heard about it later from Captain America and the rest.

If this "harmless" powder is what I think it is, we could be in a lot of trouble.

Just as she feared, the tiny grains of dust began to clump together, moving of their own accord to form gummy masses that likewise came together to form recognizable shapes: arms, legs, torsos, heads. "Ah don't believe it!" Rogue exclaimed, amazed by the miraculous process taking place before her eyes, the coalescing pink segments merging to form rudimentary bodies. "The dust—it's turning into people!"

"No," Wanda said, shaking her head. She knew precisely what these unliving creatures were. "Not people. *Humanoids.*"

The plasticform figures grew rapidly from the spilled powder, each one identical to every other: pink genderless bodies with smooth, pail-shaped heads. They had no faces as such, only a pair of white, photosensitive patches to serve as eyes. Lacking mouths, they neither spoke nor breathed; the only sound that came from them was the rustle of the congealing powder, followed by the squeaking of dozens of rubber bodies brushing against each other as they swiftly surrounded the three heroes, crowding the habitation ring as tightly as a New York subway at rush hour.

They were just as Cap described them, which could only mean one thing. "I know who made these things!" Wanda shouted to the X-Men. "I know now who is behind all this. The Leader!"

"The Leader of what?" Rogue asked, not comprehending what Wanda meant. Newly-formed Humanoids jostled against her and she tried to elbow them away, but they were already packed too tightly to make much of a difference. Colliding with their teeming counterparts, the offending Humanoids bounced back against her with equal force. "Who are you talkin' about?"

Wolverine, older and more experienced, recognized the name. "Another crackpot mad genius," he explained succinctly. He stabbed his claws into the nearest Humanoid, but its rubbery body absorbed the sharpened tines without tearing. Unable to feel pain, its elastic body stretched around the blow, swallowing Wolverine's entire fist up to his wrist. "Usually, he's the Hulk's problem," he told Rogue.

"The Avengers have had a few run-ins with the Leader, too," the Scarlet Witch emphasized. Not waiting for the fully-formed Humanoids to attack, she fired a hex bolt at the nearest cluster of artificial creatures. "Trust me, he's no one you want to underestimate."

Her hex sphere caused three or four of the humanoids to revert to powder. She smiled coldly, until she saw new bodies rise from the pink dust. Her spirits sank; she hadn't stopped them at all, only slowed them down.

The Humanoids were everywhere, knocking aside the furniture and filling the ring with hairless pink figures for as far as the eye could see. "There must be dozens of them!" Rogue declared. She clasped her arms atop her chest, tucking her bare hands beneath her shoulders and shrinking from contact with the inhuman creatures. "They—they ain't *alive*, are they?"

"Not really," the Witch called back. She quickly realized what was worrying Rogue. "You should be able to touch them without becoming like them."

"Thank goodness for that!" Rogue shouted, sounding enormously relieved. As before, Wanda got a fuller sense of just what sort of curse the young mutant had been forced to live with, and the Scarlet Witch's heart softened a bit toward her former adversary. What a tragic way to go through life, afraid to even *touch* another human being . . . !

The Humanoids gave her no time to digest this new insight. As if in response to a single invisible signal, the milling humanoids abruptly surged toward the outnumbered mutants, reaching out with plastic fingers to grab onto the escaping prisoners. "Here they come!" Rogue hollered. No longer adverse to touching the Humanoids with her uncovered hands, she charged into the oncoming tide of synthetic beings, swinging her fists enthusiastically.

Wolverine was no less aggressive than his fellow X-Man. His claws swung like machetes, trying to slash a way through the humanoid horde. "Instant cannon fodder, huh?" he grunted. "Guess you don't even need to add water."

He kicked a Humanoid in the chest, only to bounce backwards as though he had just slammed his foot into a trampoline. Snarling in frustration, he managed to slice the Humanoid's arm like salami, then gnashed his teeth as a fresh limb immediately grew from the truncated stump. "Cripes," he muttered with obvious disgust. "It's like fightin' silly putty!"

Rogue was getting equally aggravated. Her super-strong blows sent packs of Humanoids scattering like plastic dolls, yet the unfeeling creatures kept on coming. A powerhouse punch squashed an unlucky Humanoid's head, but it sprang back into place as soon as Rogue drew back her fist. She stretched, flattened, twisted, pummeled, and otherwise deformed their malleable plastic bodies, all without inflicting any permanent damage on a single humanoid. "How the heck do you stop these stupid things?" she cried out irritably, even as another wave of Humanoids flowed over her. She couldn't even use her secret weapon: her parasitic touch. For better or for worse, the Humanoids had neither minds nor lifeforce to steal.

The Scarlet Witch watched the X-Men's fruitless struggles with growing alarm; her own hex bolts were faring no better. No matter how many times she used her hex bolts to reverse the Humanoid's creation, disintegrating them back into harmless powder, the unliving beings instantly reconstituted themselves, none the worse for the experience. She searched her memory, trying to remember how the Avengers had defeated the Leader's Humanoids before; unfortunately, as she swiftly recalled, the solution had involved exposing them to the vacuum of space, which hardly seemed like a viable option under the circumstances. *There must be another way to stop them,* she thought desperately. *There has to be!*

More powder spilled from the ceiling, adding to the humanoids' oppressive numbers. They crowded against her, pressing, cramming, smothering, until there was no more room to cast any hexes and she had to use her bare hands to try to push the never-ending flood of Humanoids away from her, feeling the rubbery texture of their synthetic flesh against her sweaty palms. Plastic hands grabbed onto her arms and legs while more hands groped her face and pulled on her hair. A petrochemical reek filled her nostrils. She bit down on an intrusive finger, then spat out a mouthful of foul-tasting plastic. More fingers tugged on her lips, tak-

SEARCH AND RESCUE

ing the first one's place. She felt like she was drowning beneath a sea of anthropomorphic rubber.

Wanda braced herself against both Rogue and Wolverine. The embattled trio had been squeezed together by the relentless press of their mindless foes. Back to back to back, they faced the crushing swarm of Humanoids, whose ductile bodies effortlessly absorbed whatever force was directed against them. Wanda realized the three prisoners were fighting a losing battle and knew that the X-Men had to know that, too. The thought of going back to that sightless sarcophagus filled her with dread.

"YOU MIGHT AS WELL GIVE UP," the Leader's amplified voice informed them. "MY FAITHFUL HUMANOIDS NEVER TIRE, NEVER EXPERIENCE PAIN OR FEAR, AND NEVER, EVER STOP UNTIL THEY HAVE COMPLETED THEIR ASSIGNED TASK, WHICH, IN THIS INSTANCE, MEANS SUBDUING YOU. YOU CANNOT POSSIBLY OUTLAST THEM, SO WHY WASTE YOUR TIME AND MINE IN POINTLESS HEROICS? I DON'T KNOW ABOUT YOU, BUT I HAVE BETTER THINGS TO DO THAN WATCH A TRIO OF OUTMATCHED MUTANTS MAKE THEIR LAST STAND AGAINST THE INEXORABLE CREATIONS OF A SUPERIOR MIND."

"Then change the flamin' channel!" Wolverine barked at him, by no means ready to surrender. Sinking his claws into the pliable torso of yet another indefatigable Humanoid, he turned his head toward Rogue. "Only way out is up, darlin'. You game?"

"You kiddin'?" Rogue asked exuberantly. A half dozen Humanoids piled onto her, but she threw them back into the crushing throng of resilient pink bodies. "I'm feelin' so light on my feet I could fly to the moon." She grabbed onto both Wolverine and the Scarlet Witch by their sleeves, being extra careful not to come into contact with their skin. "Hold onto your seatbelts, y'all!"

Letting out an ear-splitting rebel yell, Rogue flew straight up with the force of a cannonball, hanging onto her two passengers with a grip of steel. Wanda felt like her arm was being yanked from its socket but Rogue's high speed blast-off tore Wanda free from the grasping hands and suffocating pressure of the Humanoids. A determined pink fist clung to her ankle, only to be stretched like taffy by Rogue's unstoppable ascent before finally slipping away.

Rogue's invulnerable skull smashed through at least three layers of ceilings before they burst free of the confining walls of the Leader's headquarters, emerging into open space at last. *We made it!* Wanda thought jubilantly. *We're free!*

Her euphoria lasted less than a second, about the time it took for her to become fully aware of their new surroundings.

Rising in the sky above them, shifting clouds veiling portions of mighty continents and oceans, the great blue globe of the Earth shined down on them, casting its reflected sunlight on a barren lunar landscape marked by still and silent craters. Peering down past her feet, the Scarlet Witch saw the perforated roof of a domed moonbase, constructed within the circumference of one of the larger craters. The atmosphere gushing from the breach in the dome blew a column of swirling debris after the rising heroes, whose lungs suddenly cried out for air.

Good lord, Wanda thought, gasping for oxygen that was nowhere to be found. Blackness rushed over her, along with a fearsome cold—or was that heat? *Rogue didn't need to fly us to the moon.*

We're already there!

Chapter Seven

The full moon shone into the cockpit of the Avengers' quinjet, waking Storm from uneasy slumber. Blinking her large blue eyes, she found herself strapped into a passenger seat to the right of Iron Man, who was busy piloting the supersonic aircraft. "Excuse me," she apologized, "I appear to have dozed off."

"No problem," he replied. "In this business, you've got to grab a nap when you can. You never know when you might get another chance." A yawn escaped his gilded faceplate. "We've been on the run ever since Wanda disappeared yesterday. I imagine it must be the same for you X-Men."

"Indeed," Storm agreed. Through the tinted windshield of the quinjet she saw the rippling surface of the Atlantic Ocean stretching beneath them and she wondered how long she had slept.

Are we almost to Scotland? She hoped, rubbing her eyes. She peered back over her shoulder and saw the rest of the rescue team, Bruce Banner and Wolverine, seated behind her. The cursed scientist, now clad in fresh clothes provided by the Avengers' butler, looked to be resting as well, while Logan stared balefully out a side window, maintaining a grim silence as he methodically polished his claws on an adamantium whetstone. No doubt he was anticipating the dire battle ahead. *As are we all,* Storm thought, fearing that the Gamma Sentinels would prove formidable adversaries. *But defeat them we must, for the sake of Kurt and the others. Bright Lady,* she prayed, *ensure that we arrive in time to protect those in jeopardy.*

"Not that I wouldn't mind a little conversation, now that you're awake," Iron Man commented. "Especially with such an attractive lady as yourself."

Storm raised an eyebrow. "Are you flirting with me, Iron Man?" she asked, amusement in her tone. Funny to realize that, only hours ago, she and this same Avenger had dueled in the skies above Niagara Falls, hurling thunderbolts and repulsor rays at each other, but such was the peculiar world in which she lived.

"Force of habit," he explained, not sounding terribly chastened. "I've always had a weakness for a pretty face." His electronically-distorted voice took on a more serious edge. "Hope you don't find that too frivolous, while your friends and teammates are in danger."

Ororo smiled and shook her head. "Not at all," she said generously. "As you suggested before, in this precarious life that we lead, we most hold onto our humanity and good humor, even in the face of overwhelming peril." She gave the armored Avenger a closer inspection and noted, with a touch of surprise, that his metal gauntlets were not upon the navigational controls but instead inserted into matching, glove-shaped depressions in the control panel. "You can link your armor directly to the ship itself?" she asked, more for the sake of small talk than out of any urgent scientific curiosity.

"Exactly," Iron Man confirmed. "I prefer a direct cybernetic interface whenever I have occasion to fly the quinjet. It eliminates one degree of instrumentality, increasing its responsiveness by a factor of .833, which never hurts in a tight spot." Clearly proud of his advanced technology, he increased the quinjet's acceleration without moving a finger. "Besides, I'm just used to flying under my own power, as you must be, too."

The increase in speed briefly pressed Storm against the back of her seat. "In truth, I also prefer flying on my own to riding in an aircraft, yet I have always relied more on the elemental power of Nature than the wonders of science. No offense intended," she added quickly.

"None taken." He sounded like he was enjoying the discussion. "Myself, though, I've always considered the human talent for technology and invention to be part of nature. Fish swim, birds fly . . . we're built to build things."

"An interesting point of view," Storm admitted, "one I had not fully contemplated before." She began to wonder what Iron Man looked liked beneath his robotic helmet. Curiously, her imagination pictured him as resembling Forge, the brilliant mutant inventor and engineer. Forge spoke just as passionately about machines and their intricacies; she suspected he and Iron Man shared a kinship of sorts, that of like souls. A stab of melancholy snuck into her heart; she and Forge had been more than friends, yet the call of their individual destinies had kept them apart more often than not. "And still, for all of humankind's unquestioned ingenuity, can any mechanical marvel truly compare in splendor to even the commonest sunset?"

"You ever seen some of da Vinci's original blueprints and sketches?" Iron Man challenged her good-naturedly. "We're talking pure elegance in design and execution." The quinjet banked to starboard, smoothly responding to the Avenger's control. "You may have a point, though."

So we agree to disagree, Storm reflected. If nothing else, perhaps this shared mission of mercy would help bridge the rift that circumstances and conflicting priorities had wrought between the Avengers and the X-Men.

SEARCH AND RESCUE

She wondered if the second team, comprised of Cyclops, Captain America, and the Vision, had arrived yet in Alberta, site of the Leader's former headquarters. The Beast had volunteered to remain behind at Avengers Mansion to coordinate the two teams' efforts; he would undoubtedly contact them as soon as there was news from Cyclops and the Avengers accompanying them.

May the Goddess grant that they find our missing comrades, or at least some hint as to their whereabouts, she thought. Every hour that passed heightened her sense that their friends faced terrible danger.

"Maybe you can clear something up for me," Iron Man said, changing the subject. "Who exactly is in charge of your team, you or Cyclops?"

"We share co-leader status," Storm explained. The group dynamics of super-powered crusaders, it occurred to her, was another subject on which they shared expertise. "We have found it the most effective arrangement."

"Really?" Iron Man sounded skeptical. "The Avengers have always worked best with a designated chairman in charge, like Captain America is now. Otherwise you end up with too many ringmasters trying to run the show." A pensive tone crept into his voice. "Ran into some problems along those lines not too long ago, when I convinced Stark to subsidize a whole new team called Force Works. Sort of an alternative to the Avengers, set up to my own specifications. The problem was, I appointed the Scarlet Witch to be team leader, but kept taking charge anyway, undercutting her authority." His helmet shook slowly atop the articulated cables of his armor's neck attachment. "By the time Force Works eventually dissolved, absorbed back into the Avengers, it's a miracle Wanda was still speaking to me."

Storm could tell the memory troubled him, no less now

that the Scarlet Witch was missing and presumed the captive of a ruthless foe. "I cannot deny that Cyclops and I have had our occasional clashes," she confided in him, "but those days are largely past. In the long run, neither of us would wish the X-Men to be deprived of the leadership abilities each of us brings to the team."

"Hard to imagine a corporation working that way," Iron Man commented, and Storm recalled the Golden Avenger was also a paid employee of billionaire Tony Stark, "but I guess there's always room for another paradigm." Storm glimpsed determined blue eyes through the slits in Iron Man's mask. "Heaven help whoever snatched Wanda if I get my hands on him, though. I owe Wanda that much, after all the aggravation I put her through."

"We shall find her, my friend," Storm said, laying her hand atop of the Avenger's recessed right gauntlet. "And Rogue as well." No matter how diabolically brilliant the Leader was, she thought, surely he could not long elude the combined efforts of the X-Men and the Avengers?

A surly voice broke into the conversation. "If you two are done yappin' up there," Wolverine said, speaking up from his seat in the rear of the cockpit, "looks like we're heading up on ground zero."

Wolverine's keen eyes had not deceived him. On the horizon, a rugged green island rose from the ocean, within sight of the distant shore of Scotland. Rocky cliffs towered above stone-strewn beaches while rural villages with names like Kilmory and Blackwaterfoot nestled in the shadow of the rolling hills carpeted in purple heather. As the quinjet zoomed nearer to Muir Island, Storm spied a futuristic complex, composed of sleek structures of steel and glass that seemed distinctly out of place among the bucolic atmosphere of the rest of the isle, poised atop a high cliff overlooking a well-maintained pier. "The Genetic Research

SEARCH AND RESCUE

Centre, I take it?'' Iron Man said, gliding the quinjet in toward an amphibious landing in the harbor below.

"Yes," Storm stated. She stared anxiously at the familiar buildings, looking in vain for conclusive evidence of what might have transpired since Nightcrawler's desperate SOS hours ago. Although it was well past midnight, local time, she spotted lights on in the primary science building, a six-story edifice at the very brink of the cliff. Forbidding steel shutters covered most of the windows in the science building, except for one of the upper floors, where the shutters appeared to have been torn asunder by some manner of explosion or energy blast. Through the ruptured shutters, bright green flashes occasionally showed, competing with the glow of ordinary fluorescent lights. "There," she pointed to the others, "something's happening in one of the labs."

Bruce Banner, roused from sleep by the activity in the cockpit, stuck his head between Storm and Iron Man, gazing out at the Centre. "I read Dr. MacTaggert's papers on genetic mutation while trying to find a cure that would rid me of the Hulk. I can see where her work might have value to unscrupulous men wanting to create artificial mutants for their own purposes. Men like the Leader." Storm gathered from his tone that, for whatever reason, he had come to abandon his quest for normalcy.

"Better settle back into your seat, Bruce," Iron Man warned the Hulk's alter ego. "We're touching down." His gaze fixed straight ahead, the Golden Avenger piloted the quinjet to a surprisingly gentle landing on the waves. Pontoons inflated from the aircraft's landing gear and the ship bounced only twice upon the waves before cruising to a halt next to a long, wooden dock. With a mechanical click, Iron Man detached his gauntlets from the quinjet's control panel. "You think the Leader might have raided the Centre just to steal her data?" he asked Banner.

The scientist's lean face, haggard and haunted at the best of times, assumed an even more somber mien. "The Leader once nuked a city of five thousand, just to create a handful of gamma-irradiated henchmen. He wouldn't pause for a nanosecond before ransacking some laboratory in Scotland, not if he thought your friend had something he could use."

A grim assessment, Storm thought, but not one she had any reason to doubt. Past experience with the likes of Apocalypse and Mister Sinister had left her with few illusions regarding the depths to which brilliant, twisted minds could sink.

"Enough flamin' talk," Wolverine snarled. His claws sliced through the seatbelt holding him in place. "Let's get on with it."

Another phosphorescent green flash came from the building above them, boding no good fortune, she suspected, for Nightcrawler, Iceman, Moira, and any others who chanced to be residing at the Centre when the Gamma Sentinels struck. Unclasping her own seatbelt, she was no less eager than Wolverine to engage the enemy. "Very well," she stated. "Follow me."

Inside the battle-scarred ruins of the once pristine laboratory, the copious sheets of ice left behind by the defeated Iceman had begun to melt, flooding the cold steel floor upon which Moira MacTaggert futilely struggled to escape her bonds. Elastic steel cables, thin as copper wire but too bloody strong, at least as far as Moira was concerned, were wrapped around her from her neck down to her ankles, pinning her arms to her sides and digging into her flesh despite the welcome padding of her labcoat and ordinary civilian wear. Shivering upon the increasingly slushy floor,

SEARCH AND RESCUE

Moira could see Bobby Drake lying equally helpless less than a meter away. No longer protected by so much as a sliver of frozen armor, the defrosted Iceman had yet to recover from the brutal electrical shock administered by the restraining wires enveloping him.

I should count m'self lucky, I suppose, that these accursed contraptions didn't judge me in need of the same sort of shock treatment they inflicted on poor Bobby, she thought.

But it was hard to feel too blessed whilst a pair of cunningly-camouflaged Sentinels helped themselves to years of her work, to say nothing of plenty of expensive equipment. . . .

Moira had deduced the true nature of the invaders hours ago, when "Doc Samson" first approached a bank of deep-frozen computers. She had watched in amazement and horror as the emerald-tressed muscleman melted away Iceman's handiwork with a set of ocular heatbeams that Moira had never known Leonard Samson to possess, but her mounting suspicions were not fully validated until Doc Samson detached the end of his left index finger, revealing a miniature electronic probe, then inserted the probe into a matching data port in Moira's main Cray supercomputer. "Recording: all files and systems," he announced mechanically at the same time that Moira had realized that Doc Samson, and presumably the "Harpy" as well, were actually machines, manufactured, for reasons she couldn't guess, in the image of well-known specimens of gamma mutation. From there, it had taken but the slightest of deductive leaps to come to the conclusion that these rampaging intruders had to be the latest and most duplicitous generation yet of the mutant-hunting mechanical monsters known as Sentinels.

Will we never learn? she had thought bitterly, appalled

to see the same hateful idea come round again. *If half the money and technical know-how that have gone into building Sentinels had been spent on something worthwhile instead, say, biomedical research, we could have surely cured the Legacy Virus by now, and Lord knows what else besides.*

Since that revelatory moment, hours past, the Doc Samson-Sentinel had not budged a centimeter. A steady hum came from his brawny chest as he took advantage of her linked computer network to prowl through years of accumulated data and theories. Many of her most important files were doubly encrypted, of course—ever since that stink with the Xavier Protocols a while back, Moira had taken care to make sure her work was unintelligible to prying hackers and other snoopers—but she had the sinking feeling that the Sentinel's electronic brain was a match for her own encryption software and computerized security checks.

The most I can hope for, she thought, *is that it slows him down long enough for help to get here.*

One thing Moira knew for certain, she sure as blazes wasn't going to provide the Doc Samson-Sentinel with any of her passwords, not that he had even bothered to ask. *That can't be a good sign,* she admitted gloomily.

While the Doc Samson-Sentinel robbed her via cyberspace, the Harpy-Sentinel took a more tangible approach. The counterfeit bird-woman flapped about the trashed laboratory, selectively placing flashing electronic tags on various items—on the hard copies of her notes and on assorted items of equipment. The tags evidently provided a signal to some variety of transporter device, since the objects selected subsequently disappeared in a flash of eerie green light. Granted, it was also possible that the items in question were merely disintegrated, but Moira considered that unlikely; the Harpy's actions were too deliberate and specific to be simple acts of destruction. If the avian Sentinel had merely wanted to destroy the objects of her search, there were doubtless easier ways to do so. Her hellbolts, for instance.

Were additional Sentinels pillaging the rest of the Centre? Moira had no idea what had become of Nightcrawler; she had not seen Kurt since he had teleported away to investigate what was happening downstairs. Since he had not attempted to rescue them, Moira had to assume that he had run afoul of a Sentinel or two. She just hoped that he'd managed to call for help before another relentless robot captured him.

Moira gave thanks, for perhaps the thousandth time, that Rahne was away from home. Had she been here to witness this assault, that dear lycanthropic lass would have felt obliged to defend Moira with tooth and claw—and would have almost certainly fallen victim to the Sentinels as well. *Be well, my sweet bairn,* she silently wished her foster daughter, in the event she never saw her again.

"Recording: complete," the Doc Samson-Sentinel announced. "All pertinent files have been assimilated." He disengaged his finger-probe from the supercomputer, then drew back a mighty fist. "Proceeding to demolition of premises," he reported, then slammed his right hand into the heart of the CPU. Metal and molded plastic tore noisily and sparks flew as his impressively-thewed arm sank into the machine up to his elbow. His fraudulent features maintaining the poker face to end all poker faces, he withdrew his arm from the violated computer, leaving a gaping crater in the side of the Cray. "Have no fear, Doc Samson is here," he intoned with nary a speck of human feeling.

Oh, give it a bloody rest! Moira thought indignantly. At this point, the Sentinel's rote attempts to maintain the imposture had become little more than an insult to her intelligence. She winced as the Doc Samson-Sentinel crushed a delicate electron microscope with his bare hands. It wasn't enough that they had stolen her data, she lamented, they had to go and wreck her equipment too?

A loud, flapping noise distracted Moira from Doc Samson's wanton vandalism. The wind from the Harpy's wings blew flecks of ice and snow against Moira's face as the flying Sentinel landed on the floor between Moira and Bobby. Bird-like talons sank into the melting slush as the human half of the Harpy leaned toward the ensnared scientist, another badge-sized electronic tag clutched between emerald fingernails. "Oh no!" Moira gasped, realizing that the Sentinel meant to tag Moira herself for transport.

Looks like I'm going to find out the hard way where all my apparatus and notes have disappeared to, she thought.

Before the Harpy-Sentinel could finish affixing the tag to Moira's person, however, a deafening crack of thunder sounded right outside the sundered metal shudders. Moira's heart leaped hopefully, especially since the daily weather report had said nothing about any nocturnal storms. *Could it be . . . ?*

Yes!

Carried by a powerful blast of wind, Storm flew into the laboratory through the shattered window. The wings of her black uniform swelled beneath her arms and her riveting blue eyes searched the icebound chamber, widening in recognition as she spotted Moira and Bobby, bound and helpless upon the floor. "Thank heavens!" Moira gasped in relief. *The X-Men were here—and Iron Man?*

So it seemed. The Golden Avenger followed Storm through the punctured metal screens. Rockets in his iron boots carried him above the floor as readily as Storm's obedient winds. Moira had no idea why the armored hero had arrived with Ororo, but she didn't much care. *Under the circumstances,* she thought, *I'm not about to look a gift Avenger in the mouth....*

Three stories below, on the ground floor of the science building, Bruce Banner and Wolverine found definite signs of forced entry; namely, a steel-framed glass door that had been ripped from its hinges. It looked, Banner thought, like the kind of excessive property damage the Hulk usually left behind, except that heavy tracks in the nearby lawn bore the unmistakable impression of something with only two toes on each foot. Banner knew of only one creature, as strong and savage as the Hulk, who left tracks like that.

"The Abomination," he said tersely.

It seemed that the Avenger's classified information was correct; the mechanized monsters allegedly attacking this isolated scientific outpost were indeed the so-called Gamma Sentinels. Banner shook his weary head in disgust. Bad enough there was already one Abomination loose in the world; why in the world would anyone want to build another one?

Not that I'm one to talk, he admitted privately. If not for his own attempts to harness gamma radiation, there would be no Hulk nor Abomination. Nor any Leader, for that matter. He could hardly sit in judgment over other scientists, not after all the heartache and havoc his own discoveries had inflicted on the world. *The best I can do now is try to clean up the mess I helped to create.*

"Not wantin' to tell you your business, bub," Wolverine said gruffly, "but maybe you ought to be changin' into your tougher half?" These were the first words the laconic X-Man had said to him since they left the quinjet down by the docks. Wolverine placed his own boot beside one of the Abomination's footprints; the disparity in size was impressive. "Don't take it personal, but I'd rather have the

Hulk backin' me up when the fur starts flyin'."

Banner looked down at the scruffy, stocky mutant, which was something of an unusual perspective. Wolverine was the only superhero he had ever met, this side of Ant-Man and the Wasp, who was shorter than the scientist in his "puny" human form. He shared enough memories with the Hulk, though, to know that Wolverine's lack of height was no reflection on his fighting abilities. Wolverine was one of the most formidable adversaries the Hulk had ever faced.

As much as Banner hated to admit it, the X-Man had a point. If there was a robotic replica of the Abomination prowling about, there wasn't much ordinary Bruce Banner could do to stop him. He would have to let his monstrous counterpart out of the box once more. "All right," he told Wolverine. "Give me a minute."

The late night air was chilly enough that he was grateful for the borrowed sweater and jacket Jarvis had provided him. Nonetheless, he stripped down to his jeans in a brisk and efficient manner, removing his shoes, socks, shirt, sweater, and polyester jacket, then placing them neatly in a pile on the off chance that the Hulk would think to retrieve them later. Goosebumps broke out all over his exposed arms and chest, but that was nothing compared to bodily changes in store.

Very well, you damn green albatross, he thought. *Come on out and play.*

Once he'd had little or no control over his transformations, but he'd learned enough biofeedback techniques over the last few years to be able to trigger the metamorphosis at will. He pictured the Hulk in his mind, remembered how the brutish creature had made a travesty of his life, destroying his career and turning him repeatedly into a hunted fugitive, and, sure enough, he soon felt his blood pressure rising, his pent-up anger and resentment initiating a metabolic chain reaction that buried the skinny scientist's scholarly physique beneath a couple tons of augmented bone and muscle, and that sank his mind and personality into the seething substrata of a more volatile and elemental identity. A narrow leather belt snapped like a rubber band as his torso expanded to fill the waistband of the oversized jeans. Goosebumps gave way to rippling layers of muscle and sinews. Massive knees tore through tough denim.

"I'm back!" the incredible Hulk bellowed triumphantly, shaking anvil-sized fists at the starry sky above.

"So much for the element of surprise," Wolverine said, scowling, irritation in his raspy voice. Shining silver claws sprang from the back of his clenched fists.

The Hulk was not at all intimidated by Wolverine's gleaming claws. "Bah!" the jade giant said. "The Hulk doesn't skulk through shadows like a sneak thief. I go where I like, and smash anything that gets in my way!" He stared down at the irate X-Man, having gained at least a yard in stature. "See you finally decided to make it, pipsqueak."

"Yeah, nice to see you, too," Wolverine snarled sarcastically. "This flamin' reunion makes me feel all warm and fuzzy inside." He spit a mouthful of chewing tobacco onto the lawn. "C'mon. Let's get this show on the road."

The door to the science building would have been too small to accommodate the Hulk's gargantuan frame had not something equally immense already busted its way through. Fluorescent lights in the ceiling spared them any need for flashlights. With Wolverine leading the way, his adamantium claws extended before him, they stalked through the deserted lobby of the building, passing an overturned cedar desk and other evidence of the Abomination-Sentinel's passage. But had the good-for-nothing robot already come and gone?

How the heck am I supposed to know? the Hulk thought grumpily. *I can bust heads, sure, but I ain't no blamed detective!*

"Hey, shorty," the Hulk addressed Wolverine. "You smell anything worth fighting?" He remembered that the feral X-Man had a nose like a bloodhound.

"Er, not at the moment," Wolverine answered vaguely, not bothering to look back at his gigantic companion. The Hulk's sloping brow wrinkled in puzzlement. Wolverine was a lot of things, he knew, but evasive wasn't exactly one of them.

"What's the matter?" the Hulk taunted. "Your sinuses clogged or something? I ain't ever known that ugly snoot of yours to let you down before."

Wolverine spun around and glared at the Hulk, his claws held up in front of him like a boxer's mitts. He bared his teeth as threateningly as his vicious namesake. Murder glinted in his cold brown eyes. "Listen, mister, I've had enough of your lip. If we didn't have a job to do, and good people dependin' on us, I'd teach you a lesson in manners right here and now."

"Oh yeah?" the Hulk answered, flexing his bulging biceps. That phony Abomination could wait; he'd like nothing better than to throw down with Wolverine more time. It had been too long since he'd last enjoyed a knock-down-drag-'em-out brawl with the scrappy Canadian. He raised his own titanic fists, his knuckles itching to knock Wolverine's block off. "I don't see anybody stoppin' you."

At the back of his mind, a squeaky little voice, sounding suspiciously like Banner's, argued that he didn't have time for this, that there were more important things at stake. *Tough luck,* he thought. The sneer on his face turned into a merciless smirk, and he swung a roundhouse punch at Wolverine's adamantium skull.

The X-Man must have seen the blow coming. He ducked beneath the swinging fist and lashed out with his claws. All three blades on his right fist skewered the Hulk right through the giant's left wrist. The Hulk roared in pain and yanked his arm back, shaking his wounded wrist free from the razor-sharp claws on which it was impaled. His gamma-irradiated flesh quickly restored itself, healing so fast that the puncture marks disappeared the instant his perforated wrist slid off the points of the claws. "Hah!" the Hulk laughed, unscathed even though the X-Man had drawn first blood. Compared to his own miraculous regenerative powers, Wolverine's mutant healing factor might as well be hemophilia.

But the feisty little mutant wasn't about to surrender. "All right, big guy," he dared the Hulk, crouched over in a defensive posture, rocking nimbly upon the balls of his feet. Emerald blood dripped from his claws. "Show me what you've got."

The Hulk wouldn't have it any other way. Arms outstretched like logs hurled by a hurricane, he charged Wolverine, who dodged to the right a split-second before the Hulk could grab onto him. A dark blue boot caught the Hulk beneath the kneecap, a blow that would have crippled any other foe. Coming up behind the jade giant, Wolverine raked his claws across the Hulk's massively muscled back, carving gouges that healed before he shed another drop of blood.

"Arrgh!" the Hulk hollered, more in fury than in pain. The little punk was fast, he'd give him that, but that wouldn't do him any good once he'd broken the pint-sized X-Man in two, adamantium skeleton or no adamantium skeleton. Turning on his opponent before Wolverine could once again slash him from behind, the Hulk connected with a backhanded swat that sent Wolverine skidding on his backside down the length of an empty hallway lined with closed office doors. The heels of the X-Man's boots left scuff marks on the linoleum floor that stretched over fifty yards before Wolverine came to an abrupt halt, slamming into an aluminum storage cabinet at the end of the hall. His back and shoulders hammered a Wolverine-shaped dent into the metal door of the cabinet.

Stop it! cried out that same tinny voice from the Hulk's undernourished superego. *Stop this now!*

The Hulk just grinned harder.

Looking dazed, Wolverine shook his head back and forth violently, perhaps to forcibly expel any cobwebs, before springing to his feet and stampeding like an enraged bull at the Hulk, who had to throw up his arms at the last minute to avoiding being stabbed through the chest by half a dozen adamantium daggers. The claws sank into the rock-solid flesh of his forearms and the Hulk stamped his bare foot down on the linoleum *hard,* igniting tremors that sent the mutant berserker staggering backwards across the quaking floor.

The Hulk stomped only once, but the tremors continued for several seconds thereafter. Momentarily distracted by the stinging scratches upon his arms, it took the Hulk a second to realize that something else was causing the floor to quiver beneath his feat. Wolverine froze in his tracks as well, also taking note of the strange phenomenon. "What the hey?" he blurted, looking from side to side.

Their brutal struggle had carried the two champions midway down the empty corridor. Now two huge figures joined them—from opposite ends of the hall. Glancing from left to right, the Hulk found himself trapped between what looked like the Abomination . . . and himself!

SEARCH AND RESCUE

"How 'bout that," the Hulk muttered. Captain America and his Avenging buddies had been right after all; somebody really had been building duplicates of the Hulk and the rest of the gamma bunch. No wonder the Leader had taken an interest in S.H.I.E.L.D.'s latest dirty tricks. This was right down his alley.

The Gamma Sentinels, each as tall as the Hulk himself, advanced on Wolverine and the original Hulk. "Identified: target designates: Hulk and Wolverine," the bogus Abomination stated. His coarse, gravelly voice sure sounded like the Real McCoy, even if Emil Blonsky, the true Abomination, had never talked like a stinking robot. "Deadly force is mandated. Take no prisoners."

"Confirmed," the other Hulk said. "Adopting termination protocols."

It was like listening to his voice on an answering machine. *Do I really sound like that?* the real Hulk wondered briefly.

A whirring sound, like a tape recorder rewinding, came from the hulking, green-skinned Sentinel. "Hulk will smash! Hulk is the strongest one there is!"

Now that's just insulting, the Hulk thought, frowning. *Who does he think he's fooling?*

"Hey, Jade Jaws," Wolverine said. "What you say we settle between us later." He kept a close watch on both approaching Sentinels. "I think these bozos just moved to the top of our dance cards."

"Fine with me," the Hulk agreed. Playtime was over; it was time to get some serious stomping in. "The Abomination is mine. You take my evil twin."

Frankly, he would have enjoyed tearing his computerized double to pieces, but that might get too blasted confusing, for Wolverine, if nobody else.

The last thing I want, the Hulk craftily considered, *is a well-meaning Canuck jabbing me with those adamantium pigstickers of his in the mistaken impression he's saving me from the clone.*

"Works for me," Wolverine grunted, then launched himself at the Hulk-Sentinel. Silver claws glistened beneath the overhead lights and a low, predatory growl issued from the X-Man's chest. The real Hulk caught only a glimpse of Wolverine's attack on the artificial Hulk before his own chosen opponent came at him, scaly green claws tearing at his face.

"Beware the Abomination!" the Sentinel bragged, as his dinosaur-like talons dug into the Hulk's scalp, right behind his ears, and tried to twist the Hulk's head from his shoulders. His reptilian face was less than an inch away from the Hulk's own primeval features. "None can escape the Abomination!"

Forget that! the Hulk decided. He'd had his neck broken once before, thank you very much, and once was enough; it had taken him literally *weeks* to recover last time. He wrenched his head from the mock Abomination's grip and shoved the Sentinel's scale-encrusted chest with both hands, with enough force to send the creature reeling backward a few steps. *Too bad it's not the real thing,* the Hulk thought vindictively. He was always up to clobbering the Abomination, especially now that he'd learned that Blonsky was responsible for Betty's death. "Tell you what," he growled at the saurian Sentinel, "I'm going to pretend you're the genuine article." He slammed his fist into the Abomination's face. "It'll be more fun that way."

He had to admit this Abomination sure looked authentic. He had the same scalloped ears and bony skull, the same scaly hide and yellow fangs. He even punched as hard as Blonsky did.

My tax dollars at work, he thought mordantly, even

though neither he nor Banner had actually drawn a regular paycheck, let alone paid taxes, for years.

His fists as rough and abrasive as a gator's skin, this Abomination pounded the Hulk with seismological force, with the original green goliath giving just as good as he got. Their exchanged blows shook the building as they grappled at close quarters. Scaly hands locked around the Hulk's bull-like neck, squeezing with enough force to reduce a diamond to dust, but the Hulk merely pummelled the Abomination's ribs until the other monster was forced to loosen his grip. The Abomination's fang-filled jaws snapped at the Hulk, trying to tear a great chunk of muscle from the Hulk's right shoulder; the sharpened incisors actually pierced green skin, in fact, yet tendons stronger than the thickest steel cable held the Hulk's flesh to his bones. He retaliated by grabbing onto the wing-like flaps of the Abomination's ears and yanking his misshapen head back so far that all the Hulk could see was his enemy's upraised chin. Seizing the moment, the Hulk butted that chin with the top of his head. The sound of his foe's teeth rattling was music to the Hulk's ears.

The homicidal monster was forced to release his deathgrip on the Hulk's throat in order to peel the Hulk's fingers away from his ears.

"Unhand the Abomination," he recited. "The Abomination cannot be stopped." One meaty finger at a time, he managed to pry the Hulk's left hand away from his ear, but the Hulk refused to release the other ear. Holding onto the membranous flap so tightly that his chartreuse knuckles turned white, the Hulk gave the ear a vicious twist. There was a harsh, ripping sound and the entire ear tore away from the left side of the Abomination's head, revealing a peek at the gleaming metallic skull beneath. Concentric circles of small blinking lights radiated out from the Sentinel's exposed auditory receptor. Shreds of synthetic skin and scales hung in tatters around the telltale glimpse of chromed silver.

Scowling in disgust, the Hulk tossed the limp ear to the floor and ground it beneath his bare heel. The Sentinel's unsightly injury spoiled the satisfying illusion that this was the real Abomination, Emil Blonsky himself, the slimy, no-good crumb who had poisoned the Hulk's—that is, Banner's—wife. *It's just another stupid robot who doesn't have enough sense to get out of my way.* the Hulk thought.

His fun ruined, the Hulk decided to get things over with. "All right," he snarled, "no more Mr. Nice Guy!" Catching the Abomination-Sentinel's thrashing form in a headlock, he spared a second to see how Wolverine was doing:

The indomitable X-Man had somehow got onto the Hulk-Sentinel's back, straddling him piggyback, his short legs locked around the Sentinel's throat, while he hacked at the duplicate's head with his flashing claws. Locks of unruly emerald hair littered the floor, but so far the other Hulk's skull seemed to be made of sturdier stuff, perhaps even some new adamantium alloy. Wolverine had to duck his own head to avoid colliding with the ceiling, probably not a problem, the real Hulk reflected, that the pint-sized X-Man had to worry about very often.

Rather than try to pull Wolverine from his shoulders, the phony Hulk bent his enormous knees, then launched himself straight up—through the ceiling and all the floors above. Peering up the newly-created shaft while wrestling with the relentless Abomination, the real Hulk spotted a satellite dish on the roof of the building, silhouetted against the full moon. Debris from every floor in-between, including, oddly enough, bits of ice and snow, fluttered down through the chasm carved out by his doppleganger's stupendous leap.

SEARCH AND RESCUE

Six stories above, a pair of overly familiar green hands wrenched the satellite dish from its housing, then heaved it at an unseen target on the roof. *Wolverine?* the Hulk speculated. *Or just Storm or Iron Man instead?* Either way, it looked like the robot Hulk had his hands full.

As did he. "Release the Abomination!" the stubborn Sentinel commanded fruitlessly. He tugged on the Hulk's arm, determined to escape the headlock. "The Abomination will destroy you all!"

"Give it up, tin man," the Hulk snorted. He could not resist giving the captured Sentinel the world's most high-powered noogies, brutally rubbing his knuckles over the bony protuberances atop the fake Abomination's cranium. "How you like them apples, robot?"

Unable to extricate his head from the crook of the Hulk's immovable elbow, the Sentinel took a page out of the Hulk's own recent playbook and stomped down on the Hulk's bare foot with tectonic force. The Hulk's toes survived the impact, but the floor did not; gravity seized hold of both green monsters as they fell into a pit of their own creation. Caught off-balance by the collapse of the floor, the Hulk let go of the Abomination as he fell, landing with a thud upon a hard cement floor one story below. Broken chunks of plaster and linoleum rained down on his head.

The basement where he had landed was dark, but enough light shined down from the hall above to let the Hulk see that his robotic adversary had also survived their crash landing. "Warning! Structural integrity of floor supports under critical strain," the Abomination-Sentinel announced belatedly. "Disintegration of immediate infrastructure imminent." One of his crimson eyes had cracked down the middle, exposing hidden circuitry. Dust and debris coated his olive-green scales. He tottered uneasily upon his two-toed feet.

Okay, the Hulk thought, rising to his feet and shaking off the residue of the collapsed floor, *now you've made me mad.*

And, as the genuine Abomination knew too well, the madder Hulk gets, the stronger he gets. . . .

Trampling fallen chunks of flooring beneath his feet, the Hulk ran across the shadowy basement and delivered a mammoth punch, backed up by all his headlong momentum, to the Sentinel's midsection. The ringing impact echoed through the basement, followed by the gratifying sound of delicate machinery breaking apart somewhere deep within the Sentinel. The robot did not fall, not right away, but it swayed drunkenly atop unsteady limbs that appeared to have lost their gyroscopic equilibrium.

"I am the Abomination . . . mination . . . mination . . . ," the Sentinel stuttered, like a scratched vinyl record, until the Hulk put it out of its mechanical misery by smashing his fist down on top of the robot's skull and driving its head halfway into its chest. The tiny lights around the Sentinel's exposed eye and ear went dead and froze in place like a wind-up toy whose spring had come unwound.

The Hulk stepped back to admire his destructive handiwork. Satisfied that the scaly mannequin was not going to start moving again, he looked around to inspect his new surroundings. *What have we got here?* he wondered.

The basement appeared to hold some sort of prison or zoo. Parallel rows of locked iron doors, each with a barred window installed at eye level, advertised the existence of at least a dozen cells, six on each side of a wide central hallway.

Looks like the X-Men's own private Alcatraz, the Hulk thought, although the cells looked comfortably furnished enough, with beds, desks, computers, televisions, and other amenities. He stomped down the corridor, peering into each cell as he passed. Most appeared unoccupied at the moment, although in one cell he spied a huge, shaggy figure lying unconscious upon the carpeted floor. A hand-written label on the door identified the inmate as "Spoor," and he looked dead to the world, snoring loudly and twitching occasionally in his sleep. Across the hall, in the opposite cell, was a bizarre, feathered creature that didn't even look humanoid. The name on the labeled identified it simply as "Unknown Mutant #9." It, too, was out cold. Probably drugged or gassed, he guessed, to keep them from escaping during the chaos upstairs.

Growing bored with Moira MacTaggert's underground mutant menagerie, the Hulk turned to leave, then heard something stirring in the last cell on the left. A voice, with a pronounced German accent, called out from behind the closed door. "Hello? *Vas is das?* Is anybody there?"

His eyes adjusting to the gloom, the Hulk peeked through the small, square window in the door. To his surprise, the cell appeared empty, even though the disembodied voice grew louder and more demanding. "Moira? Bobby? Is that you?"

Either he's invisible or he's one heck of a ventriloquist, the Hulk concluded. His beefy fingers groped along the wall beside the locked steel door until he found a manual switch.

CLICK.

Lights came on inside the cell, the sudden illumination making visible a writhing figure trapped in some kind of metallic netting. Bound but obviously not gagged, the newly revealed figure had dark blue fur, pointed ears, and a tail that was currently trying to wriggle its way free of the thin metal cables that had ensnared it.

Hah, the Hulk thought, recognizing the frustrated prisoner now that the shadows had been dispelled. If it wasn't the X-Men's resident smurf . . . !

I know Scotland is supposed to be cold, but this is ridiculous!

Zooming into the lab in Storm's wake, Iron Man was surprised to find that the spacious facility looked like it had been hit by a blizzard. Melting ice slides crisscrossed the room, along with, alarmingly dismembered pieces of Iceman. For a moment, he feared the X-Men's human popsicle had met a ghastly fate; then he realized there were enough frozen limbs around to assemble a small army of Icemen, and he surmised the nature of the ruse the real Iceman must have attempted—unsuccessfully, it appeared. The chilling effect of all that ice and snow could be felt even through Iron Man's armor, but a quick cybernetic adjustment to his internal thermostat maintained a comfortable temperature inside his iron suit.

Wary eyes, as well as on-line targeting programs, observed and evaluated the situation as he cruised below the high ceiling of the lab. Two hostages, enmeshed in wire nets, and two potential threats: Gamma Sentinels, just as Nick Fury described. The craftsmanship was impressive, Iron Man gave them that; the Sentinel impersonating Doc Samson was a dead ringer for the world's strongest psychiatrist, while the Harpy, for all her feathers and giveaway green skin, bore a noticeable resemblance to the late Betty Banner. Then again, there was no reason not to expect the Gamma Sentinels to be near-perfect replicas of the beings they were modeled after. S.H.I.E.L.D. had long ago perfected, with more than a little help from Tony Stark, the art of making believable Life Model Decoys. It galled him to think that some of his own discoveries and techniques might have gone into the creation of these destructive, mutant-hunting monstrosities.

As for the hostages, Iron Man guessed that the attractive, middle-aged woman tied up on the floor was Moira MacTaggert. By process of elimination, he swiftly deduced that the unconscious young man lying not far from her, trussed up like a Christmas tree whose branches had been tied down for easy transport, was Iceman, de-iced. One thing for sure, the downed youth didn't look at all like Nightcrawler. No tail, for one thing. His sensors picked up strong life-signs coming from both captives. *That's something to be thankful for,* he thought, although it worried him that Nightcrawler was nowhere to be seen.

Storm was more than worried. The sight of her friends, bound and left to shiver on the icy floor, while their captors despoiled Dr. MacTaggert's work at will, seemed to spark a righteous fury in the mutant weather goddess. "Sentinels," she denounced them with fierce dignity. "I know your kind too well, and I will not suffer to let you abuse these people or this place a heartbeat longer. Feel the wrath of the elements at my command!"

Thunder boomed indoors and crackling lightning wreathed her head like a halo. Radiant energy suffused her eyes, hiding their distinctive blue coloring, and jagged bolts of electricity leaped from her fingertips. Iron Man's environmental sensors instantly registered a sizable spike in the barometric pressure along with an unnatural increase in the ozone level. *Talk about storm warnings,* he thought, impressed by the lady's manifest power. Having been on the receiving end of that power only just this morning, Iron Man was glad he and Storm were on the same side now.

Twin thunderbolts singled out both the "Harpy" and "Doc Samson," striking the two Sentinels and engulfing each in a shower of sparks. With the two hostiles on the defensive, Iron Man took advantage of Storm's literal blitzkrieg to look after the defenseless hostages. Activating the vari-beam projector in his chestplate, he used a magnetic attraction ray to lock onto the metal filaments binding the prisoners and lift both MacTaggert and Iceman off the floor and draw them to his waiting gauntlets. "Don't worry, doctor," he assured the wide-eyed woman. "You're in good hands now."

His chin sagging limply onto his chest, the unconscious Iceman muttered something that sounded like "Sentinels, gotta stop the Sentinels...."

First things first, Iron Man thought. Making sure he had a firm grip on both hostages, he retreated through the shattered window into the chill Scottish night. He hated leaving Storm alone with the Gamma Sentinels, but, with any luck, he could get back to the fight before too much precious time passed. Shooting past the edge of the seaside cliff, he dove at a 45 degree angle to the pier below, then executed a last-second change in his trajectory that let him touch down on the dock rightside-up. A diamond-edged precision blade emerged from the index finger of his right gauntlet, and he carefully sliced through the wires binding Dr. MacTaggert and Iceman. "About time!" the scientist said, with a definite Scottish burr. She shook her hands and feet to restore the circulation to her extremities. "Thank you, Iron Man. I have to say, I never expected to see you here."

"The X-Men don't have a monopoly on helping mutants," he told her. "I've tangled with more than a couple Sentinels in my day. Now then, if you'll excuse me." Iron Man helped her into the quinjet, then laid Iceman across two of the passenger seats. "You should be safe here," he said. Locking the aircraft behind him with a remote-control signal, he fired his boot-jets and accelerated back toward the lab.

SEARCH AND RESCUE

Hang on a few more seconds, Storm, he thought fervently. *I'm on my way.*

When he reentered the razed and refrigerated laboratory, he found the whole place shaking like it was on top of the San Andreas fault. At least a 3.0 on the Richter scale, he estimated, and his seismic sensors quickly confirmed his ballpark figure. Crystalline ice slides vibrated to pieces, tinkling like a chorus of wind chimes, while whatever test tubes, slides, and petrie dishes had managed to survive the super-powered strife that had laid waste to what looked like a well-designed lab, succumbed at last to the violent tremors rocking the very walls of the science building.

Meanwhile, Storm was still making a valiant stand against superior numbers of Gamma Sentinels. The Harpy-Sentinel had taken to the air to fight the mutant heroine in the cramped airspace of the lab, blocking Storm's lightning bolts with her own radioactive hellbolts. Polarized filters slid into place within Iron Man's eyeslits to shield him from the strobe-like flashes being generated by the two women's respective energy blasts. Granted, the Harpy-Sentinel wasn't really a woman, but if it looked like a harpy, and acted like a harpy, Iron Man was more than willing to take the mythological she-creature on her own terms.

The Doc Samson-Sentinel added to Storm's difficulties by snatching whatever heavy objects were at hand—labstands, stools, computer monitors, even hefty fragments of ice—and throwing them with superhuman strength at the X-Man. So far, Storm's superlative aerial abilities had allowed her to evade both the Harpy's blasts *and* the Doc Samson-Sentinel's projectiles, but Iron Man knew it was only a matter of time before the dual assault overcame Storm's uncanny maneuverability. Even now, as the Golden Avenger came zipping across the lab, a flying file cabinet, propelled by the Doc Samson-Sentinel's synthetic thews, narrowly missed Storm's skull, clipping off a corner of her black, tiara-like headdress.

That was too close for comfort, Iron Man decided, making the Doc Samson-Sentinel his target.

A well-aimed repulsor ray deflected the filing cabinet back at the muscular Adonis with the flowing green hair, who batted it away with a swipe of a larger-than-life hand. The cabinet rebounded into a wall-sized Cray supercomputer that looked like it had already been bored through the middle.

What a waste of good hardware, Iron Man thought. He knew how much a Cray cost. Perhaps, when this was all over, Stark Solutions could offer the Genetic Research Centre a good price on an upgraded computer network.

Leaving the Harpy-Sentinel to Storm, Iron Man rocketed toward the other Gamma Sentinel. *This shouldn't be too hard,* he thought confidently. The real Doc Samson was, when you got down to it, just an overeducated muscleman with a natural punk hairdo and an Old Testament *nom de guerre.* No match for an Avenger, or even an X-Man.

Some of his self-assurance slipped away, though, when Iron Man spotted what the Doc Samson-Sentinel had chosen for his next piece of ammunition. No mere filing cabinet this time, the cylindrical sample containment vault was clearly marked with the universal symbol for highly biohazardous material.

Wait a sec, Iron Man thought, as the Doc Samson-Sentinel raised the dishwasher-sized vault high above his green-haired head, *hadn't the Beast said something, back at the Mansion, about Dr. MacTaggert searching for a cure for the Legacy Virus?*

Instantly, Iron Man activated the airtight seals on his armor, switching to his internal air supply, and elevating all defensive systems to Level 4 readiness, suitable for protection from all known biological organisms.

If that mechanical maniac cracks open that vault, he realized, *lord knows what sort of mutated viruses could escape.*

In theory, the deadly Legacy Virus had no effect on ordinary humans (or Sentinels, for that matter), but Iron Man didn't want to take chances. Furthermore, if an airborne form of the virus got loose, Storm and the other X-Men could be infected.

"Put that vault down—carefully!" Iron Man ordered the Doc Samson-Sentinel, increasing the volume of his vocalizer to be heard over the Hulk-induced earthquake that was suddenly rocking the building. "You don't know what you're doing!"

Unfortunately, the Gamma Sentinel seemed to know *exactly* what he was about. "Targeting: mutant designate: Storm. Calculating necessary trajectory along x-y-z axis, compensating for gravity versus momentum." Before the Avenger could raise a hand to stop him, the Doc Samson-Sentinel catapulted the vault at Storm.

"No!" Iron Man shouted. His navigational computer performed its own calculations, boosting the output of the appropriate boot-jets. The Golden Avenger shot between Storm and the pitched containment vault, which struck him squarely in the chest. Ignoring the impact, he wrapped both arms around the wide metal cylinder, hoping against hope that his chest-beam had cushioned the collision enough to preserve the structural integrity of the vault.

Upon closer inspection, he discovered that the vault had already been coated by a protective layer of solid frost. Iceman's doing, he guessed. The frozen sheath had melted away in places, but that could be easily remedied.

Let it never be said I'm too proud to appropriate another man's good idea, Iron Man thought.

A special rapid-freezing solution spurted from miniature nozzles in his gauntlets, undoing the damage that time and temperature had inflicted on the original icy casing. "That's better," he said, holding onto the vault with both arms. Now where the devil was he supposed to put the blasted thing?

He couldn't leave Storm alone against two Gamma Sentinels again. That would be pushing their luck too much. Instead, he stayed where he was, hovering several feet above the slush, and tossed the vault out through the window to the bay below. Powerful servomotors within his armor amplified the force of his throw, so that the ice-packed container easily cleared the narrow strip of land between the building and the cliff, as well as the beach and docks below, splashing at last into the sea, where the cold northern waters would surely keep the icy seal intact—at least until Iron Man had a chance to retrieve the vault later.

Then a searing blast of atomic heat caught him by surprise, scorching him even through multiple layers of armor and protective insulation. *Blast!* he thought, cursing himself for his carelessness. *I forgot about the Harpy-Sentinel.*

It seemed the winged bird-woman had not limited herself (itself?) to the division of labor that Iron Man had unilaterally drawn up among the combatants, switching her murderous attentions from Storm to Iron Man while the Avenger's concentration was elsewhere. Iron Man felt like he was being roasted alive inside his armor, a situation made decidedly worse by the fact that he had just expelled most of his primary coolant in the course of refreezing the vault of viruses. Already he could feel first-degree burns reddening his skin.

Fortunately, Storm was alert to the Harpy-Sentinel's intentions even if Iron Man had not been. A miraculous gust of wind caught the Harpy-Sentinel beneath her emerald wings, flinging her unwillingly to the opposite end of the lab. The potent zephyr also carried away much of the hellbolt's unbearable heat. The sudden cessation of the scalding radioactive hellfire, followed by the sweet relief of that cooling breeze, made for some of the best air conditioning Tony Stark had ever experienced.

I owe you one, lady, he thought gratefully.

He could think of no better way to pay Storm back than by taking care of the Samson-Sentinel, permanently. The tempest-taming X-Man had proved she could steal the wind from the Harpy-Sentinel's wings; the Doc Samson Gamma Sentinel was *his* job.

He raised his gauntlets, palms up, and targeted his pulse bolts at the long-haired LMD, who had already torn out another chunk of the vivisected Cray to use as a missile. Iron Man wasn't worried; at this range, his plasma pulses, perhaps the most devastating weapon in his armor's arsenal, would reduce the rampaging robot to a pile of nuts and bolts.

"Have no fear, Doc Samson is here!" the Gamma Sentinel bragged unconvincingly.

Not for much longer, Iron Man thought, smiling grimly beneath his faceplate. Yet before he could discharge the devastating pulse bolts, the wreckage-littered floor of the lab exploded between Iron Man and his target, as a monstrous green giant, straddled by Wolverine in his blue-and-yellow costume, blasted through the lab like a Saturn rocket heading for orbit. The leaping Hulk (or was it the Hulk-Sentinel?), along with his luckless rider, tore through the ceiling on their way to the roof three stories above, leaving an open, raggedy-edged shaft that stretched the entire height of the building. In the snowy battleground the lab had become, a yawning pit now divided the chamber in twain.

The unexpected force of the Hulk's passage sent Iron Man tumbling out of control, away from the Gamma Sentinel he had meant to blow to pieces. The Doc Samson-Sentinel recovered from the eruption faster than Iron Man, vaulting over the beckoning pit with ease and racing across the floor beneath his spinning armored adversary. By the time Iron Man restabilized his flight controls, the Doc Samson-Sentinel was waiting for him. Sensor beams shone from the Gamma Sentinel's eyes, spotlighting Iron Man and scanning his armor for weaknesses. "Analysis: Sophisticated exoskeleton housing ordinary human genotype. Tesselated armor shielding, consisting primarily of epitaxially deposited diamond and high temperature enamel over tiles of crystallized iron, with automated command and communication functions via gallium arsenide microcircuitry. Internal power generation and storage capabilities." The Doc Samson-Sentinel sounded undeterred by the varied and abundant attributes of Iron Man's state-of-the-art metal suit. "Adapting required offensive functions."

Oops, Iron Man thought. Beneath the impeccably reproduced facade of Leonard Samson, super-strong shrink, lay concealed technological resources and capabilities he could only guess at. Judging from those unexpected sensor beams, there was more to the Gamma Sentinel than met the eye.

For now, though, this "Doc Samson" relied on his powerful legs to spring at the airborne Avenger. Brawny hands captured Iron Man and dragged him down to the floor. His boot-jets scorched the ice-cold tiles, but the Doc Samson-Sentinel held Iron Man down, keeping him from blasting off again. Iron Man struggled to break free, only to find that the anthropomorphic powerhouse's brute strength was more than a match for his armor's muscle-enhancing servomotors. What's worse, he could no longer fire his pulse bolts at the Gamma Sentinel, not at this close range. The resulting explosion would obliterate him as much as the Doc Samson-Sentinel.

Then something alarming happened. The Doc Samson-Sentinel's splayed fingers magnetically adhered to Iron Man's shoulder assemblies—and began draining the power from his armor! Warning displays, projected directly onto his retinas, charted a catastrophic drain in his energy reserves. Auxiliary systems began to shut down, redirecting available electricity to primary functions, including life support and propulsion, but, at this rate, his entire suit would be out of power in less than a minute. Thinking quickly, Iron Man opened the air intake valves in his mouthpiece while he still could, before he found himself suffocating inside the sealed armor. *This could be bad,* he thought.

"Implementing conductive neutralization of obstacle designate: Iron Man," the Sentinel announced. "Power transfer 78.101 percent complete."

The deadpan recitation only confirmed what Iron Man's own internal monitors reported. At this point, the Golden Avenger doubted he could light a candle, let alone fire a repulsor ray. His armor was rapidly becoming a customized prison as the motors that gave him mobility whirred to a stop. Luckily, there was a convenient alternative power source available—if he could just get her attention.

"Storm!" he shouted. With the mike in his vocalizer out of juice, he had to rely on Tony Stark's natural lung power to be heard. Thankfully, the ear-splitting tremors had subsided with the Hulk's dynamic exit from below. "I need a boost, pronto! You know what to do. You did it before, at Niagara Falls!"

High in the air, the elemental X-Man understood. Without question or hesitation, she released her lightning, not at the Doc Samson-Sentinel but at Iron Man. The rampant electricity recharged his armor in an instant, firing up his dormant systems and leaving him with power to spare.

That's the ticket! Iron Man thought exuberantly. *I'm back in the game.*

He decided to give the Doc Samson-Sentinel a taste of his own medicine. Activating the electromagnetic energy conversion layer beneath the surface of his armor, and inverting the polarity of his protective force field, Iron Man reversed the conductivity between himself and the malignant facsimile of Doc Samson. Streaming electrons flowed out of the Gamma Sentinel and into the Avenger's armor, increasing the hero's strength and endurance. "Danger!" the Doc Samson-Sentinel's voice blurted. "Experiencing critical power loss. Unable to arrest battery depletion. Available reserves at 29.866 percent and falling—"

The Gamma Sentinel's deceptively human-looking hands attempted to disengage from Iron Man's armor, but gleaming crimson gauntlets locked onto the Doc Samson-Sentinel's wrists, stopping the robot from breaking the connection. With the combined energy of both Storm's majestic lightning *and* the Doc Samson-Sentinel charging through his circuitry, Iron Man easily overcame the gamma-powered mechanoid's efforts to escape. He leeched every volt of electricity from his enemy, until the once-powerful Gamma Sentinel was reduced to a statue of Doc Samson. Then, releasing the robot's wrists, he blasted the inert Sentinel with his chest-beam once for good measure. The repulsor ray knocked the Samson-Sentinel onto his back and shredded his stylish red vest.

Let's hear for good, old-fashioned, human teamwork, he thought. Between the two of them, he and Storm had thrown at least one Gamma Sentinel on the scrap heap.

A high-pitched squawk reminded him that the Harpy-

Sentinel remained to be dealt with. Turning his gaze upward, he discovered that Storm's galvanic intervention on his behalf had apparently left her vulnerable to a physical attack by the synthetic bird-woman. Emerald wings flapping furiously, the Harpy-Sentinel had come up on Storm from behind, clawing the X-Man's bare midriff with her bird-like talons while one of Betty Banner's shapely arms was crooked around Storm's throat, leaving her other hand free to scratch at the mutant heroine's face. Storm twisted her neck, trying to keep the Harpy-Sentinel's dark green nails away from her eyes, and flailed her arms and legs, letting the Harpy-Sentinel's wings alone bear both their weight. Wind and rain pelted mutant and Gamma Sentinel alike, but Storm's meteorological assault failed to shake the Harpy-Sentinel free from her prey. "Iron Man!" she cried out, even as the Harpy-Sentinel's prying fingers tugged at her lips. "Your assistance is required!"

One Avenger, at your service, he thought. The hovering robot, holding Storm in front of her like a living shield, presented a difficult target, but Iron Man had spent years fine-tuning his armor's tracking technology. Letting his on-line automated targeting system take careful aim, double-checking the correct coordinates via both laser and sonar sighting mechanisms, he fired a high-intensity laser beam with pinpoint accuracy, nailing the Harpy-Sentinel between the eyes. The incandescent beam burned through the Gamma Sentinel's camouflaged cranium with surgical precision, giving it a cybernetic lobotomy.

At once, the robot released Storm, who began to plummet precipitously. Less than a meter above the floor, however, a hastily-summoned wind came to her rescue, so that, moments later, she was able to spiral gracefully downward under her own power, landing softly upon the floor next to Iron Man. The Harpy-Sentinel, on the other hand, crashed into a half-melted snowdrift, where it jerked spasmodically for a few seconds before ceasing to move at all.

"A most satisfactory outcome," Storm commented, looking from the grounded Harpy-Sentinel to the immobile replica of Doc Samson. Four parallel scratches streaked her mahogany cheek but did not appear to be serious. Ditto for a few shallow gashes in her side, joining the minor cuts and abrasions she received during their tussle at Niagara Falls.

Am I the only superhero, he thought, *who actually thinks to wear armor to these rhubarbs?* Still, thanks to the Harpy-Sentinel's hellbolts, his burnt skin felt raw and sore beneath his armor, like he'd spent the whole day at Coney Island without a drop of sunscreen. *Thank goodness I didn't end up well done.*

"We make a good team," he said, hoping that Banner and Wolverine were working together as effectively.

"So it appears," she agreed. She glanced at the broken window and twisted metal shutters. "Bobby and Moira?"

"Safely tucked away in the quinjet." He instructed his armor to remind him about the sunken viruses before he left the island. It occurred to him that the very individual who had summoned them to Scotland remained among the missing. "The question is . . . ," he began.

Storm finished the sentence for him. ". . . where is Nightcrawler?"

At first, all Kurt heard was heavy footprints coming down the hall. Lying on his side upon the carpeted floor of the unoccupied containment cell, Nightcrawler allowed himself to hope that help was on the way. His right ankle still throbbed where that counterfeit Abomination had crushed his bones and the rest of him didn't feel too well either.

It could be Colossus or the Beast, he thought optimistically. He had managed to send out an SOS, after all, before that mechanical Hulk caught up with him. The monster's mighty fists had left him with a pounding headache and a ringing in his ears, but he figured he had gotten off lucky. *Good thing these Sentinels wanted me alive.*

"Hello?" he called out, although his throat was dry and parched. "*Vas is das?* Is anybody there?"

The footsteps, too heavy to be any X-Man but Colossus, came closer. Chances were, it was just another bulky Sentinel, but Nightcrawler was not the sort to abandon hope. Rocking back and forth, his arms, legs, and tail tightly wrapped by the ersatz Hulk's snare, he managed to roll over onto his back. Alas, he discovered, he was still in no position to see who was at the door. It was always possible, he supposed, that the thunderous tread had drowned out the footsteps of less ponderous visitors. "Moira? Bobby? Is that you?"

An ominous silence stretched on for longer than he liked, and it occurred to Nightcrawler that the shadowy confines of the cell would render him completely invisible to anyone in the corridor outside. *Is that a good thing or a bad thing?* he wondered.

Just as he was about to speak again, the lights came on overhead, blinding him. Then he heard the armored door of the cell fly open. A mountainous shadow fell over him, turning him invisible once more, until a powerful hand seized him by the collar and yanked him roughly off the floor.

"Aiee!—*Nein!*" he shouted, the sudden movement jarring his fractured ankle. His bound legs, squeezed tightly together by his restraints, dangled above the floor while the massive arms, which almost certainly did *not* belong to his dear friend Colossus, turned him around so that he ended up face-to-face with an all-too-familiar jade countenance.

The Hulk. Again.

"*Ach*, so it's you, *Herr* Sentinel." Nightcrawler tried to keep the disappointment, to say nothing of the pain, from his voice. He was determined to maintain a brazen demeanor to the end, in the best swashbuckling tradition, yet couldn't help wondering what had brought the mechanical monster back to the very cell the Sentinel had personally tossed Kurt into mere hours before. Was he now to be transported to an even more heinous captivity, or was a cursory execution on the agenda? *Farewell, sweet world,* he thought grandly, just in case. *'Tis a far, far better thing I do—*

"You got that wrong, elf," the great green troglodyte informed him brusquely. His hot breath hit Kurt like an open furnace. "I ain't no cheap imitation. I'm the real McCoy."

Luminous yellow eyes widened. The real Hulk? *Here?* Nightcrawler was dumbfounded; he couldn't imagine what might have brought the original gamma-spawned goliath to Muir Island. If this was true, however, then it was, as the Americans were prone to say, a whole new ball game.

"What?" he asked, flabbergasted, the pulsing ache in his ankle forgotten in the excitement of the moment. "How?" He looked up at the ceiling, thinking at once of the friends he had left behind three stories above. "Moira and Bobby?"

But the Hulk wasn't interested in answering Nightcrawler's questions. "Let's go," he said. "I got things to do." Tucking the tightly-wrapped X-Man under his arm like a load of groceries, he stepped out of the cell and marched down the corridor to the far end of the hall. Light from the floor above filtered down through a haze of drifting dust and plaster. "*Mein gott,*" Nightcrawler gasped at the destruction, catching a glimpse of the gaping breach in the ceiling. *What have I missed?*

Every lumbering step the Hulk took sent a fresh pang of agony through Nightcrawler's ankle. The pain would even be worse, he thought, were his legs not tightly bound together, turning his unfractured leg into a splint of sorts. "Please, *Herr* Hulk," he entreated. "A little more gently, if you please. My right ankle, I'm afraid it is broken."

"Sorry, elf," the Hulk replied gruffly. He gazed speculatively up through the gap in the ceiling. "Last I saw, your pal Wolverine was tacklin' that cast-iron copy of me on the roof, so that's where we're goin' next." He squatted down on his powerful legs, preparing to jump.

"Wait!" Nightcrawler cried out in alarm. "My ankle!"

The Hulk ignored him, springing into the air. A short, excruciating leap brought them out of the basement onto the ground floor. Nightcrawler bit down on his lip, fighting back waves of nausea; the last thing he wanted to do was vomit over the ill-tempered man-brute's feet. His vision blurred momentarily, then came back into focus. Kurt realized he was in shock, and very close to passing out.

Wolverine? he thought, as the Hulk's remark sunk in at last. *Wolverine is here, too?* It seemed as though his long-distance SOS had been well and truly answered. *What about the rest of the X-Men? Are they here also?*

The Hulk gave him no time to recover from that first, jolting jump. Directly overhead, a greater chasm stretched all the way from the ground floor to the roof. "Hold on to your stomach," the jade goliath said by way of warning, then cleared six stories in a single bound. He landed heavily onto the roof of the rectangular building, his bare feet smacking soundly against the granite floor of the observation deck. He grabbed Nightcrawler by the collar again and, with one swift motion, ripped the metallic netting off the dazed mutant's body. "There," he rumbled. "You're on your own now."

He casually dropped Nightcrawler to the rooftop. Kurt landed on both feet, but his injured leg would not support his weight and he fell to his knees, gasping for breath. The world blurred again, growing dark around the periphery of his vision, but he held onto consciousness through sheer willpower. He couldn't give out now, not until he knew Moira and Bobby were safe. *"Unglaublich!"* he whispered. The pain and fatigue were almost overwhelming.

Clutching his aching ankle with both hands, he looked up to see the Hulk flying away from the building, brilliant orange gouts of flame shooting from the soles of his feet. No, wait, he realized groggily; that couldn't be the Hulk, that had to be the Gamma Sentinel disguised as the Hulk, taking advantage of a hitherto-concealed mode of transportation.

The jet-propelled Gamma Sentinel rapidly disappeared into the horizon, where the starry sky met the moonlit surface of the Atlantic. Returning his gaze to the rooftop, he saw the real Hulk shouting at Wolverine, who was standing at the edge of the observation deck staring out at the sky into which the counterfeit Hulk had vanished. Judging from the greenish saliva spraying from the real Hulk's enormous jaws, the towering monster was not at all happy about this latest turn of events. "I can't believe it!" he bellowed at Logan. "You let him escape!"

Wolverine shrugged, unintimidated by the irate ogre. "Sorry, bub," he said, walking away from the guardrail around the perimeter of the observation deck. A crumpled satellite dish lay nearby, folded over like a crepe. "He got away." He retracted his claws with a decisive *snikt*. "It happens."

Nightcrawler had to admit he was a little startled too. Logan let a bad guy get away? That wasn't like him. Still,

SEARCH AND RESCUE

Kurt was in too much pain to obsess over Wolverine's apparent lapse. "Excuse me, *mein freunds,*" he called out. Two heads, one masked, one chartreuse, turned in his direction. "If it's not too much trouble, could someone kindly take a look at my ankle? And perhaps inform me *vas* in the world is going on?"

Chapter Eight

The Columbia Icefields in Alberta, Canada, are one of the largest accumulations of ice and snow outside the Arctic, covering nearly four hundred square miles in area. The last enduring remnant of an ice age that had covered most of Canada some twenty thousand years ago, the huge frozen mass, over a thousand feet thick at points, had carved out three valleys via a trio of conjoined glaciers.

Hard to imagine that anyone could live here, Cyclops considered, *let alone an entire underground city.*

Yet the Hulk had sworn, in his incorrigibly ill-tempered fashion, that just such a city had been erected by the Leader only a few years ago, shortly before the malevolent mastermind's apparent death. Cyclops glanced out the window of a chartered SnoCoach at a snowy plain riddled with deep blue crevasses. The customized bus rolled across the icefield on large, balloon-like wheels. Could it be, the somber X-Man wondered, that Rogue and the Scarlet Witch were somewhere beneath them at this very moment? *Let's hope so,* he thought fervently; otherwise, they had come a long way on a wild-goose chase.

Flying west from New York had gained them a few more hours of daylight. The sun had not yet set behind the Canadian Rockies, casting a twilight glow over the snow. Nevertheless, Captain America, behind the wheel of the SnoCoach, switched on the vehicle's headlights, the better to watch out for treacherous cracks and crevices in the ice. Unwilling to risk the Blackbird by landing upon ice of uncertain stability, Cyclops had parked the X-Men's aircraft several miles away in Jasper National Park. He envied the ease with which Cap's Avengers I.D. had allowed them to commandeer the tourist coach for the rest of their journey.

If the X-Men tried that, they'd probably sic a pack of Mounties on us, Cyclops mused. Working alongside the Avengers felt like traveling first-class instead of steerage, with all the special privileges and amenities that entailed.

The third member of their party, the Vision, flew on ahead of them, searching for a hidden entrance to the Leader's buried city. Dr. Banner had provided the android Avenger with a specific set of coordinates, but Cyclops was impressed that the Vision could navigate at all amidst this glacial desolation, even with the looming presence of Mount Athabasca to use as a landmark. Contemplating their surroundings from the heated interior of the coach, it was easy to imagine that they were at the South Pole instead, approaching the cavernous tunnels that led to the Savage Land.

I hope Jean is okay, Cyclops thought, taking a moment to think about his absent wife. He reminded himself that Phoenix was perfectly capable of defending herself from any irate dinosaurs or cavemen.

The snowbound landscape outside also reminded him of Iceman, currently menaced by Sentinels in Scotland, along with Moira and Nightcrawler. Had Storm and her team come to their rescue yet? Muir Island was so many time zones away that Cyclops found it hard to calculate when the Avengers' quinjet would have delivered its reinforcements to the island.

"Almost there," Captain America announced from the driver's seat, interrupting the X-Man's calculations. The

SnoCoach came to a halt somewhere astride the Athabasca Glacier, a few yards away from a deep crevasse that stretched across their path for at least a mile or so. From where Cyclops was sitting, this gap in the ice looked no different from any of a dozen others they had passed. Could they be sure this was the right place?

Pulling on fleece-filled parkas over their respective uniforms, Cap and Cyclops disembarked from the bus and trudged through the snow to the edge of the ravine, where the Vision patiently waited for them. Cyclops could not help noticing that the immaterial synthezoid left no tracks in the snow, unlike him and Captain America. "According to Dr. Banner," the Vision reported, "the entrance to Freehold lies through this trail, ingeniously camouflaged as a natural fault in the glacier. A preliminary reconnaissance indicates that the crevasse is indeed reinforced with artificial support beams constructed of super-hard translucent plastic."

"Good work," Captain America said to his teammate. His hot breath fogged the frigid air. With no room beneath his parka for his shield, Cap carried the concave steel discus in his right hand.

Cyclops peered over the edge of the ravine. He spied a sloping pathway starting at about a hundred feet below the surface of the icefield. *Good thing Storm joined the expedition to Scotland instead,* he reflected; her claustrophobia would have made this trek difficult for her. The idea of dropping down into that deep fissure gave him the creeps and he didn't have any particular problem with enclosed spaces. *I just hope the Vision is right about those concealed support beams. I wouldn't want this thing closing up on me before we find the Leader's former residence,* he thought.

"Let me go first," he volunteered. Cybernetic controls

in his visor lifted the ruby quartz lens just a fraction, and he used his eyebeams with careful precision, chiseling out a series of handholds and footholds in the icy wall of the crevasse. Once that task was finished, he stepped over the edge of the ravine and swiftly climbed down to the top of the inclined pathway.

Not quite as nimbly as the Beast, perhaps, he graded himself, *but good enough, I guess.*

"Watch your step," he called to Captain America as the Star-Spangled Avenger began his own descent, tossing his shield to the Vision before starting down. "It's slippery down here."

It was cold, too. Flanked by rising walls of ice that seemed to suck the heat from his body, Cyclops rubbed his hands together. Despite his yellow gloves, his fingertips were already starting to feel as numb as his toes. He pulled the hood of the parka over his ears, and found himself hoping that the Leader's so-called city came complete with central heating. Captain America dropped lightly onto the ice behind Cyclops, then signaled the Vision to throw him the shield, which he caught one-handed on the first try.

The Vision had no need for a parka, of course, nor for Cyclops' improvised ladder. He merely floated silently to the floor of the ravine. "The frozen surface of the pathway indeed appears conducive to slips and other mishaps," he confirmed upon landing. He increased his mass so that his yellow boots sank deeply into the packed ice and snow. "I recommend that you both walk in my footsteps to avoid accidents."

Stepping into the android's deep tracks proved a good idea, and the trio of heroes descended the slope much faster and less precariously than they might have otherwise. The trail soon led, however, to an apparent dead end: a sheer wall of blue ice stretching nearly five hundred feet above their heads.

Now what? Cyclops wondered, growing increasingly cold and impatient. *I hope we don't find Rogue and Wanda frozen in a glacier somewhere.* Rogue might be invulnerable enough to survive such an ordeal, but he had his doubts about the Scarlet Witch.

"Vision?" Captain America asked.

The synthezoid required no further instruction. Turning intangible once more, he passed through the solid ice, disappearing from sight. Mere seconds later, he reemerged from the face of the frozen wall. "Dr. Banner's directions were correct," he reported. "There is an artificial tunnel continuing downward beyond this camouflaged barrier, which consists of a layer of real ice over a glazed plastic gate. By my estimation, the entire barrier is approximately 15.62 inches thick."

"Sounds like we've come to the right place," Cap said. "In theory, there should be some sort of concealed locking mechanism, unless the whole operation is automated, in which case the gate may be waiting for a verbal password." He glanced over his shoulder at the way they'd came. "The Leader certainly didn't make it easy for people to find their way here."

"When you have access to trans-mat technology," Cyclops pointed out, "you don't really need a driveway or front door. Besides, I imagine he didn't want to encourage visitors." He stepped ahead of the two Avengers. "Let me ring the doorbell."

Crimson energy poured from eyes, merging to form a single beam that smashed through fifteen-plus inches of reinforced ice and plastic like an incandescent battering ram. Stepping beside him, the Vision added his own thermoscopic beams to the endeavor, melting away any chunks of ice that collapsed onto the path before them. The combination of extreme heat and concussive force quickly exposed the man-made tunnel beyond. Cyclops stepped off the slick surface at the bottom of the crevasse and onto a paved walkway that sloped away into the distance. A dusting of snow fell upon his hood and shoulders as he passed beneath the blasted entrance of the tunnel. Overhead lights, perhaps activated by pressure-sensitive pads in the pavement, came on automatically.

Stealth, they had all decided on the way to the icefield, was not an issue here. If the Leader was as near-omniscient as his reputation would have it, then he doubtless already knew they were here. And if, against all expectations, he really was dead, then he wasn't likely to object to their forced entry.

While the Vision soared above their heads, just beneath the curved ceiling of the tunnel, Cap and Cyclops jogged downhill, pacing each other. The further they descended, the warmer the tunnel became and soon the two heroes gratefully discarded their parkas, although Captain America kept his shield at hand rather than strap it onto his back. Like Cyclops, he obviously wanted to be ready for anything.

By the time they reached the end of the tunnel, Cyclops guessed that they were well below the icefield. He was surprised therefore when he ran out from beneath the overhanging ceiling and saw a clear night sky above him.

How is that possible? he wondered; they had to be hundreds of feet below the glacier at this point. He could tell by Captain America's startled expression that the veteran Avenger was puzzled as well.

Closer inspection, however, revealed that the starry indigo sky was nothing more than a fraud, an elaborate and highly realistic simulation, complete with shining crescent moon, installed upon the underside of an immense, city-sized dome.

Shades of The Truman Show, Cyclops thought; Jean had dragged him to that movie on one of her periodic campaigns to get him to relax. Like Jim Carrey, he felt as though he had just stepped onto the world's largest soundstage. The illusion was convincing enough that it might even have fooled Storm's claustrophobia.

Beneath the phony sky, a shimmering city rose toward the purely decorative stars. Cyclops spotted skyscrapers, monorails, even what appeared to be a full-sized cathedral, adorned with lavish stained-glass windows. Streetlights, posted at regular intervals, supplemented the cool radiance of the counterfeit stars and moon. The path through the tunnel opened out onto a main thoroughfare that led to the very heart of the city: an open plaza spread out around a central fountain. Sparkling water, no doubt melted from the glacier above, sprayed fifty feet in the air, then cascaded down into a foaming pool surrounded by low marble steps. No litter or graffiti marred the pristine and elegant design of the plaza, nor any other visible part of the city. The streets and buildings were all spotless and in good repair. At first glance, the entire city looked remarkably clean, civilized—and empty?

"Where are all the people?" Cap asked, voicing the same question that Cyclops was silently asking. According to Banner, Freehold was populated by hundreds of refugees from the outside world, many of them suffering from cancer or radiation poisoning. Cyclops had to assume that the Leader had possessed his own nefarious reasons for creating this haven; still, he could think of worse places to live. In some ways, Freehold reminded Cyclops of Avalon, the orbital sanctuary Magneto created for his mutant followers. Like Avalon, Freehold seemed proof that even the most ambitious and power-hungry of would-be conquerors could sometimes create an oasis of peace and beauty, no matter how unworthy their intentions.

"Listen," Captain America said. "I hear something, I think. An alert—about us."

Cyclops heard it, too, but not with his ears. The announcement came not from any conventional loudspeaker, but via some manner of telepathic public address system. He heard an unfamiliar voice inside his head, the same way he had so often communicated with Jean or Professor X.

"Attention, citizens of Freehold," the voice commanded. "Strangers from the outside world have entered our city, but there is no cause for alarm. All non-powered citizens are requested to stay indoors until further notice. The Riot Squad is on the way."

"Correct that," a younger voice declared, the old-fashioned way. "The Riot Squad is here!"

Cyclops turned toward the source of the second voice. Four unusual figures stood between the three heroes and the fountain plaza, having apparently materialized out of thin air, thanks to the Leader's trans-mat beams. Three of the newcomers bore the unmistakable evidence of gamma mutation: complexions and tresses colored in varying shades of green. The fourth was a black man, whose entire body seemed encased in a craggy block of brownish-gray stone, so that only his face could be seen through an aperture in the levitating boulder. He hovered in his granite shell a few feet above the marble steps leading down into the plaza.

That has *to be Rock,* Cyclops deduced without too much difficulty. Banner had briefed the X-Men and the Avengers on the so-called Riot Squad, Freehold's own team of super-powered defenders, created by the Leader through the ruthless expedient of exploding a stolen gamma bomb in the middle of a small city in Arizona. Thousands had died, but a select few had survived, endowed with a variety of gamma-spawned traits and abilities; those lucky (?) survivors had been recruited by the Leader to fight for Freehold against such foes as the Hulk. According to Banner, the Riot Squad's powers were not to be underestimated.

"We mean you no harm," Captain America insisted, lowering his shield. "All we want is information."

"Is that why you smashed your way in here?" challenged the same young man who had spoken earlier, whom Cyclops identified as Hotshot. He looked like he couldn't be more than nineteen years old, tops, and wore a dark purple uniform identical in hue to his two nonpetrified teammates. His pale green hair, a few shades lighter than his jade-colored skin, was neatly cut above his ears. His youthful appearance and brash attitude reminded Cyclops of the X-Men's earliest days, when they were just a bunch of overenthusiastic kids. *He even looks a bit like Bobby did then,* Cyclops thought, *minus the ice, that is.*

"We don't much care for uninvited visitors here in Freehold. They've never brought us anything but trouble," said Hotshot.

"I don't know, Lou," said the attractive young woman at his side. She looked even less mature than Hotshot, which might be why she called herself Jailbait. Cyclops shook his head as he remembered her unlikely appellation; *super hero codenames just aren't what they used to be,* he thought.

Dark green tresses, the color of tropical ferns, fell to her shoulders, while her purple uniform could have passed for a supermodel's swimsuit. "Maybe you shouldn't be talking to him like that. I mean, it's *Captain America,*" she said, breathing the name in an awestruck hush.

Hotshot was considerably less impressed by Cap's status

as a living legend. "So what?" he countered bitterly. "Captain America, the Avengers, the Fantastic Four... none of them stopped the Leader from nuking Middletown, killing all our friends and family—and turning us into freaks." He glared at Cap angrily, as if daring the Avenger to refute his accusation. "We're not Americans anymore, Jess. We have a new home, Freehold, and we're not about to let anybody walk all over us again!" Hotshot eyed them skeptically. "Besides, how do we even know that he *is* Captain America? Probably just another Hydra trick; they want to steal our technology again, force us to work for them."

Sounds like these kids have seen some rough times, Cyclops thought. It was a pointed reminder that branded-at-birth mutants weren't the only people whom life had dealt a tough hand. He decided to let Captain America continue as the spokesman for their joint expedition; despite Hotshot's hostility, Cap still presented a more trustworthy appearance than either a fire-eyed mutant outlaw or a spooky android.

"I sympathize with your loss," Captain America said gently. "What happened to Middletown was a terrible tragedy. But you have to believe me when I tell you that we wouldn't disturb you or your city unless it was a matter of life and death." He held his shield at his side, in a non-threatening fashion. "We come in peace, I promise you that."

The fourth and final member of the Riot Squad answered Cap not with verbal threats or accusations, but with a deep-throated roar like a bull gorilla's. Ogress, as she was now known, was the biggest woman Cyclops had ever seen, if she could still be called a woman. She was taller than the Hulk or Colossus, and her gigantic muscles bulged with power and menace. Tufts of shaggy emerald fur bristled along her arms, and her misshapen face made her look like the Missing Link; beady green eyes glowered from beneath sloping brows, while her prognathous jaw was crammed with oversized yellow incisors. Lacking anything resembling a neck, her elephantine skull merged with her massive shoulders, which strained the overstressed fabric of her king-sized purple uniform. Her matted, unkempt mane looked like it hadn't been combed since the day she first came to Freehold.

According to Banner, this grotesque, growling giantess had once been a polished and articulate attorney. If so, Cyclops observed, little trace of that prior existence remained in the Ogress that now faced them across the deserted thoroughfare. *That poor woman,* he thought; her monstrous transformation made Banner's look like a makeover.

"Maybe we don't care about your stupid problems," Rock said harshly, a mean-spirited sneer upon his face. Unlike his teammates, he had not been caught in the gamma blast that destroyed Middletown; instead, Samuel John La Roquette was a disgraced former college professor and Hulkbuster, whom the Leader had surgically modified through his own insidious super-science. He had thrown his lot in with the Riot Squad even before the Leader was presumed dead. "You may be big shot super-heroes up top, but down here we're bigger than the Avengers and the Fantastic Four put together, and, like Hotshot said, we don't stand for surprise visits."

Jagged spikes, like stalactites, sprouted suddenly from the great stony mass enclosing Rock, demonstrating his Leader-given ability to control the shape of his granite shell. Before Captain America could argue the heroes' case any further, Rock charged the heroic Avenger, scooting over the pavement like some sort of mineralogical hovercraft, his foot-long spikes aimed straight at Cap.

SEARCH AND RESCUE

"Wait!" Jailbait called out. "Maybe this isn't a good idea!" Her words held little sway over her less peaceable teammates, however, as both Hotshot and Ogress took Rock's preemptive strike as their signal to rush into battle. "Oh, drat!" the green-skinned teenager cursed and bit her lip. She hurried after her comrades, apparently giving in to the inevitable.

Cyclops knew just how she felt. *Here we go again,* he thought, pinpointing Rock with his visor. *Another clash of titans. Another senseless fight...*

Captain America brought up his shield just in time to avoid being impaled upon Rock's spiky exterior. The shield, composed of an unbreakable alloy unlike any on Earth, blunted the jagged points of the spikes, but the force of the human boulder's charge knocked Cap flat on his back. "Stop this!" he called out as he fell, stubbornly determined to prevent any unnecessary violence. "We don't have to fight each other."

"You're wasting your breath," Rock replied. He retracted his stony spears, then turned the bottom of his shell into an enormous hammer, with which he began pounding away at Captain America's shield. The indomitable shield resisted the blows, but the impact of each hammer strike jarred Cap to the bone. "I didn't like you self-righteous hero types calling the shots back when I worked for the Feds, and I like you even less now. This is our city—ours!—and nobody's taking that away from us, not even Captain God-Bless-America!"

We don't want your city, Cap thought, grunting as another blow from the hammer squashed him between his shield and the pavement, but it seemed that Rock didn't want to hear that.

All right then, he decided with steely resolve. *Nobody*

can say we didn't try to do this the peaceful way.

He counted the seconds between each hammer strike, then, with perfect timing, rolled out of the way during the pause between blows. The hammer came swinging after him, but Cap was already halfway to his feet by the time he blocked Rock's latest attack with his shield. The red-white-and-blue discus rang like a bell beneath the hammer, yet its patriotically-painted surface was not even scratched.

"What the devil is that thing made of?" Rock complained, frustration evident in his voice. "I'm the Rock. I'm the hardest thing there is!"

You may be wrong there, friend, Captain America thought, proud of the lost wartime ingenuity that created his decades-old weapon. Not even the Hulk's vast strength, nor Wolverine's adamantium claws, had overcome his shield's durability. He had no reason to expect that Rock's granite appendages would fare any better. *Not that Rock himself won't be a tough foe to bring down*, he reminded himself; apparently the shape-changing Squad member had given the Hulk a run for his money on a couple of occasions.

Cap readied himself for Rock's next move, while watching carefully for a chance to go on the offensive. Adrenalin flooded his body, mixing with the Super-Soldier Formula in his blood and raising all his well-honed reflexes to peak performance levels. But before Rock could strike again, a crimson beam blindsided the monolithic assailant, sending his rocky form tumbling head over hammer. Cap's eyes followed the luminous red beam back to its obvious origin: Cyclops's open visor. "Thanks for the assist, mister," he called to the X-Man.

"No problem," Cyclops stated, taking the fight to Rock, and Cap paused to take a breath before diving back into the fray. Then a red-hot fireball slammed into his shoulder.

What in blazes—? He clutched his shoulder with his free hand. *That smarts,* he thought, wincing. *I don't want to take many more of those if I can help it.*

Looking away from Rock and Cyclops, Cap saw Hotshot running toward him, with Jailbait chasing after him. *In my day,* he thought, *Jailbait was not a name any young woman would voluntarily assume for herself.* Then again, things had changed a lot since the Forties. . . .

"You should have left when you had the chance!" Hotshot shouted angrily. Apparently his temper was just as fiery as his codename, not to mention his trademark fireballs. A volcanic glow suffused his palm as another burning projectile formed within his grip.

Just like the Human Torch, Cap noted.

"Listen, son," he tried again, keeping one eye on the nascent fireball and another on Hotshot's expression. He didn't think the youth was evil at heart, just cocky and quick to fight, like many other boys his age.

Hawkeye used to be the same way, Cap thought, recalling many dustups with the Avengers' boisterous bowman before he had picked up a little hardwon maturity. Cap felt inclined to give Hotshot the same benefit of the doubt he had always given Hawkeye. "Think again before you do anything you might regret later. You don't want to do this," Cap said

"Oh yeah? You don't have the slightest idea what I want. You don't belong here!" Hotshot shot back, punctuating his retort with a flying fireball that came whizzing through the air at Cap.

The fireball exploded against Cap's shield in a shower of bright red sparks. "Maybe not," he agreed, running to meet Hotshot, "but you ought to learn not to shoot first and ask questions later, especially when you're not under attack." A third fireball came at his legs, but Cap deftly hurdled the sizzling globe which landed on the pavement behind him, scorching it. "That's three misses in three pitches," Cap pointed out. "If I were you, son, I'd think twice about trying out for the Yankees just yet."

Cap came within an arm's length of the green-skinned pyrokinetic. "This is no game," Hotshot sputtered indignantly and swung a glowing fist at Captain America's head as it rose above the outer rim of the shield. "I'm fighting for my city!"

The Avenger easily parried the punch with his shield; despite the youth's gamma-induced energy powers, he was no Joe Louis. "That's an admirable sentiment," Cap said, even as he rammed his fist into the boy's mid-section. He took care to pull his punch; he didn't want to batter Hotshot into unconsciousness, just knock the wind out of him. "First, though, you need to learn *when* to fight."

Dazed, Hotshot lay sprawled on the marble steps of the plaza. His fingers sparked like firecrackers as he blinked his blurry eyes and tried to shake the fogginess from his head. "Just a lucky punch," he gasped defiantly. "Just give me a sec, and we'll see who's got a lot to learn."

The kid's got spunk, Cap noted with approval. *Who knows? He might actually make a decent hero someday.* He reached down to help Hotshot up.

"Don't you touch him!" Jailbait shouted, misunderstanding his intentions. "Nobody beats up my boyfriend as long as I'm around."

A shimmering cage enclosed Cap, cutting him off from his recovering opponent. Crisscrossing lines of scintillating energy, crackling with restless electrons, formed a radiant dome above the Star-Spangled Avenger. Cap experimentally tried to step through the coruscating bars, only to receive an intense electrical shock the instant he came into contact with the energy lines. Cap clenched his teeth to keep from crying out and stepped back from the bars. He stared through the gaps in the cage at Jailbait, who stood a few feet away, her green hands extended before her, palms out.

"Good work, Jess!" Hotshot praised, springing to his feet with all the resilience of youth. He held a hand over his bludgeoned abdomen, though, as he joined his girlfriend. "That's the way to do it. I'll bet he wasn't expecting that."

Actually, I should have, Cap castigated himself. Bruce Banner had warned them all about Jailbait's ability to create webs of highly-charged energy, but Cap had overlooked the mild-looking teenager, possibly because she never sounded too enthusiastic about fighting in the first place.

Never underestimate an adolescent girl whose sweetheart is in trouble, he concluded. The smell of ozone filled his nostrils.

Even now, though, she didn't seem very committed to the battle. "Are you sure we're doing the right thing, Lou?" she asked Hotshot.

"Remember the Hulk?" he reminded her. "Remember Hydra? Heck, remember the Leader?" He placed a comforting arm over her shoulder. "The whole world wants what we've got here, wants to exploit us and steal our technology. We can't trust anyone."

"Not even Captain America?"

"Not even," he insisted. "It's us against the world, just like always."

"That's not true," Cap said from within the cage. "You should listen to that young lady, son. She's the only one of your bunch who is not declaring war before checking the facts."

He tried to appeal to Jailbait, even if he couldn't bring himself to call her by that name. "Look, miss, I'll bet we can work this whole mess out if we just talk it over for a few minutes. All we want is information about the Leader. Call off your teammates, let us make some inquiries, and we'll be on our way. You have my word on it," Cap said

"Don't listen to him, Jess," Hotshot warned her. "He's trying to trick you." He expressed his anger by hurling a fireball through a gap in the cage, but, despite his cramped circumstances, the Avenger deflected the flaming sphere with no difficulty. Cap was worried more about Hotshot's obvious influence over his girlfriend; it was going to be hard to get through to her as long as Hotshot was worked up.

He had to try, though. "Where's the harm in a cease-fire?" Cap asked her. "Why not give us a chance to explain?"

"Shut up!" Hotshot shouted at Cap. "Stop messing with her head." He lowered his voice to plead with Jailbait. "Think about it, Jess." He pointed at Cyclops, now squaring off against Rock. "What's the real Captain America doing with one of the X-Men? An Avenger hanging out with a mutant criminal? That doesn't makes sense. This guy's got to be a fake!"

"You think?" Jailbait asked, eyeing Cap more suspiciously than before.

"For sure!" Hotshot said confidently. "He's probably not even human. Just an adaptoid wrapped in a flag."

Cap sensed he was losing ground in his campaign to strike a peace initiative with Jailbait. *I might get her to come around eventually,* he thought, *but we don't have that much time to spare.* His blue eyes probed beyond the confines of the glimmering cage, searching for an alternate strategy. Looking around the plaza and its surroundings, his gaze lit upon Freehold's impressive cathedral. That imposing edifice stood several stories above the level of the street, its stained glass windows looking out over the plaza. Cap noticed in particular a marble ledge running along the second story of the cathedral. He hefted his shield and calculated the correct angle. *Yes,* he thought. *That looks like just what the doctor ordered.*

He lifted his shield until it was parallel with his chest, then aimed it at an open space between two crackling lines of electrical energy. "Jess, watch out!" Hotshot yelled, spotting Cap at work. "He's trying something!"

Captain America flung his shield like a frisbee and it went spinning out of his hands. At the same time, Jailbait mentally tightened her cage so that it fell like a net over his head and shoulders, delivering painful electrical shocks wherever the lines of the snare came into contact with him. Cap stiffened in pain, nearly biting his own tongue off, but his shield had escaped the net, soaring out over the heads of the two mutated teenagers.

"Hah!" Hotshot crowed. "He missed us by a mile." He hugged Jailbait to his side. "You did it, Jess! You stopped him!"

Cap watched as his shield flew gracefully toward the waiting cathedral, striking the correct corner of the sturdy ledge, and ricocheting back toward the unsuspecting teenagers. Without a single wobble, the metal disk slammed into Jailbait from behind, knocking her onto the pavement. *Sorry about that, miss,* Cap thought sincerely, *but your hot-headed boyfriend didn't give me much choice.* He knew the shield hadn't hit her hard enough to do any permanent damage; after several decades of constant practice, he could gauge the force of a rebounding shield to the nearest ounce.

With Jailbait's concentration broken, her luminescent net flickered for a split-second, then disintegrated entirely. Cap seized his freedom with breathtaking speed. Hotshot was still staring aghast at the prone figure of his girlfriend when

Captain America barreled into him. Hotshot was sent tumbling down the steps even as Cap retrieved his shield from where it had landed after knocking Jailbait unconscious.

Flying toward the hypertrophic organism known as Ogress, his synthetic body lighter than air, the Vision experienced a peculiar sensation that it took him approximately 1.73 seconds to identify as trepidation. The mere sight of the jade giantess was apparently sufficient to induce a disturbing fluctuation in his synaptic functions. *How unusual,* he thought, ascending higher, out of reach of even Ogress's exceptionally long arms. Better to delay his conflict with the mutated attorney while he performed a hasty self-diagnostic in hopes of isolating the cause of his uncharacteristic consternation.

Vivid images sprang from his memory banks, of his intangible right arm plunged up to the elbow in the broad green chest of the Hulk, of the extreme discomfort he had experienced when the atomic structure of the Hulk's organic substance refused to be displaced by the Vision's own rapidly solidifying limb, and of that indelible moment when the Hulk tore the Vision's arm from its socket, throwing his entire system into the cybernetic equivalent of shock. The Vision found he could not dismiss these disruptive memories, despite a concerted effort to do so. A human being, he suspected, would label such persistent and counterproductive recollections as "post-traumatic flashbacks"; the Vision preferred to think of them as an unwanted perturbation of his artificial thought processes.

The reason these freshly-recorded memories were resurfacing now was readily apparent; obviously, some portion of his analytical faculties had equated his present antagonist, Ogress, with another hostile green brute: the Hulk. Hence, his previously inexplicable trepidation at the prospect of engaging in hand-to-hand combat with Ogress. A predictable consequence of his recent dismemberment, perhaps, but not one that he could permit to interfere with the proper execution of his duties as an Avenger.

My course is clear, he resolved. *Captain America and Cyclops require my aid.*

"Grrr!" Ogress roared at him, shaking her immense fists at the unreachable android. Even from high above, she looked much larger than the Hulk and arguably more bestial in manner and appearance. Unable to lay her hands on the flying Avenger, Ogress turned her attention to targets closer at hand, scanning the vicinity with a predatory gleam in her eyes. The Vision realized he needed to intervene immediately, before Ogress could unleash her considerable wrath upon either Captain America or Cyclops.

"You are unwise to look away from me," he warned as he swooped down at her, increasing the mass in his outstretched fists enough to accelerate his descent along the desired approach vector. His thermoscopic beams preceded him, specialized lenses in his eyes focussing the discharged solar energy upon the distracted Ogress. "Do not attempt to harm my companions or I will be forced to take further action against you."

Neon-red heat rays fell like a spotlight upon Ogress. Her transformation having reportedly rendered her mute, she could respond only by howling in pain and anger; discouragingly, the Vision believed he detected more of the latter than the former. Her coarse green hide showed no sign of blistering beneath the thermoscopic barrage, but the furry tufts upon her bare arms and legs began to smoke and smolder. She snarled at the Vision, baring her brick-sized teeth, then loped across the plaza to the cooling relief of the spewing fountain. Like a prison searchlight, the Vision's heat rays chased her down the low marble steps, but the intense photonic bombardment did not even slow her down; hurdling the raised curb of the fountain in a single leap, she splashed into the churning pool. Cascading streams of water rained on her, providing partial protection from the burning thermoscopic beams, which raised dense clouds of steam, concealing Ogress from the Vision's visual receptors.

Floating silently above the pool, his saffron cloak billowing above him, the Vision extinguished his heat rays and considered his tactical options. He could narrow the focus of his eyebeams, significantly increasing their laser-like intensity, but he was reluctant to employ potentially deadly force against an opponent who was merely defending her homeland from unwanted intruders. True, the circumstances hardly warranted the excessive animosity and violence with which he and his traveling companions had been greeted, yet the Riot Squad could not reasonably be considered villains on the level of, say, the Masters of Evil or the Sons of the Serpent.

The sheltering steam dissipated, revealing the titanic form of Ogress. Bending over, she dug her mammoth fingers into the base of the fountain, tearing loose a huge chunk of cement that she hurled at her android attacker. The washing machine-sized cement fragment shot like a cannonball toward the Vision, only to pass harmlessly through his spectral form.

"I cannot fault your accuracy or endurance," he informed her, "even if you have failed to take into account the full difficulty of defeating an intangible foe with such a crude physical attack."

Unfortunately, the Vision realized, that same intangibility limited his ability to subdue Ogress long enough for the three heroes to complete their mission. To achieve anything more than a stalemate with this female goliath, he would have to become solid enough to touch and be touched.

With that in mind, he descended to the floor of the plaza, experiencing yet another surprising surge of apprehension as soon as his yellow boots touched down on the pavement. For exactly .753 seconds, his basic self-preservation subroutines threatened to override his higher cognitive functions. A photographic afterimage of the Hulk, triumphantly flourishing the Vision's sundered arm superimposed itself over the daunting sight of Ogress, waiting impatiently for the Vision beneath the spray of the fountain. For .753 seconds, his legs malfunctioned, unable to take one step nearer the fountain despite his deliberate intention to do so.

Ogress is not the Hulk, he told himself emphatically. *That she is is a false equation.*

Or was it?

His cybernetic synapses still firing off nonstop signals to retreat, the Vision walked purposely into the fountain, passing like a ghost through the raised concrete curb. Ogress, watching him approach, cupped her gargantuan hands over the fountain's central spout, redirecting the full force of the pillar of water at the Vision so that it jetted into the Avenger like a liquid battering ram. The Vision increased his mass and density, however, becoming hard as diamond and as heavy as neutronium. The high-pressure spray broke harmlessly against his immovable form.

Physically, the watery cannonade could not deter him; psychologically it was another story. The surging torrent only raised more associations with his catastrophic encounter with the Hulk amidst the driving currents of Niagara Falls. He remembered the cataract carrying his broken body over the edge of the Falls, and his motor functions froze once more, leaving him standing immobile at the edge of the circular reservoir. *Not again,* he thought, feeling an alarmingly human sense of panic.

Ogress was neither frozen nor afraid. Tiring of her trick

with the waterspout, or maybe just disappointed with its results, she pulled back her hands, then charged straight through the resulting column of sky-high water. A savage roar drowned out the thunder of falling water as she grabbed onto the Vision with Hulk-like strength. A single massive fist wrapped around both of the synthezoid's legs, while her other hand ripped the yellow cape from his shoulders, letting it flutter to the pool around their feet where it floated like a yellow oil slick atop the water. She raised the Vision like a club and began hammering his head and shoulders against the concrete curb of the fountain. Again and again, she lifted the android Avenger high above her head, then brought him slamming down onto the paved plaza. With each blow, his super-hard body reduced the solid cement to powder.

The Vision felt like he was repeatedly hitting the bottom of Niagara Falls. Then, as each jarring collision with the ground rattled his synthetic enamel teeth, another memory inserted itself into his fading consciousness. He saw a woman, blue-eyed and auburn-haired, reaching out to him from the past, a past they once had shared.

"Wanda," he murmured, remembering with renewed intensity the cause that had brought him first to Niagara Falls, then to this uncharted realm beneath the Canadian ice. There was more at stake here than simply the continued existence of one malfunctioning synthezoid. Wanda was in danger. *Wanda!*

Confused and contradictory directives came together in his computerized mind. Priorities were assigned, files rearranged, and counterproductive programming discarded as irrelevant. An immediate course of action presented itself as clearly as any other step-by-step procedure:

1. The Vision shed his accumulated density, slipping easily between the atoms of Ogress's clenched fist until he was completely free of her grip. A befuddled expression supplanted the animal fury on her simian face. She snatched fruitlessly at the Vision's immaterial form, her grasping paws seizing only empty air.

2. The Vision turned his thermoscopic vision on the spout at the center of the fountain. The tremendous heat melted it into slag, sealing the nozzle. The towering plume of water collapsed into the pool.

3. The Vision eyed Ogress with a look of implacable calm upon his plastic features. His body still intangible, he stepped entirely *inside* Ogress's enormous frame before beginning to become solid once more. There was more than enough room inside the mutated lawyer's vast torso, but less so as the Vision's own unstable molecules started to occupy space formerly occupied by Ogress's flesh and bone.

As the Hulk's tissues had before her, Ogress's gamma-enhanced body resisted his incursion, fighting his accumulating substance for every nanometer of available space, competing with him on a molecular, if not an atomic level. But the Vision's revised programming would not permit him to terminate this procedure until its ultimate objective was achieved. The face of his former wife, the one and only Scarlet Witch, lingered like a hologram in his mind's eye, providing him with all the software he needed to override obstacles both within and without.

Even an android, it seemed, could be inspired by a vision.

"I know you," Rock accused. "You're one of those renegade mutants. One of the X-Men." He glared at Cyclops with a contemptuous look on his face, the only part of him that wasn't concealed within a lumpy gray shell. "Back when I worked for the military, I saw contingency plans for dealing with you freaks."

Look who's talking, Cyclops thought. Electrodes attached to Samuel John La Roquette's forehead linked him to the bulky chunk of rock from which he drew his new identity. Banner had described Rock as the most dangerous member of the Riot Squad, as well as the least innocent. Unlike the luckless survivors of Middletown, Rock had bought into the Leader's agenda more or less willingly, motivated by years of bitterness and resentment over his personal and professional failures. Cut off from humanity in more ways than one, Rock had retreated like a hermit crab into his forbidding stone carapace.

How can he live like that? Cyclops thought, appalled at the idea of spending the rest of your life encased in a floating boulder.

After being sent tumbling through the air by Cyclops's eyebeams, Rock swiftly regained control of his own orientation and locomotion. He coasted above the pavement in a manner that reminded Cyclops of Charles Xavier's anti-gravity wheelchair. He suspected a similar form of technology was at work within Rock's monolithic cocoon. How else could Rock pilot himself so freely without any visible means of propulsion?

"Thought you'd thrown me for a loop with that sneak attack, did you?" Rock challenged Cyclops. "Tough luck, mutie. You just moved to the top of my hit list."

The roughhewn granite that enclosed the man hardly looked very malleable, but in this case appearances were deceiving. Through the ruby lens in his visor, Cyclops saw Rock extrude a pair of gigantic concrete claws from his shell. Craggy fingers, sharp and jagged at their tips, reached for the X-Man, who threw himself backwards to avoid their clutches. His eyebeams lashed out at the grasping stone talons, blasting the points off the nearest of the claws so that they looked more like stumps than stalagmites.

"Arrgh!" Rock cried out, evidently sharing a psychic link with his prosthetic appendages. Having successfully declawed one stony hand, Cyclops aimed his force beam at the remaining claw, breaking it off at the wrist. La Roquette's face contorted in pain, and Cyclops allowed himself to hope that the hostile cyborg might have learned his lesson.

"Had enough?" the X-Man asked. Banner said Rock was a bad apple, but maybe he could be made to see sense. "We don't need to fight you. Just tell us what we want to know and we'll go."

"You're not going anywhere but down!" Rock spat at him, saliva spraying from his lips. The truncated claws regenerated, growing new talons just as deadly as before. Rock zoomed across the wide thoroughfare at Cyclops, intent on skewering the mutant hero with his rocky projections. "I've speared the Hulk with my claws, so I'm not going to take any lip from some mutie troublemaker."

Cyclops watched Rock speed toward him like a sentient asteroid.

I wonder if it's too late to borrow Captain America's shield, he wondered as he dropped to the pavement only a second before Rock's claws would have impaled him. Rock's momentum carried him over the prone X-Man. *A closer shave than I want or need,* he concluded, thankful as ever for all the hours he'd spent training in the Danger Room. He scrambled to his feet while Rock slowed to a stop, then spun around to face the X-Man once more. Noting the vengeful gleam in Rock's dark eyes, Cyclops suddenly felt like a matador missing both his cape and his sword.

"Pretty slick move," Rock conceded, "but you can't

keep dodging me forever." He retracted his concrete claws, replacing them with sharp-edged spikes that protruded from his cocoon in every direction. "Get ready to bleed, mutie."

Cyclops knew better than to argue with this sort of unreasoning malice. Rock was right, though; it was only a matter of time before one of those spikes ran him through, unless he took out the man inside the shell. *Forget the stone,* he advised himself. Rock could regenerate his lethal appendages indefinitely. Instead Cyclops aimed his visor at Rock's achilles' heel: his exposed face.

A crimson beam shot from Cyclops's unshielded eyes, but Rock was way ahead of him. The levitating boulder began spinning like a top, carrying La Roquette's face out of the line of fire. Flaky chips of stone flew off the rotating Rock as Cyclops's beam struck home, but his petrified adversary had become a blur. Whirling like a dervish, or perhaps the Tasmanian Devil in an old Bugs Bunny cartoon, Rock came at the X-Men's stalwart co-leader. His cyclonic rotation whipped up a fierce wind that raised a swirling cloud of dust beneath him. Cyclops held his ground, firing blindly at the twirling juggernaut, but trying to hit La Roquette's face under these conditions was like playing roulette with eyebeams; the odds were against him.

Cyclops was forced to retreat, running back the way he and the Avengers had come. *Rock can't possibly see where's he's going while he's spinning like that. He's going to have to stop twirling sometime, just to find out where I am. That's my chance,* Cyclops theorized, so the X-Man zigzagged back and forth across the deserted street, finally taking refuge beneath the awning of a six-story apartment building.

Moving at random over the wide paved road, Rock came unnervingly close to the X-Man's hiding place. The wind generated by the whirling cyborg threw dust in Cyclops's face, but his visor protected his eyes from the abrasive particles—and vise versa. Cyclops held a gloved hand over his mouth and nose to keep from coughing or sneezing, and thus alerting Rock to his location.

He couldn't be sure at first, but he thought that the spinning boulder was slowing down. His head leaned forward, his neck taut, as he waited tensely for an opportunity to strike. This was what a sharpshooter felt like, he imagined, right before he pulls the trigger. "Come on," he whispered. "Give me a clean shot."

Rock was definitely spinning slower now. Cyclops glimpsed La Roquette's features as they whipped past him every other split-second, still moving too quickly to pose a viable target. Finally, the rotation slackened enough that Rock and Cyclops were able to lock eyes across a narrow strip of sidewalk.

There you are! they both must have thought simultaneously. Cyclops centered the cyborg's scowling visage within his sights. *Ready, aim . . . fire!*

He let loose his eyebeams, which streaked toward their target, but Rock had already formed a shield from his carapace of living stone, raising it in time to block the crimson forcebeam. Granite crunched beneath the impact of eyebeams, yet La Roquette's vulnerable countenance was spared. Cyclops attempted to fire past the rectangular shield, which was connected to the core boulder by a thick gray pseudopod, only to find himself parried once more. "Not so fast, mutie," Rock mocked him from behind his protective curtain of stone. "You didn't think I was going to make it easy for you, did you?"

I guess not, Cyclops thought. Rock then proved he could attack and defend at the same time by extending a well-aimed spike at the cornered X-Man. The petrified spear tripled its length in a heartbeat, hurling at Cyclops like a jouster's lance. His eyebeams darted downward, intercepting the deadly javelin before it could pierce his abdomen. Already, however, another spike was stretching toward him. How was he ever going to fend off all of Rock's vicious jabs, let alone get past the murderous cyborg's homegrown shield?

"Cyclops! Over here!" a deep voice cried out. Cyclops spotted Captain America several yards away, off to one side of Rock. The living legend of World War II held his own shield up high, catching the moonlight—and La Roquette's reflection. *Got it,* Cyclops thought swiftly, comprehending at once the Avenger's strategy. Twisting his body violently to one side, to avoid yet another oncoming stone pike, he fired his eyebeams at Captain America's shield. The crimson rays caromed off the polished surface of Cap's shield and back at Rock's face.

From where he now stood, Cyclops couldn't see the beam hit La Roquette where it hurt, but he could imagine the wide-eyed look of shock and alarm the man must have displayed just before several dozen foot-pounds of extra-dimensional energy wiped the sneer from his face. The X-Man heard a single shouted obscenity disturb the moonlit tranquility of Freehold, then the entire levitating boulder hit the pavement like, well, a rock. The spike-covered shell, looking something like a petrified porcupine, rolled back and forth for a moment or two, breaking off many of the concrete spines on its underside, before ceasing to move at all.

Cyclops ducked under a protruding spike and prodded Rock with his foot. The boulder continued to squat lifelessly on the pavement, suggesting that its animating intelligence was indeed out for the count. "Thanks for the use of your shield," the X-Man called to Captain America. "Your timing couldn't have been better."

"Just glad I could return the favor," Cap said warmly, prompting Cyclops to recall that he had first fired his eye-beams at Rock to defend the Avenger. Cyclops stepped away from the fallen rock and surveyed the vicinity. The two super-powered teenagers, Hotshot and Jailbait, were both sprawled limply on or near the steps to the plaza. They didn't look like they'd be giving anyone a hard time anytime soon; Hotshot, in particular, had a bruise on his chin that was getting darker by the moment.

"Those two give you any trouble?" he asked Cap.

"Nothing I couldn't handle," the Avenger said, with neither arrogance nor false modesty in his tone. He wasn't bragging, just stating the facts. "Once you get past their specialized tricks, they're still only a pair of inexperienced kids, with not much skill or training in hand-to-hand combat." He flexed a set of sore knuckles beneath his scarlet gloves. "Hotshot's got a bit of a glass jaw, to tell the truth."

That left Ogress, Cyclops realized, who appeared to be having problems of her own. The mammoth she-creature stood ankle-deep in the basin of the fountain, where once a towering plume of water had leaped toward the sky. Inexplicably, the last Squad member still standing seemed gripped by some kind of seizure. Her marble-sized eyes, too small for the rest of her face, bulged from their undersized sockets while convulsive palpitations shook the enormous timbers of her legs and arms. Greenish foam frothed at the corners of her ape-like jaws, and she clawed at her chest with meaty fingers, shredding the front of her purple uniform, as if trying to extract the source of her agony from somewhere deep within her mighty frame.

Good Lord, Cyclops thought, experiencing a moment of panic, *what if she's having a heart attack?* It was a terrifying idea; how in the world could you perform CPR on such a behemoth?

"Wait a minute," Cap said beside him. The veteran hero glanced around the street with a puzzled expression. "Where is the Vision?"

Cyclops noticed for the first time that the synthetic Avenger was missing. Had the android, so recently reassembled, been demolished again? If the Hulk could commit such an atrocity, why not Ogress as well? The worried X-Man hastily scanned the plaza for any evidence of disaster, such as bits and pieces of the artificial hero, and quickly spotted the Vision's yellow cloak, floating in the fountain not far from Ogress's quivering legs.

What does that mean? Cyclops wondered anxiously. If his latex cape had ended up discarded and drifting in the basin, like a greasy film upon the water, what had become of Vision himself?

"GRRR!"

A final, wrenching spasm shook Ogress, and her eyes rolled back so that only the bloodshot whites, streaked with grisly green veins, could be seen. She collapsed, toppling forward in a heap. The ponderous weight of her falling body smashed the rim of the basin and shook the ground beneath Cyclops's feet. Water from the shattered fountain spilled out onto the plaza, drenching the marble tiles around the stricken giantess and lapping at the heroes' boots.

Captain America rushed to Ogress's side and placed a hand where her neck should have been. "I feel a pulse," he reported with audible relief. Cyclops was glad to hear it, even if he remained unsure what had happened to the Riot Squad's ferocious answer to She-Hulk. "She's still breathing, too."

An unexpected shudder rocked the unconscious monster, and Cap stepped back warily from her colossal form. Cyclops backed away, too, only to watch in surprise as a phantasmal green figure emerged from Ogress's broad back without even rustling the fabric of her uniform. "You need not be concerned, Captain," the Vision informed him calmly. "Ogress has suffered no permanent damage, merely a neurological shock sufficient to render her insensate for the time being."

"I see," Captain America said, nodding. He took the Vision's startling reappearance in stride; having seen the immaterial android perform many similar stunts before. "Good work."

I wonder if he can teach Shadowcat that trick? Cyclops thought. Like the Vision, the X-Men's most precocious recruit could phase through solid objects, although Cyclops had never seen young Kitty Pryde incapacitate a living being as devastatingly as the android Avenger just had. Then again, he recalled, Shadowcat's phasing invariably disrupted electronic equipment—like androids, perhaps? *Hmm, you've got to wonder who would prove most dangerous to whom, the Vision or Kitty?*

That was a question for another day, however. Here in Freehold, the night was not getting any shorter. Cyclops looked around the plaza, from which an entire underground city spread. There were altogether too many buildings to search effectively for the answers they sought. "Now what?" he asked his Avenging companions, daunted by the task ahead of them. "Go door to door?"

"I don't think that will be necessary," Cap said. Eyes widening, he pointed past the X-Man's shoulder.

Cyclops spun around in time to see a peculiar optical phenomenon only a few yards away. Beneath the moonlight and the soft glow of streetlamps, a man-sized column of air shimmered above the marble tiles, like the ripples one sometimes saw above the blacktop on a hot day. The seeming mirage took on color and definition, presenting the image of a humanoid figure swiftly coming into focus. *A hologram,* Cyclops speculated, *or the Leader's matter transporter at work?* He suspected the latter, and aimed his visor just in case.

In a matter of seconds, the figure looked as real and tangible as the rest of them. "That's quite enough," he stated decisively, his mild, phlegmatic voice sounding more bored than annoyed.

Was this the Leader? He looked much as Cyclops recalled the gamma-mutated mastermind was supposed to appear: a slight figure, with skin green as malachite, whose most predominant feature was a skull large enough to house an unusually well-endowed brain. The man's elongated forehead rose twice as high as the rest of his face and his hairless cranium was not so much a dome as a silo with a rounded top. All in all, the implied cerebral capacity of the man's head made Professor X look like a troglodyte.

Aside from the distinct green tint of his flesh, the rest of the man was unremarkable. He had a thin, unathletic build and, if not for his towering cranium, would have stood less than six feet tall. A purple nehru jacket and violet trousers echoed the color scheme of the Riot Squad's uniforms and his hands were clasped before his chest in a meditative pose. Frankly, the man did not present a very threatening appearance, but Cyclops did not lower his guard. "Is this him?" he asked Captain America. "The Leader?"

"No," Cap said, "although the resemblance is striking, especially to the way the Leader looked when he first fought the Avengers." Cyclops recalled that, in recent years, the Leader's mutated skull had continued to swell, taking on mushroom-like contours, or so Banner reported.

"Great minds think alike and look alike, I suppose," the

newcomer said. He seemed unoffended by the comparison. "You may call me Omnibus. I'm in charge of this city."

"Omnibus?" Cap asked.

The image shrugged. "I was once an encyclopedia salesmen, before my transfiguration. As the late, unlamented Leader once quipped, it was that or name me Britannica." He rolled his eyes at the very notion. "He had a peculiar sense of humor, you see."

"Right," Cyclops commented brusquely, unconcerned about the idiosyncracies of the Leader's funnybone. "The Hulk mentioned you earlier."

"The Hulk!" Omnibus reacted negatively to the name. Much of his diffident manner slipped away as he regarded Cyclops anxiously. "That monster's not coming back here, is he?"

"Not unless there's a reason," Captain America stated, his shield at his side. "Our apologies, by the way, for whatever damage your city sustained during our altercation with the Riot Squad, but you should know that your people started the fight."

Omnibus looked unconcerned by the recent violence. "No harm done." He coldly surveyed the vanquished Squad members, making *tsk*-ing sounds with his tongue. "Obviously, our security forces are in need of additional combat experience."

Cyclops got the impression that Omnibus had deliberately sicced the Riot Squad on them, simply to test their fighting abilities. "For what purpose?" Cyclops asked, suspicious.

"Why, to better defend Freehold, of course," Omnibus replied, perhaps a touch too quickly. Cyclops found himself doubting the man's sincerity; could it be that he had other plans for his super-powered storm troopers? "But you have yet to explain your own reasons for visiting our isolated and reasonably inaccessible domain," Omnibus pointed out, effectively changing the subject.

"Fair enough," Cap admitted. "Let me get straight to the point. We have reason to suspect that two of our respective teammates, the Scarlet Witch and Rogue, have been abducted by the Leader. Evidence of gamma-based teleportation technology, of the sort formerly employed by the Leader, was found at the scenes of both disappearances. And, according to a reliable source, this city of yours is the Leader's last known address."

"That's true enough," Omnibus conceded, "but Freehold's singular founder has not been seen alive since that terrible occasion, over a year ago, when a Hydra assault team invaded our city, in tandem with the Hulk. I myself personally saw the Leader cut down by gunfire during the resulting chaos, shortly before his laboratory was consumed by a dreadful conflagration." He dipped his lofty forehead in memory of the dearly departed. "I'm afraid there's no way he could have survived."

Spoken like someone who has never seen Magneto or the Shadow King return from the dead a dozen times, Cyclops thought, then asked. "But you never actually saw his body?"

The Vision sounded equally skeptical. "The Leader has been reported dead on many previous occasions, but such pronouncements have always proved premature."

"Let me assure you," Omnibus said, shaking his head, "after the battle we searched every square inch of the wrecked laboratory. All we ever found were minute traces of his blood. Green blood, naturally. Like my own."

Cyclops could not miss the note of pride in his voice. *Just what the world needs,* he thought dourly. *A self-appointed successor to the Leader.*

"I can't help noticing that you've helped yourself to the

Leader's trans-mat technology. Perhaps the Leader isn't the guilty party after all. *You* could have beamed our friends away,'' Cyclops said.

"That's a plausible hypothesis," Omnibus admitted, unfazed by the accusation. "I can't deny that I have inherited many of the fruits of my predecessor's genius. But what would be my motive? Naturally, I have heard of the two remarkable ladies the Captain mentioned—since the . . . unfortunate . . . incident at Middletown, I've become a veritable fount of information—but I certainly have no compelling reason to abduct either woman, let alone bring down the combined wrath of the X-Men and the Avengers on our humble community. Please believe me, the people of Freehold, myself included, wish nothing more than to be left alone and in peace." He assumed a benign, smugly serene expression, like that of a pale green *bodhissattva*. "Furthermore, as far as we know, the mortal remains of the Leader were completely incinerated in the fire. For better or for worse, he is no more."

Times like this Cyclops wished he was a telepath like Jean or the Professor. *I'd like to read Omnibus's mind right now, find out what's he hiding.* He didn't buy the man's peace-loving act for a minute; Cyclops had met too many self-important, would-be dictators not to spot one more when he saw one. Omnibus's ambitions would not be confined to Freehold forever, that was for sure. In his gut, however, Cyclops sensed the man was telling the truth about one thing: he had nothing to do with yesterday's kidnappings in New York.

They would not find Rogue or Wanda here.

Chapter Nine

"*En vain pour eviter les réponse amères...*"

The Beast sang along with his favorite recording of Bizet's *Carmen* as he held down the fort at Avengers Mansion. Just as Carmen herself passed the time reading her fortune in the cards, the shaggy blue mutant perused the latest reports from S.H.I.E.L.D., searching for a hidden pattern that would reveal the malevolent purpose at work behind recent events, events that had brought the X-Men and the Avengers together, then sent them spreading out across the globe.

UFO sightings. Kidnapped super-heroines. Stolen Sentinels. Gamma rays. The Beast had to admit, it was quite a puzzle. He crouched atop the circular meeting table, sorting through freshly-printed hard copies of the reports with his toes. A pitcher of hot coffee sat dangerously close to the piled papers, along with a tray of finger sandwiches that Jarvis had generously provided before retiring for the evening. A pair of wire reading glasses perched upon his nose, the Beast nibbled on a cucumber sandwich while perusing his handwritten notes one more time.

In truth, he had made some little progress already. According to his estimations, two of the UFO sightings reported by S.H.I.E.L.D. corresponded almost exactly with the abductions of, first, the Scarlet Witch, then Rogue, which seemed to confirm everyone's assumption that the aerial assault on the Helicarrier, conducted later that same day, bore a direct connection to Wanda and Rogue's enigmatic disappearances.

A third UFO sighting, made much further upstate, troubled him, primarily because he had yet to link that appearance of the elusive aircraft to any contemporaneous event. Surely, the mystery ship had not been out joyriding on that particular occasion! No, he had to assume that the UFO had been about some business of which he as yet remained unaware. *What, pray tell, could that be?* the Beast wondered. Last he'd heard, no one up in the hinterlands had reported any missing mutants or purloined hunter-robots.

The Beast glanced at the silent communications console. He did not resent being left behind—*someone* had to stay here to monitor communications and coordinate the two teams' activities—but he was anxious to receive word from his farflung friends and colleagues. The imbroglio at Muir Island particularly disturbed him, since there seemed little doubt that Bobby, Kurt, and Moira were in immediate peril from the ominously-named Gamma Sentinels. Granted, he was quick to remind himself, Iceman and Nightcrawler had each survived numerous encounters with various generations of Sentinels, so there was no reason to assume the worst in this instance, not until he had a compelling reason to do so.

A color photo of a bizarre green countenance, freshly downloaded from the Avengers' database, caught his eye. The infamous Leader, he decided, certainly lent new and very literal meaning to the hackneyed phrase "a swelled head." The Beast did not believe for a second that this virtuoso of villainy had gone to his eternal reward as reported; the Leader was surely sequestered in some obscure location, far from prying eyes and inquiring minds.

Indeed, the Leader's bulging file revealed an inveterate

fondness for hidden strongholds in unexpected and remarkably inaccessible locales. A desert lair in New Mexico. A hidden city beneath a glacier. A cloaked space station in orbit above the earth. *Where, I wonder, might he be hiding nowadays?*

He looked again at those intriguing UFO reports. He felt sure the answer lay in those cryptic accounts of aerodynamic hijinks. He could practically feel his impatient unconscious nudging him toward some waiting revelation, had he but eyes to see it.

Is there anything about their flight plans, he speculated, *that might point to a common point of origin?* Earlier calculations along those lines had proved unrewarding, yet he felt compelled to noodle with the data again.

Counting the forcible boarding of the Helicarrier by those fraudulent X-Men, somewhere over Montana, he had four documented sightings of the UFO, complete with precise readings of its speed and heading each time it appeared and disappeared from surveillance. Trying to track all four flights back to a single location, in the continental United States or elsewhere, had led to naught but to a dispiriting sense of futility.

But what if he was losing the forest for the flight plan trees? Maybe the answer lay not in the particulars of all the sightings, but only in the UFO's first and final manifestations. *Yes!* he thought enthusiastically, taking another gulp of liquid caffeine.

Let's assume the UFO came a long way from anywhere, as the Leader's proclivities presuppose. Then wouldn't its pilots have wanted to take care of all their inequitable errands in one trip, before returning to the Leader's exclusive enclave? Of course! the Beast concluded, energetically endorsing his own supposition.

In which case, the UFO would have zoomed first to New

SEARCH AND RESCUE

York City, to pick up the Scarlet Witch and Rogue, then zipped upstate for who knew what, before flying west to intercept the S.H.I.E.L.D. Helicarrier over the great state of Montana. Then, and only then, its felonious scavenger hunt completed, would the UFO have returned to its home berth—wherever that might be.

So, he silently asked the empty conference room, *given the trajectories reported by Nick Fury's assiduous agents, from whence did the UFO come and to where was it homeward bound?*

He did the calculations in his head first, then scribbled with a pencil over the napkins left behind by the sandwiches he had consumed. "Oh, my stars and garters!" he exclaimed, lifting the spectacles from his nose to peer at the surprising results with his naked eyes.

His hypothesis had yielded two probable locations for the launching pad of the busy UFO, and hence the Leader's secluded abode: downtown Duluth, Minnesota. Or the moon.

The former hardly fit the Leader's *modus operandi,* but the *moon . . .* ! You could hardly get more remote than that. The Beast somersaulted across the table, clapping his feet together in glee. Intuitively, he *knew* he had arrived at the truth. The Leader was on the moon!

And so, presumably, were Wanda and Rogue.

He bounded from the table, eager to share his epiphany with his fellow X-Men and Avengers. But just as his sasquatch-sized soles smacked against the floor, within easy reach of the communications console, a seismic jolt vibrated the very walls of the venerable mansion.

An earthquake—in Manhattan? he marveled, before hearing ponderous footsteps stomping up the stairs from the foyer below. The Beast gulped nervously. *Please,* he beseeched the fickle Fates, *let this merely be our old friend Hercules, with a bit too much wine in him.*

Instead a monumental green figure filled the doorway, casting a shadow the size of a lunar eclipse. *Carmen* continued to play, reaching its violent climax as Don Jose stalked the streets of Seville, driven to hot-blooded murder while the roar of the *corridia* provided a sanguinary accompaniment.

"Hulk?" the Beast asked uncertainly. Every one of his bushy blue bristles seemed to be standing on end. "What are you doing here? Where are the others?"

"Identified: mutant designate: Beast," the jade giant stated implacably. He stepped into the conference room, rattling the floor with his heavy tread. "Threat assessment: minimal. Immediate priority: termination."

Carmen screamed her last aria. The Beast knew exactly how she felt.

Chapter Ten

The sun was rising over Muir Island as Iron Man inspected the stiff, unmoving form of the Doc Samson-Sentinel. *A pretty good likeness,* he decided, *all the more impressive when you consider all the nasty surprises they built into this baby.*

Thanks to some super-powered teamwork, the third floor laboratory of the Genetic Research Centre no longer looked like the interior of an old-fashioned icebox. The Hulk, not surprisingly, had declined to help out at all, instead slouching against the butchered Cray and shooting dirty looks at Wolverine. The irritated brute had yet to forgive the Canadian X-Man for letting his mechanical doppleganger escape the island.

Iron Man regretted letting one of the Gamma Sentinels get away, too, but bowed to the inevitable. These things happened; he'd be lying if he said he snagged the bad guys every time himself. Sometimes you just had to be satisfied with chasing a dangerous felon off before too many innocents got hurt.

We'll catch up with that Sentinel eventually, Iron Man resolved. How long could a mechanical Hulk remain hidden anyway?

Speaking of blameless people getting hurt, Nightcrawler limped toward Iron Man, an aluminum crutch under his right shoulder. Dr. MacTaggert had already applied a cast

SEARCH AND RESCUE

around the blue-furred mutant's fractured ankle and given Nightcrawler something for the pain. Despite his injury, the hobbled X-Man seemed in admirably good spirits. *Is that the painkillers,* Iron Man wondered, *or just his natural personality?*

"*Mein gott,* that thing is realistic," Nightcrawler said of the Doc Samson-Sentinel, "although not nearly as ugly as the mechanical Abomination that chased me around downstairs." He poked the inert figure with his tail. "*Ach,* I think I liked it better when a Sentinel looked like a Sentinel. At least you always knew where you stood."

Iron Man recalled that the Abomination-Sentinel still rested lifelessly at the bottom of the pit the Hulk-Sentinel had torn through the floor. Given that the armored Avenger was the strongest person present, excluding the steadfastly uncooperative Hulk, Iron Man realized he'd have to personally retrieve the mock Abomination from the basement before returning the damaged Gamma Sentinels to S.H.I.E.L.D., where they would promptly become Nick Fury's problem.

First, though, he wanted to take a closer look at Doc Samson-Sentinel's internal mechanisms. Technically, that was probably classified technology, but Iron Man felt he had a right to know just how much of it was lifted from Tony Stark's patented research and inventions. *Lord knows,* he thought, *it wouldn't be the first time those cloak-and-dagger types at S.H.I.E.L.D. had twisted my own discoveries to dubious ends.*

"Excuse me," he said to Nightcrawler, gesturing for the German mutant to step away from the Sentinel while Iron Man subjected it to an exploratory scan along the entire electromagnetic spectrum. His multipurpose sensor beam radiated from his chest projector, probing beneath the Sentinel's crimson uniform and synthetic skin for vital data, such as the composition of the various alloys composing the Sentinel, the structure of its cybernetic nervous system, the amount of available memory in its central processor, its primary and secondary operating systems, and so on. He was both amused and distressed, but more the latter than the former, to discover that the sophisticated microcircuitry maintaining the Sentinel's artificial intelligence bore a suspicious resemblance to his own ground-breaking HOMER technology, otherwise known as a Heuristically-Operative Matrix-Emulation Rostrum. *I think Tony Stark needs to have some serious words with the bigwigs at S.H.I.E.L.D., after we've taken care of the Leader.*

A dense layer of lead shielding enclosed the portable gamma reactor that theoretically provided the Gamma Sentinels with the atomic energy that powered them. Turning his most sensitive instrumentation upon the reaction chamber, which was located, with a fine sense of verisimilitude, just where Doc Samson's heart would be, Iron Man expected to find the reactor shut down entirely, its radioactive isotopes cooling into unreactive slag.

Instead he registered a gamma spike of over 500 kiloelectron volts—and climbing. "Good Lord!" he exclaimed, the shock in his voice catching the attention of every human, mutant, and gamma-spawned behemoth in the demolished laboratory.

"What is it, my friend?" Storm asked him, soaring over the open pit to join Iron Man and Nightcrawler by the supposedly inactive Sentinel. The breeze her flight generated blew bits of shattered plaster and circuitry across the lab. "Is there something wrong?"

"You could say that," Iron Man said tensely. He rapidly recalibrated his instruments, but the results were no better. The gamma emissions coming from the Sentinel's interior had already increased 32 percent. Within the shielded heart

SEARCH AND RESCUE

of the robot, he realized, electrons and positrons were colliding at a geometric rate, annihilating each other in subatomic reactions that spewed out quantities of gamma radiation proportional to the mass of each electron destroyed. The discharged radiation subsequently energized more electrons and positrons, leading to further collisions, resulting in yet more unleashed gamma rays. "It's a chain reaction building inside the Gamma Sentinel," he said to the others, his hushed voice struggling to convey the magnitude of what his sensors were recording. He stepped back from the Doc Samson robot duplicate, knowing all the while that he wasn't getting nearly far enough away to survive what was coming.

On the other side of the lab, Moira MacTaggert hastily waved a handheld radiation sensor over the feathered remains of the Harpy-Sentinel. "Iron Man," she called to him desperately, "I'm pickin' up a gamma surge, too. Over 600 keV and heatin' up fast!"

The same thing must be happening inside the third Sentinel as well, Iron Man guessed. The Abomination in the basement. He clicked off his sensor beam as the full horror of his inadvertent discovery sunk in.

"They're not just Sentinels!" he announced to the X-Men and their associates. "They're walking, talking Gamma Bombs—programmed to detonate upon defeat!"

That got even the Hulk's attention. . . .

To be continued . . .

Greg Cox is the author of the Iron Man novels *The Armor Trap* and *Operation A.I.M.* In addition he was the author of *Star Trek: The Q Continuum* trilogy as well as the co-author of two *Star Trek* novels (the *Deep Space Nine* novel *Devil in the Sky* with John Gregory Betancourt and the *Next Generation* novel *Dragon's Honor* with Kij Johnson). Greg served as coeditor of two science fiction/horror anthologies (*Tomorrow Sucks* and *Tomorrow Bites* with T.K.F. Weisskopf), and he has also published many short stories, in anthologies ranging from *Alien Pregnant by Elvis* to *100 Vicious Little Vampire Stories* to *The Ultimate Super-Villains* to *OtherWere*. Greg lives in New York City.

George Pérez, one of the most renowned artists in comics, is best known for his stints on *The Avengers, Fantastic Four, Justice League of America,* and *The New Teen Titans* (which he also cowrote and coedited). Other noteworthy efforts include his work on *UltraForce, The Silver Surfer* (as writer), *Isaac Asimov's I-Bots, Sachs & Violens,* and *The Incredible Hulk: Future Imperfect.* He coplotted and drew *Crisis on Infinite Earths,* and wrote and drew the revamp of *Wonder Woman* (both for DC). Recently, George returned to the series that made his career, Marvel's *The Avengers,* where he collaborates with writer Kurt Busiek. George lives in Florida.

CHRONOLOGY TO THE MARVEL NOVELS AND ANTHOLOGIES

What follows is a guide to the order in which the Marvel novels and short stories published by BP Books, Inc., and Berkley Boulevard Books take place in relation to each other. Please note that this is not a hard and fast chronology, but a guideline that is subject to change at authorial or editorial whim. This list covers all the novels and anthologies published from October 1994–October 2000.

The short stories are each given an abbreviation to indicate which anthology the story appeared in. USM=*The Ultimate Spider-Man*, USS=*The Ultimate Silver Surfer*, USV=*The Ultimate Super-Villains*, UXM=*The Ultimate X-Men*, UTS=*Untold Tales of Spider-Man*, UH=*The Ultimate Hulk*, and XML=*X-Men Legends*.

X-Men & Spider-Man: Time's Arrow Book 1: **The Past** [portions]
by Tom DeFalco & Jason Henderson
Parts of this novel take place in prehistoric times, the sixth century, 1867, and 1944.

"The Silver Surfer" [flashback]
by Tom DeFalco & Stan Lee [USS]
The Silver Surfer's origin. The early parts of this flashback start several decades, possibly several centuries, ago, and continue to a point just prior to "To See Heaven in a Wild Flower."

CHRONOLOGY

"In the Line of Banner"
by Danny Fingeroth [UH]
This takes place over several years, ending approximately nine months before the birth of Robert Bruce Banner.

X-Men: Codename Wolverine ["then" portions]
by Christopher Golden
"Every Time a Bell Rings"
by Brian K. Vaughan [XML]
These take place while Team X was still in operation, while the Black Widow was still a Russian spy, while Banshee was still with Interpol, and a couple of years before the X-Men were formed.

"Spider-Man"
by Stan Lee & Peter David [USM]
A retelling of Spider-Man's origin.

"Transformations"
by Will Murray [UH]
"Side by Side with the Astonishing Ant-Man!"
by Will Murray [UTS]
"Assault on Avengers Mansion"
by Richard C. White & Steven A. Roman [UH]
"Suits"
by Tom De Haven & Dean Wesley Smith [USM]
"After the First Death..."
by Tom DeFalco [UTS]
"Celebrity"
by Christopher Golden & José R. Nieto [UTS]
"Pitfall"
by Pierce Askegren [UH]
"Better Looting Through Modern Chemistry"
by John Garcia & Pierce Askegren [UTS]

CHRONOLOGY

"Side by Side with the Astonishing Ant-Man!"
by Will Murray [UTS]
"Assault on Avengers Mansion"
by Richard C. White & Steven A. Roman [UH]
"Suits"
by Tom De Haven & Dean Wesley Smith [USM]
"After the First Death..."
by Tom DeFalco [UTS]
"Celebrity"
by Christopher Golden & José R. Nieto [UTS]
"Pitfall"
by Pierce Askegren [UH]
"Better Looting Through Modern Chemistry"
by John Garcia & Pierce Askegren [UTS]

These stories take place very early in the careers of Spider-Man and the Hulk.

"To the Victor"
by Richard Lee Byers [USV]

Most of this story takes place in an alternate timeline, but the jumping-off point is here.

"To See Heaven in a Wild Flower"
by Ann Tonsor Zeddies [USS]
"Point of View"
by Len Wein [USS]

These stories take place shortly after the end of the flashback portion of "The Silver Surfer."

"Identity Crisis"
by Michael Jan Friedman [UTS]
"The Doctor's Dilemma"
by Danny Fingeroth [UTS]
"Moving Day"
by John S. Drew [UTS]

CHRONOLOGY

"Out of the Darkness"
by Glenn Greenberg [UH]
"The Liar"
by Ann Nocenti [UTS]
"Diary of a False Man"
by Keith R.A. DeCandido [XML]
"Deadly Force"
by Richard Lee Byers [UTS]
"Truck Stop"
by Jo Duffy [UH]
"Hiding"
by Nancy Holder & Christopher Golden [UH]
"Improper Procedure"
by Keith R.A. DeCandido [USS]
"The Ballad of Fancy Dan"
by Ken Grobe & Steven A. Roman [UTS]
"Welcome to the X-Men, Madrox..."
by Steve Lyons [XML]

These stories take place early in the careers of Spider-Man, the Silver Surfer, the Hulk, and the X-Men, after their origins and before the formation of the "new" X-Men.

"Here There Be Dragons"
by Sholly Fisch [UH]
"Peace Offering"
by Michael Stewart [XML]
"The Worst Prison of All"
by C. J. Henderson [XML]
"Poison in the Soul"
by Glenn Greenberg [UTS]
"Do You Dream in Silver?"
by James Dawson [USS]
"A Quiet, Normal Life"
by Thomas Deja [UH]
"Livewires"
by Steve Lyons [UTS]

CHRONOLOGY

"Arms and the Man"
by Keith R.A. DeCandido [UTS]
"Incident on a Skyscraper"
by Dave Smeds [USS]
"A Green Snake in Paradise"
by Steve Lyons [UH]

These all take place after the formation of the "new" X-Men and before Spider-Man got married, the Silver Surfer ended his exile on Earth, and the reemergence of the gray Hulk.

"Cool"
by Lawrence Watt-Evans [USM]
"Blindspot"
by Ann Nocenti [USM]
"Tinker, Tailor, Soldier, Courier"
by Robert L. Washington III [USM]
"Thunder on the Mountain"
by Richard Lee Byers [USM]
"The Stalking of John Doe"
by Adam-Troy Castro [UTS]
"On the Beach"
by John J. Ordover [USS]

These all take place just prior to Peter Parker's marriage to Mary Jane Watson and the Silver Surfer's release from imprisonment on Earth.

Daredevil: Predator's Smile
by Christopher Golden
"Disturb Not Her Dream"
by Steve Rasnic Tem [USS]
"My Enemy, My Savior"
by Eric Fein [UTS]
"Kraven the Hunter Is Dead, Alas"
by Craig Shaw Gardner [USM]

CHRONOLOGY

"The Broken Land"
by Pierce Askegren [USS]
"Radically Both"
by Christopher Golden [USM]
"Godhood's End"
by Sharman DiVono [USS]
"Scoop!"
by David Michelinie [USM]
"The Beast with Nine Bands"
by James A. Wolf [UH]
"Sambatyon"
by David M. Honigsberg [USS]
"A Fine Line"
by Dan Koogler [XML]
"Cold Blood"
by Greg Cox [USM]
"The Tarnished Soul"
by Katherine Lawrence [USS]
"Leveling Las Vegas"
by Stan Timmons [UH]
"Steel Dogs and Englishmen"
by Thomas Deja [XML]
"If Wishes Were Horses"
by Tony Isabella & Bob Ingersoll [USV]
"The Stranger Inside"
by Jennifer Heddle [XML]
"The Silver Surfer" [framing sequence]
by Tom DeFalco & Stan Lee [USS]
"The Samson Journals"
by Ken Grobe [UH]

These all take place after Peter Parker's marriage to Mary Jane Watson, after the Silver Surfer attained freedom from imprisonment on Earth, before the Hulk's personalities were merged, and before the formation of the X-Men "blue" and "gold" teams.

CHRONOLOGY

"The Deviant Ones"
by Glenn Greenberg [USV]
"An Evening in the Bronx with Venom"
by John Gregory Betancourt & Keith R.A. DeCandido [USM]

These two stories take place one after the other, and a few months prior to The Venom Factor.

The Incredible Hulk: What Savage Beast
by Peter David

This novel takes place over a one-year period, starting here and ending just prior to Rampage.

"Once a Thief"
by Ashley McConnell [XML]
"On the Air"
by Glenn Hauman [UXM]
"Connect the Dots"
by Adam-Troy Castro [USV]
"Ice Prince"
by K. A. Kindya [XML]
"Summer Breeze"
by Jenn Saint-John & Tammy Lynne Dunn [UXM]
"Out of Place"
by Dave Smeds [UXM]

These stories all take place prior to the Mutant Empire *trilogy.*

X-Men: Mutant Empire Book 1: **Siege**
by Christopher Golden
X-Men: Mutant Empire Book 2: **Sanctuary**
by Christopher Golden

CHRONOLOGY

X-Men: Mutant Empire Book 3: **Salvation**
by Christopher Golden
These three novels take place within a three-day period.

Fantastic Four: To Free Atlantis
by Nancy A. Collins
"The Love of Death or the Death of Love"
by Craig Shaw Gardner [USS]
"Firetrap"
by Michael Jan Friedman [USV]
"What's Yer Poison?"
by Christopher Golden & José R. Nieto [USS]
"Sins of the Flesh"
by Steve Lyons [USV]
"Doom^2"
by Joey Cavalieri [USV]
"Child's Play"
by Robert L. Washington III [USV]
"A Game of the Apocalypse"
by Dan Persons [USS]
"All Creatures Great and Skrull"
by Greg Cox [USV]
"Ripples"
by José R. Nieto [USV]
"Who Do You Want Me to Be?"
by Ann Nocenti [USV]
"One for the Road"
by James Dawson [USV]

These are more or less simultaneous, with "Doom^2" taking place after To Free Atlantis, *"Child's Play" taking place shortly after "What's Yer Poison?" and "A Game of the Apocalypse" taking place shortly after "The Love of Death or the Death of Love."*

"Five Minutes"
by Peter David [USM]

CHRONOLOGY

This takes place on Peter Parker and Mary Jane Watson-Parker's first anniversary.

Spider-Man: The Venom Factor
by Diane Duane
Spider-Man: The Lizard Sanction
by Diane Duane
Spider-Man: The Octopus Agenda
by Diane Duane
  These three novels take place within a six-week period.

"The Night I Almost Saved Silver Sable"
by Tom DeFalco [USV]
"Traps"
by Ken Grobe [USV]
  These stories take place one right after the other.

Iron Man: The Armor Trap
by Greg Cox
Iron Man: Operation A.I.M.
by Greg Cox
"Private Exhibition"
by Pierce Askegren [USV]
Fantastic Four: Redemption of the Silver Surfer
by Michael Jan Friedman
Spider-Man & The Incredible Hulk: Rampage (Doom's Day Book 1)
by Danny Fingeroth & Eric Fein
Spider-Man & Iron Man: Sabotage (Doom's Day Book 2)
by Pierce Askegren & Danny Fingeroth
Spider-Man & Fantastic Four: Wreckage (Doom's Day Book 3)
by Eric Fein & Pierce Askegren
  Operation A.I.M. *takes place about two weeks after* The

CHRONOLOGY

Armor Trap. *The Doom's Day trilogy takes place within a three-month period. The events of* Operation A.I.M., *"Private Exhibition,"* Redemption of the Silver Surfer, *and* Rampage *happen more or less simultaneously.* Wreckage *is only a few months after* The Octopus Agenda.

"Such Stuff As Dreams Are Made Of"
by Robin Wayne Bailey [XML]
"It's a Wonderful Life"
by eluki bes shahar [UXM]
"Gift of the Silver Fox"
by Ashley McConnell [UXM]
"Stillborn in the Mist"
by Dean Wesley Smith [UXM]
"Order from Chaos"
by Evan Skolnick [UXM]

These stories take place more or less simultaneously, with "Such Stuff As Dreams Are Made Of" taking place just prior to the others.

"X-Presso"
by Ken Grobe [UXM]
"Life Is But a Dream"
by Stan Timmons [UXM]
"Four Angry Mutants"
by Andy Lane & Rebecca Levene [UXM]
"Hostages"
by J. Steven York [UXM]

These stories take place one right after the other.

Spider-Man: Carnage in New York
by David Michelinie & Dean Wesley Smith
Spider-Man: Goblin's Revenge
by Dean Wesley Smith

These novels take place one right after the other.

CHRONOLOGY

X-Men: Smoke and Mirrors
by eluki bes shahar
This novel takes place three-and-a-half months after "It's a Wonderful Life."

Generation X
by Scott Lobdell & Elliot S! Maggin
X-Men: The Jewels of Cyttorak
by Dean Wesley Smith
X-Men: Empire's End
by Diane Duane
X-Men: Law of the Jungle
by Dave Smeds
X-Men: Prisoner X
by Ann Nocenti
These novels take place one right after the other.

The Incredible Hulk: Abominations
by Jason Henderson
Fantastic Four: Countdown to Chaos
by Pierce Askegren
"Playing It SAFE"
by Keith R.A. DeCandido [UH]
These take place one right after the other, with Abominations *taking place a couple of weeks after* Wreckage.

"Mayhem Party"
by Robert Sheckley [USV]
This story takes place after Goblin's Revenge.

X-Men & Spider-Man: Time's Arrow Book 1: **The Past**
by Tom DeFalco & Jason Henderson
X-Men & Spider-Man: Time's Arrow Book 2: **The Present**
by Tom DeFalco & Adam-Troy Castro

CHRONOLOGY

"Sidekick"
by Dennis Brabham [UH]
Captain America: Liberty's Torch
by Tony Isabella & Bob Ingersoll

These take place one right after the other, with Soul Killer *taking place right after the* Time's Arrow *trilogy,* Venom's Wrath *taking place a month after* Valley of the Lizard, *and* Wanted Dead or Alive *a couple of months after* Venom's Wrath.

Spider-Man: The Gathering of the Sinister Six
by Adam-Troy Castro
Generation X: Crossroads
by J. Steven York
X-Men: Codename Wolverine ["now" portions]
by Christopher Golden

These novels take place one right after the other, with the "now" portions of Codename Wolverine *taking place less than a week after* Crossroads.

The Avengers & the Thunderbolts
by Pierce Askegren
Spider-Man: Goblin Moon
by Kurt Busiek & Nathan Archer
Nick Fury, Agent of S.H.I.E.L.D.: Empyre
by Will Murray
Generation X: Genogoths
by J. Steven York

These novels take place at approximately the same time and several months after "Playing It SAFE."

Spider-Man & the Silver Surfer: Skrull War
by Steven A. Ronan & Ken Grobe
X-Men & the Avengers: Gamma Quest Book 1: **Lost and Found**
by Greg Cox

CHRONOLOGY

X-Men & the Avengers: Gamma Quest Book 2: **Search and Rescue**
by Greg Cox
X-Men & the Avengers: Gamma Quest Book 3: **Friend or Foe?**
by Greg Cox
These books take place one right after the other.

X-Men & Spider-Man: Time's Arrow Book 3: **The Future** [portions]
by Tom DeFalco & eluki bes shahar
Parts of this novel take place in five different alternate futures in 2020, 2035, 2099, 3000, and the fortieth century.

"The Last Titan"
by Peter David [UH]
This takes place in a possible future.

Comics

star in their own original series!

 MARVEL®

BP Books, Inc.

❏ **X-MEN: MUTANT EMPIRE: BOOK 1: SIEGE**
 by Christopher Golden   0-425-17275-9/$6.99
When Magneto takes over a top-secret government installation containing mutant-hunting robots, the X-Men must battle against their oldest foe. But the X-Men are held responsible for the takeover by a more ruthless enemy...the U.S. government.

❏ **X-MEN: MUTANT EMPIRE: BOOK 2: SANCTUARY**
 by Christopher Golden   1-57297-180-0/$5.99
Magneto has occupied The Big Apple, and the X-Men must penetrate the enslaved city and stop him before he advances his mad plan to conquer the entire world!

❏ **X-MEN: MUTANT EMPIRE: BOOK 3: SALVATION**
 by Christopher Golden   0-425-16640-6/$6.99
Magneto's Mutant Empire has already taken Manhattan, and now he's setting his sights on the rest of the world. The only thing that stands between Magneto and his conquest is the X-Men.

®, ™ and © 2000 Marvel Characters, Inc. All Rights Reserved.

Prices slightly higher in Canada

Payable by Visa, MC or AMEX only ($10.00 min.), No cash, checks or COD. Shipping & handling: US/Can. $2.75 for one book, $1.00 for each add'l book; Int'l $5.00 for one book, $1.00 for each add'l. Call (800) 788-6262 or (201) 933-9292, fax (201) 896-8569 or mail your orders to:

Penguin Putnam Inc.
P.O. Box 12289, Dept. B
Newark, NJ 07101-5289
Please allow 4-6 weeks for delivery.
Foreign and Canadian delivery 6-8 weeks.

Bill my: ❏ Visa ❏ MasterCard ❏ Amex _____ (expires)
Card# _____
Signature _____

Bill to:
Name _____
Address _____ City _____
State/ZIP _____ Daytime Phone # _____

Ship to:
Name _____ Book Total $ _____
Address _____ Applicable Sales Tax $ _____
City _____ Postage & Handling $ _____
State/ZIP _____ Total Amount Due $ _____

This offer subject to change without notice.   Ad # 722 (3/00)